A House of Stone is Forever

A House of Stone is Forever

STORIES

GARY GRIFFITH

iUniverse, Inc.
Bloomington

A House of Stone is Forever
Stories

This is a work of fiction. All of the characters, names, incidents, organizations, and dialogue
in this novel are either the products of the author's imagination or are used fictitiously.

iUniverse books may be ordered through booksellers or by contacting:

iUniverse
1663 Liberty Drive
Bloomington, IN 47403
www.iuniverse.com
1-800-Authors (1-800-288-4677)

Because of the dynamic nature of the Internet, any Web addresses or links contained in
this book may have changed since publication and may no longer be valid. The views
expressed in this work are solely those of the author and do not necessarily reflect the
views of the publisher, and the publisher hereby disclaims any responsibility for them.

Any people depicted in stock imagery provided by Thinkstock are models,
and such images are being used for illustrative purposes only.

Certain stock imagery © Thinkstock.

ISBN: 978-1-4759-6245-1 (sc)
ISBN: 978-1-4759-6246-8 (hc)
ISBN: 978-1-4759-6247-5 (e)

Library of Congress Control Number: 2012921590

Printed in the United States of America

iUniverse rev. date: 1/23/2013

To my father.

CONTENTS

FOREWORD

In Walden, Thoreau reminds us of the benefits that can come from building our own homes: Not only can we save money and resources, but, more importantly, the poetic faculty can be awakened in each of us—That we can begin to see the world in a better way, as the poet sees it, with harmony and integrity in the landscape, which leads to even grander things in our soul. These lofty thoughts appeal to the romantic in me, and I would like to believe that my family in some way measured up to this. That is why I am dedicating this book to my father, Carl Griffith, because he built a house of stone during those lean, hard years of The Great Depression, and also because he always had my back when I was growing up. And also to my mother, Gladys Griffith, a strong, tireless woman who stood by us through it all.

The idea for this collection came to me during a writers' conference I attended at The University of Nebraska, Lincoln, during the summer of 2004. The University was impressed with my recently completed novel and offered me a merit scholarship, which afforded me an opportunity not only to meet with agents, but also to study under a Pulitzer Prize winning author. This author soon crushed my dreams of publishing, when he told me to destroy my novel. He told the gathering of budding novelists that he often told aspiring authors to do this. I did not take his advice, but I did refocus my attention on the current collection of stories, some of which date back to my earliest attempts at writing.

My first published story, entitled "The Original Love Story," appeared in my hometown newspaper, The Antrim County News, in December of 1972. A few years later I submitted another story to them, which was rejected. That story, "Legends," is included in this collection. It became the first of a long series of rejections that would continue to this day. This brings me to the obvious; writing involves rejection, and you must keep at it, no matter what, because writing also brings about an immense satisfaction and pleasure.

Great writers have always been an inspiration to me, and now with humility, I must mention America's best, William Faulkner, whose works taught me to look inward for inspiration as well as outward to my origins. Thus, the stories in this collection are rooted in the woods and two tracks of Northern Michigan, which will always be my true home.

A big thanks to my mentors and supporters: To the late Richard Erno, one of Michigan's finest novelists. Thanks to the entire Bread Loaf community at Middlebury College, Vermont, especially novelist extraordinaire, David Huddle and the late Ken Macrorie. Also thanks to the Antioch, Los Angeles community, especially Jim Krusoe, Leonard Chang, Susan Taylor Chehak, and Alma Luz Villanueva. Thanks to Arizona poet Miles Waggener for his continued support as well as editor Steven McDermott of Storyglossia for publishing my work and believing; and of course, thanks to Paula Griffith and Pauline Bechtold for always believing. Thanks to Sharon Creek for the extraordinary cover design. Sharon also designed the cover for The S-Virus. Lastly, thanks to all of the many legends of Northern Michigan, both living and deceased, who shaped me during those rough, coarse years.

Gary Griffith
December, 2012

A House of Stone is Forever

PART ONE

What is it about Welshmen? Why does our imagination run so wild? With a name like John Dee, I am no exception. I share that name with you, Father. We are both dreamers. One incongruity inevitably leads to another. That has always been our problem. We wander from person to person and place to place. Time loses its meaning. Only space remains. Anything is possible.

Today the March sky is full of gray clouds and bitter wind. I will honor your request. I will bury the past for the future—these archives with the insignias and intricate details on the outside, just as you had made them. I am a few years late. I know you will forgive me for that. You had insisted that it happen on the first day of spring. That promise I have kept. You were like that—a star gazer and a stone gatherer, always paying attention to the solstices and reading your almanac. I spear my shovel into the hard earth, but then pause. I have kept a few things out—your picture for one; it continues to captivate me. It has faded with time. A white pasty effect seeps in from all sides and has changed the grass where you stand to ashes.

It is the spring of 1922, your eighteenth year. An old, red-brick schoolhouse is in the background. You are clad in dark trousers, corduroy shirt, and sport jacket. The school is the old, turn-of-the-century style, typical of government buildings during that era: tall and narrow of design with a steep, sharp-angled roof, haunted windows, and a portico entryway.

You present a tall, lean figure for the camera's eye. I imagine it to be graduation day, a fine spring day in May. The morels must have been pushing their way up through the pungent floor of the North Woods. But I know this is no graduation day. Mother always made it abundantly clear that you never finished high school. "Just remember, John Dee," she would tell me, "any brains you received came from my side of the family, not his."

1

But I refuse to believe that. Not now, at least, holding your picture out at arm's length like this. Your dark hair is long on top and combed straight back, like Michael Douglas, giving a boyish roundness to your face that accentuates your prominent nose and ears. You are looking into the sun. Shadows fill your sockets, yet I can still detect your gaze, dark and amused, just as it always was right up to the end—when you no longer recognized anyone, and they dressed you in that special orange vest and sat you daylong by their antiseptic window.

A sturdy looking woman stands next to you. She is not my mother. She wears a dark skirt and white knit top. A brooch can be seen just to the left, slightly beneath her throat and above her ample bosom. Her pose is much more reserved than yours. Her right arm hangs straight down, as if paralyzed. Her left hand hides at midthigh, deep in the pocket of her coat. Only her nervous smile gives the situation away.

Her brother, Hoyt, is taking the picture. He stands twenty feet in front of you, looking into the black Kodak. At first, you are wearing a porkpie. "John, put your hat on Ailda," he says. You grin and take it off and plop it on Ailda's head. She wears her hair fashionably short. Hoyt comes over and turns the hat to the right in a rakish angle. A breeze gently passes through the maples and makes soft sibilant sounds. I can tell by the way that your shadows have merged into a short, inverted V that it is just past noon. The moment is set forever, frozen.

The two of you make a handsome couple. You look Gatsbyesque, but you are no Gatsby by any means. Your left foot reveals the truth. You are leaning back slightly, striking the pose, causing the cuff to move up a little, exposing the thick heavy laces that run high up your foot, past your ankle. The toes are worn and need polish. They form the left point of the shadow, the one that points toward the north. They tell the story of the hard work you have known already at eighteen years—standing there that warm afternoon in May, the month you were born, on the threshold of summer and the rest of your life, and they foretell the hard years ahead.

Elbowdeep in guts and blood, you will work the slaughterhouse and bring home the meager pay that will keep everyone eating during those lean, Depression years. Killing the animals in such a brutal fashion takes an iron will and goes against your gentle nature. You will lean up against the damp cement walls and watch the frightened cattle nervously step down from the trucks, prodded along by the hard poles in the driver's hands.

Sometimes you will step outside for a smoke and listen to the C&O blow in from Hitchcock, or you will think about the cool blue waters of Cartlett Pond, where the rainbow trout lurk.

I take a closer look at the picture. It is your right hand that interests me, so nonchalant next to your pants pocket with your thumb hooked in. Only a "bird's eye" like mine would have noticed it. At first I thought it a meaningless gesture, or possibly you were giving the "okay" sign to the camera, until I got out the magnifying glass. Your forefinger encircles it, a smooth dark stone, and the same one that now sits on the mantel piece in the living room of the stone house. Your shadow points north, toward the site a short distance away, where across the field, up the knoll and beneath the box elder tree, you will one day build your house of stone. Another woman will enter your life for fifty years—a woman so mixed with the elements, so full of strength, kindness, and rage that she will overshadow your presence to the six children you will have together.

C.P. is the firstborn—Calvin Prescott if you use the full name that mother gave. Mother will give names to all the children, a trait that I will one day inherit. She will give the girls plain and simple names, but the boys will have a high-minded names—except for me. You aren't much for that Calvin Prescott business. You are a man who gets down to the essence of things. In no time at all Calvin Prescott will become C.P., and C.P. it is. Calvin Prescott will appear on his gravestone, but in everyday life, it will be C.P.

Later on, there will be the twins, Andrew and Alfred—identical in looks but not in action. You will take care of that, too. Drew and Alfie it will be. But with the girls, Mother will name them Marie and then Janet. There will be no need for you to intervene on that one. Plain and simple are always fine with you.

"I never had much luck with my girls," you will say, when referring to their untimely deaths. Little Janet will be first, taken one spring day by the Michigan cellar—that crawl space you would eventually add to the stone house—the storing place for potatoes, jams, and jellies. This will be the project that involves everyone digging and carrying and reinforcing—working those long hours to stay ahead of the Michigan winter, while the children play. Into it she will fall, emitting her small, fragile scream, banging her head and cutting her delicate arm on a rusty nail. "Little Janet with the Dripping Curls" is what you will call her. You have your own way with names, too.

2

C.P. and his pa are walking up the path that cuts through the apple trees, tall grass, and hollyhocks. C.P. likes pushing the old, rusted out wheelbarrow. It is a real test of his muscle. He wants to be big and strong like his Pa. His Pa strolls along beside him. Neither is in any particular hurry. The bees are droning a sleepy, lazy tune to the apple blossoms. The wheelbarrow is filled with palm-sized stones that are shaped like prehistoric eggs. His pa says to him, "We'll use them later on for the porch, but for now they'll be markers." C.P. labors to keep the load even because he is the first born. One day he will be the eldest, and all responsibility will lie with him to watch over the rest of us.

He leans into the load of stones and looks at his arms, searching for those big-man-muscle-veins like he has seen in his Pa's arms, but there are none, not now, least-ways. Pa strolls alongside in that long-legged, easy manner of his, swaggering slightly in the rhythm of things, one hand knuckle-deep in his britches, the other dragging the shovel behind. He looks at the stones as if they aren't really stones but something else, like buried treasure or something. Pa says, "Stack a pile over yonder, C.P.," pointing toward the northeast corner. "That will be the First Stone."And he runs back and forth like the jackrabbit he was, trying to please his pa, until every last one of them are in place. There are the First Stone, the Second Stone, Third and Fourth. All formed into a pyramid just like Pa wanted, shaped on three sides with one on top. He keeps sending him for another and another and another, until everything is laid out.

Then C.P. says to his pa, "Pa, why is there four stones?"

And Pa says back to him, "Time will take care of that. You will know in due time. A good home is built on four stones. That's all you need to know for now."

Just then the courthouse bell begins sounding. Twelve times it rings in those clear tones. C.P. can almost see the belfry, being up high and behind things like this, on the knoll that his ma picked out. The only thing keeping it from sight is the maples, thick and green and moving slightly in the summer air. There are trees beneath them layer after layer, running down toward the valley, where town is.

His stomach is gnawing away, but he knows his ma has her own ideas about when everyone can eat. She is still going over things with August Polawski. They stand there beneath the box elder tree that divides itself in a Y just perfect for riding. Ma has the same apron on she always has, white with little blue dots all over it, faded. It has big pockets in the front intended to cover up her big belly. Grandma says she is "with child," which means, C.P. will have a little brother or sister sometime in November.

Ma and August have the maps and papers out. Ma has her hands in her apron pockets where she always keeps the money for the tooth fairy and other things. She has worked him to agree, one dollar a month for a year. That is, if Pa can get down and sign up for the WPA, like he's supposed to. August is hot and uncomfortable in his dark suit. His shirt is rumpled at the belt where his belly hangs out. His blue tie is too short and way up on his chest. It is the first hot day of summer and August has to mop the side of his bald head and his neck with his handkerchief. Ma is doing all the talking and from time to time she half turns her back on him and shrugs her bony shoulders slowly and lets them back down again. Finally he shakes his head yes and she pulls a dollar out of her apron pocket and hands it to him. One dollar a month for twelve months. That's what they settle for on the land.

Meanwhile Pa has taken the wheelbarrow and shovel back down to the field and started digging again up next to the bluff. C.P runs to him as fast as he can.

"Pa, we got the land. Now we can have our own house."

His shovel is cutting through the dry field grass and forming an "O" in the hillside. He keeps digging and pawing at the earth with the blade of the shovel, until it hits up against something sharp and hard.

"Hear that?" he says. He continues prodding and prying. Pa is always digging for something it seems like, if not stones then worms or potatoes in the garden.

"What's that?" C.P. says. "What'd you find?"

He is on his knees now pulling and tugging until he's unearthed a white, smooth stone, perfect and symmetrical, the size of a squash or maybe bigger. He rolls it down the side of the hill.

"See this, C.P. This is what we're going to build our house of." He wipes the sweat from his face with his sleeve. "We're going to build a house of stone and it will stand for a thousand years, C.P. A thousand years. Long enough to see and survive the next ice age."

"Let's go eat, Pa. I'm hungry." August's big black Buick is rolling down the makeshift trail. "Let's have Ma fix us something to eat."

3

The ties are stacked up like jackstraws. Rory says they can have them if they want, because they aren't doing anybody any good just sitting there like that. They were supposed to be used for the second line they was planning to put in to run a train up to Chirk, "but you can forget that," he says. We'll be lucky to keep what we got with this Depression going on the way it is. He speaks to them through his green visor from behind his desk at the ticket counter. "You'll have to cut them to size." He has a toothpick in one corner of his mouth that he keeps working back and forth from one side to the other. Then he says, "Them ties is ten feet long. We'd a had to cut 'em too if we kept them because they's too long for the ballasts. So you better make up your mind because come Friday, them ties will be gone for sure." Pa is none too good at negotiating and Ma can't be here, as much as she'd like to, because of the puking. She's laid up with a hot water bottle pressed to her belly. She says the baby inside her likes the heat and it eases the pain.

Pa looks down at C.P. as if he's waiting for an answer. He adjusts his porkpie. C.P. can't keep his eyes off the train tracks outside. Everything is silent as though breath was held up inside a chest just waiting to let itself out, because at any moment the next train will be coming. You just know it by the stillness in the air and the way people are sitting about in the lobby with nothing to do. It's coming and everybody knows it. C.P. strains his ears, hoping to catch the faint sound of its whistle, but all he can hear is the rattle and tap of Rory's telegraph.

"How much you want for them, Rory?" Pa finally says.

"They're free."

"Free?"

"That's right," Rory says. "Even you can afford that, John. Take as much as you want by Friday, cause like I said, after that we got a freight coming in to haul 'em back to Grand Bay."

The poison violence seeps into C.P.'s veins. Just like that, I can feel it through the synapses of time—the ancient curse of the earth—puffing up the adder and closing off the pipe. "Even who can afford what, Mr. High and Mighty?" C.P. wants to say, but doesn't.

Rory stands up and walks through the side door of the office to join us. He presents a tidy picture with his white shirt, green armbands and black vest. He walks lively across the tiled floor, clicking his heels, and whistling a nonsense tune. C.P. has half a mind to trip him as he passes, but he doesn't because then he would have to face the even greater wrath of Ma. Rory steps through the glass door into the morning sunshine, and the others follow.

"How many you need, John?"

That's one thing Pa isn't very good at, figuring with numbers. "Oh, I don't know. Maybe a hundred. Maybe a little more."

C.P. thinks about what Ma said about all the smarts coming from her side of the family. He'd heard the same story as me. He didn't believe it either. Pa's not dumb. He's just got his own way of doing things. He's gentle with animals and handy with a saw. He was our pa.

Rory pulls a watch out of his pants pocket and checks it. Then he gives a little whistle like a falling bomb. "What you need a hundred ties for?"

"I'm building a house," Pa says.

"You building a house with railroad ties?" C.P. starts getting mad again about the way he's making fun of Pa with his voice and trying to pretend that he's not.

"It will last a thousand years," Pa says. "I'm covering the ties with stone. It will be here long after we're gone, when the ice comes."

Rory gives that wheezy laugh, the kind that heavy smokers often have, like his lungs are a worn out accordion. "I'm sure it will, John. I'm sure it will."

C.P. feels more than a little embarrassed. He wishes Pa wouldn't say these things, at least not in public. People already think he's a little crazy, digging in the ground for stones and such, and now building a tie house and covering it with fieldstone. The kids at school sing this song, "John Dee, Crazy as Can Be." I wish he had said the truth—we're too poor for anything else, and that's why I'm using ties and fieldstone.

Rory checks his watch again and then pulls a baggage car out of a side door and wheels it up next to the unloading platform. The people begin to come out of the station and stand beneath the long awning. There is a mother with her babies, three of them all hanging on to her hand. She wears a blue bonnet and is still young and pretty with no gray hairs in her head like Ma does. A well-groomed man with gray hair is next. He totes two small suitcases. He is dressed in a dark, mail-order Sears and Roebuck suit and tie. He opens one bag and tries to sell Pa a cigar, Johnny on the spot. Pa reaches in his pocket and gives him a nickel for two of them and asks him for a light. "Kindly sir, most kindly indeed," he says and scratches a long match on the floor and watches it flair up for a few seconds before applying it to the Cheroot, which Pa draws on, turning his head at an angle and stooping down.

By this time C.P. can already hear the whistle in the distance, and his heart begins to do a dance. He wants to stay and see the train but Pa's had enough.

"Remember, Friday is the last day," Rory says.

Monday is already half over so they had four days at best to move the ties. C.P. can see the train up yonder on the tracks bearing down on them, slowing some with great clouds of steam and smoke belching out both above and beside.

Pa doesn't feel like bothering with the ties right now. He's got something else on his mind right now. Although he don't come right out and say it, he wants to go to The Smith Crick Tavern for a cold one. It is one of the oldest businesses in Blackwood and just reopened a few weeks back after being shut down as a speak easy. Most of the locals just call it Smitty's after the owner, George Smith, a Canuck who migrated down here. It would be a family-owned business for years to come. Old George, the owner, decided to name the place Smith Crick because up in Canada that's how they pronounce creek. He thought he was being real funny, and so he named the joint, Smith Crick Tavern. There really is a fine trout stream near here that originally was called Smith Creek, but that is another story.

Pa says now the taverns can all reopen again because of something called the Twenty-first Amendment. C.P. heard him arguing with Ma about it. Ma is real strict about alcohol. She said she grew up with one no good drunk, her father, and that was one too many, and she would never tolerate another. At church she belonged to something called The WCTU, and sometimes they came to the house they were renting from Cletus Shoemaker (if you want to call it a house; it was his garage that he made into a room with a sink, a little wood-fired cook stove, and a outhouse attached outside) and had their meetings. It wasn't a good thing to cross Ma about these matters or anything else because she was quick with the stick.

C.P. and Pa walk toward town and then duck down behind the alleyway out of sight, until they get to the backdoor of Smitty's. Pa doesn't say anything to C.P. about keeping things quiet. All of us always protected our Pa. In the old days when Pa took C.P. fishing for the evening's dinner, he would get a bottle of bootleg from Doc Hibbard, and C.P. would never say anything. It was the only time he had a happy face on and that was a good enough reason in itself to keep quiet.

The willow trees are hanging over both sides of the street, and C.P. would just as soon stay outside and play marbles with Fred Dickson or go down by the river and skip stones with Floyd Ward; but Pa makes him go inside with him and sit by the pool table while he gets himself a draft with a one-inch creamy head of foam on the top, which he sips off before getting into the real thing.

4

Well they moved those ties, every one of them, thanks to the help of Grandpa Dee. He came with his wagon and two horses. Ma didn't like C.P. being around Grandpa Dee because he says things that young boys shouldn't hear, at least in her mind anyway. One time she overheard him asking C.P. if he had any hair on his privates yet, except he used other language that I can't repeat. Now Pa, he just smiled when he heard him say things like that. But Ma would get plenty mad. Ma has a bad temper sometimes and she's not afraid to let it show.

There were plenty of other things that Grandpa Dee said and done that would have made Ma fighting mad, if she had known. He always was talking about boys and girls' private parts. I can't repeat that story either, too much.

Grandpa Dee had a big square head that had gone bald in his old age and he wore thick black glasses and an Amish-style hat. At that time he was on his third marriage. His third wife C.P. didn't call her Grandma. He just called her by her real name, Nellie. Later on, we all did the same with his fourth, fifth, and sixth wives.

For the rest of the summer and on into the fall they worked on the house, while Ma's stomach grew bigger. They were trying to hurry because like I said, she was due in November. On into the early part of the evening they would work and C.P. would watch Pa sawing away at those ties, cutting each one to length by hand, and using one of Grandpa's bucksaws. It was an awful straining task, but Pa would keep right at it, not stopping, once he put the saw to it. He'd go right after it, while C.P. held the lantern, which cast the shadow of him against the wall, the right arm going back and forth and his head curved over the top. C.P. would count the strokes and stop after fifty or so because that was as high as he could without starting over. Pa would slow up a little but he'd never stop. That was how he done it. One right after the other, day after day, until those ties were all cut to size, and they were standing them upright into the holes they dug and filling them with cement. Then C.P. would slather more mud in between the ties because his hands were the smallest. He would pack the mud in between with old nails to make sure everything held.

Next they cut the rafters from a stand of maple saplings in the woods behind us. By Labor Day the roof was on and all the outside walls were standing. Then Pa began the stonework. This was when he slowed down and took his time. Pa would handle each one like they was babies needing special care. He would pick one up and turn it in his hands, rubbing his palms over the smooth surfaces. "Look at this one, C.P.," he would say. "This one is older than Moses, I'll bet, formed from the womb of the earth." He would talk like that sometimes, saying things like "in the womb of the earth," or "in the bosom of time."

They finished the stonework and got most of the flooring in before the first snow began to fly. Grandpa brought in a Franklin woodstove and enough wood to get make it through the winter. It was just before Thanksgiving on the second of November, 1934, that Ma gave birth to her second child, a girl that she named Marie.

It was the spring after the first mushrooms appeared in the woods, and C.P. and Pa were out cutting firewood and picking morels when Pa did something very peculiar. After he had felled a pine tree, he sawed off a thin slab and peeled away the bark. Then he took his chisel and made and inscription, which he later burned and sealed with a hot nail. The inscription read, A HOUSE OF STONE IS FOREVER. Then he hung it over the mantle of stone fireplace. He was then ready to tell C.P about the archives.

"What's an archive, Pa?" C.P. said, bending down to pick up a moist, brown morel, three times the size of his thumb.

"It's a time capsule, son. It's a living testimonial meant to preserve the past and carry on to the future for those who survive the final test."

C.P. should have known better than to ask him about this because whenever you asked Pa anything about what he was saying, it always ended up being more complicated than when you started.

It wasn't until he showed him the chest that C.P. began to slowly understand. Evidently Pa had someone over at the foundry in Advance make it for him. It was solid steel and double-lined and heavier than all get-out. Across the top someone had etched the following: John Dee Family 1935-1968.

"We have to carefully collect our artifacts, C.P." C.P. knew better than to ask what an artifact was.

"Sometime between 1965 and 1968, it must be buried in the northwest corner of the property."

They were standing out behind the house where he kept the chest covered with a tarp. Later on that year, he would build a shed to store it in.

"Why 1968, Pa?" 1968 seemed like a date that was so far in the future that it would never occur. It was a number that meant nothing.

Pa was gazing at one of his small stones. He had them collected around the place and kept them in glass jars and cans. This one was flat and smooth and just right for skipping, a lime-colored gem that he had polished. He was holding it up toward the sun so it was a little transparent or glowed some.

"I can't be exactly sure, but sometime between 1965 and 1968 will be the turning point. It could be as early as 1965. That is why we must have the archives. Because one day someone will unearth it and want to know why and how things were, and here is the first thing that will go in there."

He brought out from somewhere the family Bible with all of our names in it and the names of our ancestors for a couple of generations back. Before he put it in the chest he made C.P. put his hand on it and swear that he would make sure the chest was buried in the spring of the year, in 1965 or shortly thereafter and in March if possible, but certainly no later than 1968.

March, C.P. said to himself, 1965. That was thinking about the impossible: him and a date in the future, called March 1965.

C.P. did some quick figuring. In 1965, he would be thirty-six-years-old, an old, old, man. He couldn't imagine such. He decided to just let it happen, and when it happens to take what would come. C.P. closed that thought off and filed it away in a drawer that he would open later, much later. Old age was something he didn't want to think about.

"Ma, I don't want to get old," he said to her at bedtime that night. She was in one of her good moods, when she was the mother I knew she wanted to be, but for some reason couldn't.

"Don't worry about that," she said. "You've got plenty of time."

She lied.

I drop the picture into box and start to fasten the lid down, but then remember the other thing—the manuscripts. They are bound in the old dark leather of Grandma's Bible. I toss them in for good measure. What good are they? You didn't know about those, but I don't think you would care. This isn't 1965. It's not even 1968, but it's close enough. I'm a few years late. Close enough.

I slowly begin to shovel in the dirt and finish the job that C.P. never lived long enough to finish.

Awakening

C.P. was the oldest and the most deserving of my father's name. Maybe that was why he never trusted me through the years. As if I was one up on him from the get-go. They say that on the day I was born he was hunting those woods up behind the stone house, searching for the beloved whitetail, the coveted venison that would one day be brewing on the stovetop, helping to feed a family of seven, and soon-to-be-eight.

Mother surrounds me. It is only through sleep that I can escape, but she will not let me sleep. Just when my eyelids begin their heavy fall, another contraction ripples through me. Throughout the years, my drowsiness will vex her. She believes it a wanton sign of slovenliness. With each thrust of her hips, she pushes me further away; the soft pressure against my face like pink gum tissue, gives way. She squeezes me out and through the narrow chasm, the tight fit, the tug and push, the heave-ho, the grunt and groan. Her nails dig into the tick mattress.

They say her heart may have given way a little that day, the tissue scarred in the struggle. It may have been at the moment when her watery blue eyes went to the ceiling, where the cheap tiles were. Hatred wells up and then dies down, like the kettle of hot water Grandma has boiling on the stove. It was the life of hard work, what Reverend Terry called God's plan of suffering for redemption, the sorrow that would remind us to care for others. Not so. Not so. Because this sorrow made her mean and guilty, this sorrow would cause her to bring the rod down across my neck and make me cry out and the tears come flooding into both of our eyes, her looking down at me, much in the same manner as she now looks at the ceiling. I knew it wasn't me she hated, not me, really, but God and His plan, the plan that kept her in servitude all these years.

Yet C.P. sat on, oblivious to all, waiting up beyond The Icy Pines, in the gray, chill November twilight. It was the day I was born, the month my older sister Marie was born, too. Me and her, both November's children— her first, then fourteen years later—me , on this day. C.P. sat next to the dark curtain of woods, waiting for something to emerge. Snow drifted down from those low skies, and a pallor spread over things, in what was to be the metaphor of me for the first fifty years or so: damp, cold earth, leaden skies, short days, long nights, waiting to be born; the picture will be framed on my face throughout the ages in the scattered remnants of photos at a place I sometimes call home.

He waited for the buck that never came, until he finally walked toward home. The air was damp with approaching winter, this dark day, the twentieth of November, the early part of the evening. I was still inside Mother, trying to break free, my emancipation causing her to wail and turn her head from side to side. Her thin hands clutched the sheets. She still wore the thin white gold band, that which had kept her with my father all these years, as he slipped into drunkenness and forgetfulness.

The courthouse bell struck seven times, as C.P. made his way back, walking down past the gravel pit that yet remained, playground of my early years; walking was he, down one of the many Pembroke County two-tracks, 30-30 slung over his arm; he was a young man of seventeen, flat top, dark-eyed, handsome, sturdy. Past mother's window he went, but not before pausing to listen to her groans, as I awakened to life.

Grandma held me up as if I were a prized chicken and gave me my first swat, bringing the first of my tears.

"He's such a skinny thing," she said.

"Yes," Mother said. "Just a little bird. Give 'em here."

"What did you call him?" my father said. "You can't call him that. I ain't gonna have no bird in my family. Let's call him John. Name him after his poor ol' pap."

By this time, C.P. had stomped the snow off his boots and was standing there in the doorway, peering in, and catching the tail end of the conversation. "You can't call him that, Pa. I'm the oldest. That should've been my name."

"Never you mind," Mother said.

Grandma handed me to Mother. She took me and hooked me up to her breast. "You can call him whatever you want, but he's always going to be my little bird. My bird."

"John Dee will be his name," my father said. "My last and my first."

"The last shall be first and first shall be last,' Grandma said.

Mother ran her coarse, dry finger across my cheek. She said it again, "Bird."

I closed my eyes. I smoothed my face. I fell back to sleep. I tumbled headlong into the chasm. There I would remain, hopefully.

The Other

These tall ceilings have stories to tell, even through the angel's eyes of a baby, flat on my back (I was) in the adjacent room, already separated from the other. This was my "good Grandpa," as Mother called him. My other Grandpa was good, too, but this Grandpa, my good Grandpa, was divine.

We are at this place. They must have been having lunch that day so long ago. Their language suggests as much, the warble of it all, the unintelligible melodies (like birds in a dark tree). Back and forth it goes, the banter of humans; the exchanges, the rise and fall of scales. Then come the busy footfalls and the metallic rattle of drawers opening and closing, the digging through, and the separation: pots and pans. The aroma drifts my way. Around corners and through darkness it goes. Something chicken it is. The unmistakable blandness, the flavor that is almost not a flavor, sustained by salt.

That's Marie's voice. She is my older sister. Her song is an octave above the other. It floats and dances and can feed the hungry or clothe the poor. It is her eighteenth year and decades before her cancer. She has just become engaged. Each of her moments runs to the next. There is no tomorrow. She must suffer and die a horrible death. How can I tell her? I can't. When she dies she will weigh only 90 pounds. They say she looked young again, like she did on this day, with her ankle strap sandals, waist cincher girdle and hourglass figure. Her hair is parted on the side with those straight bangs falling down.

The space between us pulls me. I am drawn to the other. I turn my head to and fro and suck my fist. The pressure builds, pushing out at the frontal lobe and wrinkling my infant forehead. Sputtering and coughing, I register my protest, until a face appears over me, shattered with a web of fine wrinkles, hair prematurely white, blue eyes full of the slow, low burn and sometimes-love, Mother.

At eye level, I compare mine to his. Grandpa's is bigger. His emits a dribble; mine a jet stream. I squeeze mine between thumb and forefinger like the stub of a balloon, restricting the flow, producing the infinity sign, one yellow strand weaving through the other, jettisoning and then slowly receding, until just his is going. The two dark eyes of the outhouse stare up at us. I hear the wash and run of things down below, the soft stink of earth and excrement. I breathe through my mouth. This is not a place to tarry.

Outside, the huge umbrella of the box elder rattles in the breeze. This is a large, dirty, annoying tree that gives good shade in the summer, but coats your house with creepy crawling bugs.

We step out onto the dark boards that line the pathway. Why Grandpa and Grandma have put them there, I'll never know. When it rains, they are slick and shiny and have sent me more than one time skidding on my behind. Beneath them are the tender juicy worms and beetles, so alluring to the trout that my father covets.

I take Grandpa's hand in mine. I feel their stiff, arthritic texture, the little finger and ring finger permanently bent into the palm. He holds my hands gently but firmly as he leads me out of the dark shadows and through the narrow pathway that separates the tall grass and eventually leads to the stone house, my home.

The hollyhocks are tall and mixed in with the grass. They appear as miniature trees within my four-year-old world, their violet matches the spangled sky and sets off Grandpa's snow white hair—the head of my gentle and powerful giant, my lord protector, looking down on me.

This Grandpa has a full head of hair, parted left to right. It is a perfect match for his square features. He even has a bit of a cowlick in the back. He eclipses the sun. His face is the dark spot. Everything is aural about him. His dark eyes make a perfect contrast. They are flat and full of wisdom, with an underlying mirth and kindness. He is a good Grandpa.

We pass beneath the crabapple tree; the drone of bees fills the air. We step into the tall grass. Ordinarily, such an adventure would have frightened me. There are snakes in there. Often times I have heard them pass on either side of me when I walk this way alone. I can feel their black eyes on my broken images through the tall thistle, their fleeting tongues testing the air. But no serpents can harm me when I'm in the strong hands of my grandpa.

He lifts me into the crotch of the tree, which is really a giant palm with four large fingers running up. We take a rest while he finishes his pipe. I listen as the bees hum overhead. And then...

"John Dee!"

The spell is broken.

"John Dee!"

Mother is calling me. She has her mad voice on, but it is tempered a little because Grandpa is with me. I have wandered off again.

Grandpa lifts me off the tree. Thus begins one of our oldest games, the race home. I am delighted because I always win. Grandpa can't really run. He scoots along and not far because he must always rest, taking deep breaths, his face flushed. That is one trait I have inherited from him, as well as his height.

I always gave him a good head start, then I would speed by him, a tempest on the breeze, waiting for his recovery. Then off I would go again.

Today I give him an extra long head start because I'm in no hurry to get home. Mother is mad and cross today. I can tell.

She is exhausted and irritable. Half of her family is raised. C.P. , her oldest boy, my brother, is away in the Army. Marie has graduated and is away most of the time. Drew and Alfie are both in seventh grade. They are identical twins—born only minutes apart. Everybody is always getting them confused, and they always take advantage of this in various ways. Sometimes they copy each other's tests in school. Drew is the smarter of the two of them. I can always tell them apart though by their eyes. Alfie's right eye always wants to turn inward toward his nose, especially when he is mad or tired. Mother got him some special lens to help with the problem. They are both nothing but a bunch of frog eyes looking out through thick lenses. Add to that a head full of curly hair, and I think you get the picture.

Then along came me, an accident, as they say. Mother was almost forty when she had me. Forty is no age to be starting over, especially with the likes of me. I was still having a tough time with potty training. Pooping my pants at age four.

Maybe that is why I let Grandpa get such a huge lead, because I have to go. I can feel that awful pressure beginning to build, and my muscles becoming all taunt. My natural instinct is to hold it back, and that is where trouble begins.

I am still standing in the tall grass at the foot of the crabapple tree. I can hear the black snakes moving in on me. I should be off like the jackrabbit I am, but I hold back.

She is good and mad, but she won't show it fully around Grandpa. She likes Grandpa. He gives her money for things, just like he gives us kids money. He and Grandma carry large rolls of money with rubber bands around them. Dad tells us kids that Grandpa and Grandma have money hidden throughout their house. It is an intriguing thought.

Grandpa has gotten far ahead of me now, too far ahead, I'm afraid. It is difficult for me to run because I have to concentrate on "the other." It takes all of my will to hold that back, this growing pain that wants to pass through me and in me. I break the spell and start to run after him.

"Wait!" I scream, but he isn't waiting. He is walking toward my mother. She has stepped out of the stone house, poor little dark structure that it is, with its narrow confining rooms. Her hair is as white as his, as if she could be my Grandma.

"Wait!" Hot tears are running down my cheeks. I am furious, furious as Mother sometimes is with all of us after she has cooked dinner and Dad has gone fishing instead.

I am crying and running as fast as I can. It is a terrible feeling to lose. Grandpa is nearly at the top of the little knoll at the end of the path. He is smiling and saying something to my mother. He is tapping the pipe out on the heel of his shoe.

I am full blown in my fury and terror. "I hate you! I hate both of you." I try to kick his leg and swing at him.

She cuffs me hard on the back of the head. "You stink," she says. She sends me into the house. I can tell that this matter will be further discussed later.

I go into the little room I share with Alfie and dive on the bed kicking and screaming.

He is on the other bed sorting baseball cards. He looks at me disapprovingly. "What's a matter with you, dumb ass!"

The whole room stinks. I can feel the whole massive presence in my pants, where it itches and burns.

Alfie gets up and leaves the room. "You're disgusting."

I like days like this, when Grandpa takes me to work with him down at Deep Water Point. He's a handyman and can fix anything. Seems like half my family is here today though. Mother has come along to clean cottages. Rich people are always hiring her because she has a nose for dirt. Our home is always spotless. As my father always proudly declares, "You could eat off our floors." For some reason, my older brother Drew has decided to come along too. I think I know why. It has to do with a crushed up pack of Lucky Strikes I found the other day next to his heap of clothing. He has suddenly become best buddies with the owner's son, Vinnie Page. Vinnie is a hood and older than Drew. He shackles his pants and wears black engineer boots. His hair is always slicked back with Brylcream. He has long sideburns like Elvis. Vinnie always wears his cigarette pack tucked up beneath the arm of his tee shirt, where the red badge that says Lucky Strikes shines through the material. I have a suspicion about why Drew has suddenly become best friends with him, but I don't tell Mother this. That would get me in big trouble.

Me and Gramps are down by docks painting a rowboat. I can't tell you how happy I am to be here; it is something like Christmas morning or maybe like your best birthday, except it isn't about you but about him and being a part of the adult handyman's world of tools and fix-it-gadget-tasks. But the lazy rhythm of this brush going over and over the same spot has hypnotized me and made me sleepy. The paint is pretty, a light sky-blue with hints of gray. Grandpa must have finished his side already. I can't see him. He must have laid himself down and taken a nap. I haven't been paying attention again. But I think I can hear him. He is making a different noise, like he is snoring. I think I will join him. It is the lazy time of the day, just after lunch, when time always seems to stop. I am sleepy too. We will take a nap together, me and Gramps. This is the perfect spot, right up next to the docks. The water is making soft lapping sounds against the brown sand but is otherwise still.

The sun slips behind a cloud. A dark shadow moves my way. It passes over the water and turns it a deeper blue. In the sky two black birds doggedly chase a lazy hawk, which circles aimless round and round, up and up, as they pursue.

I put my brush down and decide to race the shadow. I want to be with Grandpa when it passes over. I scramble around to the other side of the boat. I must hurry before it gets here.

I lay down next to him. He is cold and clammy. The back of his ears has turned a light blue, the same color as the boat. He is still snoring and rattling, like something is caught in his throat. He looks at me, but he's not really there.

"Grandpa?" I say. I know the answer to my question. A new sensation comes over me, like something has suddenly switched on inside. My breath comes in short little puffs. "You wait here," I say. "I'll be right back."

Running comes so easily. I could be in a dream, the way my red sneakers fly over the grass, one after the other. It is effortless. The frog pond tempts me to stop; I do, just for a minute. There are a million places to play here and the pond is just one of them. It reminds me of a giant platter, the way it is shaped, kind of long and narrow. The water is elbow-deep at the most and just right for seizing the bullfrogs that lurk along the bottom. It may have been a fountain during the early days of the hotel. The cement edges are old and moss-covered. The waters are still and green. My face looks back up at me through dark, murky leaves. The frogs move along the shadows of the bottom. I would like to stay and catch one, but I promised Grandpa I'd be back.

At the hotel I find Tony, the cook, in the kitchen. Tony is big, fat, and jolly. He wears a chef's hat. "Tony, you seen Drew?"

He is busy dicing onions in that musical pattern, the sharp knife going choppity-choppity-choppity against the carving board.

"Drew? Why you wanna see Drew?"

My run has caught up with me. I am out of breath and have trouble talking. "I gotta tell him something important."

"You gotta tell him something important?"

Tony always repeats everything anybody says. He thinks he's being funny. Usually I play along, but right now I don't feel like playing along. I keep thinking about Grandpa's ears and how blue they were. And I don't like crying like this. I don't really want to scream, but I can't help myself. "Where's my brother, you fat fuck!"

Tony begins to waddle around the kitchen in his nervous manner, drying his hands on a towel.

"I think he's upstairs with that Vinnie. You be careful going up there."

I take the stairs three at a time calling out Drew's name as I go. When I get to the third floor, there is a sign that says closed for remodeling. I know they can't be far because I see Vinnie's cat Ginger leaning up against the wall. I stop and give her a pet. It is a long hallway with a single window at the end that beams a fiery white eye at me. I go down the hallway. The old boards squeak beneath my feet. Ginger walks along with me and slips inside the end door on the left, which is partly open. The brass letters on it read 333.

"Drew, you in here?" I say. The room is nearly dark. The shades have been drawn on the windows, but enough light has bled through so I can see outlines and shadows. I can hear a siren going off in the distance and drawing near. I smell burnt wax and then I see the candles burning, three of them.

There is Drew tied to the high back wooden chair, taken from the dining room below. His shirt is off and so are his glasses, which make him half blind. "Come on in and join us, Bird-Brain." I know that voice, deep, dark, edged with sarcasm. There are tools spread out on the floor and I step back for a minute and pick up a hammer.

"What are you doing in there?" I say.

"Playing a game. Want to play?"

"Get lost, Bird!" Drew says.

"Drew, something's wrong with Grandpa."

"Something's wrong with Grandpa," the other voice says, mocking me.

"Shut up," I say. I am closer now and I can see him standing in front of Drew with his shirt off. The muscles on his chest stand out, and his belly is flat. He steps toward me and I haul off and swing at him with the hammer. I aim for his head but am only able to connect with his bottom lip, where the teeth are. I get him good and he goes down, screaming.

"You leave my brother alone!"

I'm wanting to hit him again and finish him off, but I hear the ambulance pulling up and car door slamming. I drop the hammer and run.

This is a special night. C.P. is back from the Army. We are all going to watch ringside wrestling from Chicago with Russ Davis. I will sacrifice my Saturday night movie to do so, but Gramps will not hear of it.

"But I don't want to go to the movie," I say.

He gives me a fifty cent piece. I rub my thumb over the eagle.

"Get yourself some buttered popcorn," he says.

Wow! Buttered popcorn. I never get that.

So me and Alfie go to the movie, a Disney double-feature, *Johnny Appleseed* and *The Littlest Outlaw*. Movies can have a real affect on you. Later on, I will tell my Methodist Sunday school teacher, Mrs. Stein, that Johnny Appleseed was greater than Jesus. She will ignore my Swendenborgian nature. Denis Day's catchy whistle and song bring tears to my eyes: "The Lord is good to me, and so I thank the Lord. I wake up every day, as happy as can be." The animals all love Johnny. The ending is disturbing. Johnny doesn't want to die, but his guardian angel leads him off to an apple blossom sky. Just then I feel a strong hand on my shoulder. It is C.P. He gestures for me and Alfie to follow him.

He doesn't take us directly up to the stone house because by that time the hearse is there. Instead, he takes us into Uncle Herald's place. Most of the family is already there, and everyone is bawling and carrying on. Even Alfie begins to cry. I couldn't believe it.

I slip out the door and head over to Grandpa's house. Mother is inside trying to talk to Grandma. She had to wake her up and give her the news. They stand inside the kitchen window, beneath the single light bulb that hangs from a thick, industrial cord from the ceiling. Grandma looks spooky, with her hair down like that; it is a gray-rust color and falls beneath her shoulders. She has her teeth out and her face is caved in toward her mouth, and her face is full of lines and folds.

I don't like what I am seeing and decide to walk out back and breathe in some of the night air. The hollyhocks are standing in the tall grass. Their blossoms have closed for the night. They seem all aglow in the moonlight. I step out into the taller grass, next to the tallest ones. I wonder about the snakes, if they sleep at night. Grandpa would know the answer to that question, but Grandpa is gone. Another light goes on in Grandma's bedroom. Her shades are drawn. Next door, Uncle Herald's place is all lit up, where the others are. They are there, and I am here. Forever it will be that way. I lay down in tall grass amidst the hollyhocks and among my enemies.

Grandpa would have wanted it that way.

Held Back

Mrs. Jacques has us walking in single file, and as usual, in alphabetical order. Our feet make a tramp-tramp-tramping sound against the sidewalk. It's like we're prisoners or something, but all of us know better. We'll only have to be prisoners for a little while longer, until after the picnic. Then we'll be free for the summer. Some of us try to step on the leaf shadows that are moving every which way like crazy critters across the sidewalk or like ghost hands trying to cast spells and scare us in broad daylight. Mrs. Jacques tells us to stay in a straight line, but we know she doesn't really mean it, not in the strictest way like she would if it was the middle of school year instead the last day. The teachers can't keep us quiet. We've been penned up long enough.

I'm a D, a *D-e-e*, the first of my grade section, near the front with only the C's, B's, and A's in front of me. At first I thought she might put me with the "B's," since even Mrs. Avery sometimes calls me Bird. But no, she has me with the D's, which is where I belong. Some of the other kids have tried teasing me about that (including my own brothers), saying that's a perfect name for you, John Dee, meaning that I get mostly D's and E's on my report card. But they know better than to push their luck too far with that. I don't take much of that. Sometimes I get real mad, so mad that I don't see things right. I get teased enough at home and one thing I learned early was that I was a whole lot bigger and stronger than most others. God may not have given me much of a brain, but he gave me a strong body. I can whip most of the boys two grades above me.

We are passing by Judge Bradford's big house. It sits back behind a big lawn and a long walkway with tulips all in bloom on either side. I break line and snatch up one of the tulips and bite its head off, munching it down like a marshmallow. Sharon Cuthbertson, who is one up in front of me, makes a face at me. She wears braces and her hair hangs straight down shiny and dark—around a narrow face, small nose, and a neat mouth with chapped lips that always look like they are sore. Some of the other guys behind me thought it was pretty funny. I hear the special laugh of David Kosac. It reminds me of a pheasant taking flight—smooth and even, but building up to a point, then disappearing. It is a laugh that I will take risks for, a laugh that knows me and doesn't make fun of me.

Up ahead, the white steeple of the Methodist church rises up to a ball on top. After that, comes the park. There is a long line of us, first through sixth grade, stretching almost the whole the length of the block. Our moms are all ahead and busy preparing the fixings: deviled eggs, potato salad, hotdogs, hamburgers, and strawberry shortcake. It's going to be a real feast. My mother is supposed to bring her specialty—fried chicken and baked beans.

Since I'm a fourth grader, I'm in the middle of the pack. Next year I will move up one to fifth grade, and after that I will be in the front of the line in sixth grade. The seventh graders don't have to march. They get to ride their bikes or just walk in groups however they want.

Mrs. Jacques is a big woman—head and shoulders above the rest of us, and she walks with a funny gait, like a penguin, rocking back and forth. We all make fun of her behind her back. I guess she's got bad knees or something that makes her walk like that. None of us give her any lip though. She's a little mean. She's strict and I guess that's okay, but not really okay. She's not as strict as my mother, so I guess she's pretty easy, come to think of it.

Richardson Pond is warm enough for swimming and it's only May. I am chumming along with Harris, Luke, Barkley and Sammy. I see Ann Marie Buffman and Janey Jones coming our way. Janey lives next door to me. We all have our swimsuits with us, but nobody's changed yet. Now I was smart enough to wear mine under my pants so changing is a snap. In nothing flat I have my clothes off and lying in a pile next to the bank and I take a big run and do a cannon ball off the dock there and come up in time to catch the last of the splash. I look over and Harris and the rest of them are laughing—but Janey, she is pretending that she never saw a thing. She does finally manage to scold me a little in front of the others.

"John," she says, "you better hope Mrs. Avery doesn't see you or Mr. Shumberg. You'll get another paddling. I don't care if it is the end of the year." She never calls me Bird. That much I'll give her. But she is always trying to act like a goody-goody girl, but I know better. She can't keep the smile off her face either. None of the others had the nerve to do what I did. Mrs. Avery is busy with the rest of the teachers and moms putting food out on the picnic tables. And old Mr. baldy, Shumberg, isn't here yet. So I fooled them all again. I hurry and get out of the pond because the water is a little chilly, end of May or not. All the others have gone over to the change station to get into their suits. That leaves just me and Janey and Sammy standing there alone.

We walk out on the dock and I begin to skip stones across the water. The water is calm and is the color of blue, like ink, framed in green from all of the foliage hanging over the sides. My first one is a skimmer, and goes five times before it finally glides along and sinks.

Janey is looking at her report card. "I have all A's," she proudly announces. "Where's yours?" I let another one go toward a circle of ducks that's out there a ways. It falls way short of them, as I knew it would.

"My mother picked mine up," I say.

"Well what did you get? Did you pass?"

"I know I passed. I just haven't seen it yet."

Now Sammy is tagging along too. He is the class brain and I know why he isn't getting his suit on. I gave him the nickname of "Snake" because he has all these flaky scales over his arms and back. Mother told me there's a name for his condition, but I forget what it is called. Sammy holds his report card high in the air. "Not only did I get t all A's, but Mrs. Avery has asked me to give a speech to the PTA."

I have just let my last stone fly. It takes one big skip in a high arching curve and buries itself in the water. "A speech?" I say. " About what?"

"About school and good grades, and the merits of being a good citizen."

"How about the merits of this," I say, and act like I accidentally have lost my balance and bump him into the water, report card and all.

Sammy comes up spitting mad, like I knew he would. He has a bad temper too. "You're just jealous, Birdbrain. I.Q." Sammy has a few nicknames of his own. I.Q.? This is a new one. He is soaking wet and looks like a half-drowned rat coming out of the water. He says to me, "You're going to spend your whole life wanting to be something that you're not."

"Oh yeah, and what's that?" Sammy doesn't get a chance to answer. By that time, Harris and the others are back. This time they are getting a good laugh out of this, but Mr. Shumberg appears out of nowhere and of course he doesn't think it is so funny. He takes me by the ear and leads me off, though for some reason he isn't as mean as he could have been or has been in the past.

Pretty soon he lets go of my ear and walks me over to my mother's car. He actually has one hand on my shoulder and it isn't squeezing me like he'd like to kill me or something. His hand is just resting there in a funny way, like my dad's hand sometimes does, when we are walking along and he's taking me hunting or fishing. "Wait here," he says and opens the front rider's side door for me.

"My Mom won't like me sitting on the seat with a wet suit," I say.

He has a towel in one hand. "Here, take this." He hands me the towel and I don't know what to say exactly. "I'm sure she won't mind this time," he says. His voice is actually kind of friendly, and I am caught completely off guard because Shumberg and me have never gotten along. I feel real uneasy with him acting so friendly. I jump in and he closes the door.

Mother is standing over by one of the picnic tables talking to Mrs. Avery. Everybody is getting ready to eat and here I sit. They're probably going to send me home. She will be good and mad about this one. I can expect the yardstick across my butt and shoulders for sure this time. All the food is laid out but she is still talking away to Mrs. Avery. The sunlight shines on mother's silvery white hair and makes her looks like an angel; it is all aglow. She looks much older than the other moms. Pretty soon she walks my way, carrying my report card in her hand.

"You didn't have to come, Mom," I tell her. "I was just joking around with Sammy. That's all. I didn't mean nothing by it. He's always bragging about what a brain he is, so I thought I'd let him cool off a little in the water. That's all. I didn't mean nothing by it, honest."

She has that kind of faraway look with her eyes half-closed that I've seen only a few times before, usually when she's getting ready to deliver a knockout punch. Like when she had to tell us that my older brother C.P. was in the slammer because he was caught being a minor in possession of alcohol. I knew that look well and I gripped the side of the door where the armrest was and got ready.

"No, I want to take you home with me. There's something I have to show you." She puts the Chevy in reverse and backs out and then angles around until we are heading home at a slow pace. This has the same feel as when my grandpa died. That same sort of eerie, dead weight, ache-in-the-gut-feeling when you know bad news is coming but you don't know what. I begin to wonder who might have died?

She pulls out my report card and hands it to me. It is in a brown manila envelope with a little copper colored safety clasp over the hole. I open it up and stare at it. Reading, Arithmetic, Art, Penmanship, Geography, Science. All E's.

Then at the bottom of the card comes the hammer. X marks the spot:

The student shall be promoted to fifth grade or X retained in fourth grade.

"Does this mean I flunked?"

"It means that you will be held back for a year."

I hate crying about anything, and if I have to do it I don't want anyone seeing me.

"Sammy was right," I say.

"What's that?" she says. It's like my question brought her back from daydreaming.

"What did Sammy say?"

Words come out of me, but I must keep clearing my throat. It's like poison is seeping into my veins, an IV of bile and bitterness. I try to fight it. I hate losing to this. I begin taking deep breaths, long deep breaths to neutralize the toxins. I keep clearing my throat because it feels like it is closing or maybe swelling shut, though I keep telling myself that this isn't possible. Mother starts the car and begins backing out.

"This will be better for you. You can have a nice summer to swim and play and next school year you get to start again." She lights up a Viceroy and the stale smell of smoke drifts my way.

Some of the other brats are starting a softball game. I try to concentrate on the so called action, the blooping high pitches and the failed swings. Yes, the failed swings. I'm not the only failure, but I did fail. If I was at bat it would be different.

"We can get some ice cream, if you like. How about a chocolate milk shake?" She eases the car into drive, and I rest my head against the dash. Wow, this is my lucky day. This never happens, but it is too late. Not even chocolate can save me today. I am still taking deep breaths, except now they come out more as snorts through my nose. My legs are stiffening out. I am stretching without trying, an electric current running through me. I could tip over cars. I begin tapping the dash. I just tap out a little rhythm with my fist as she pulls away from the park. The taps become blows. The blows become an all out assault.

I don't want to damage it, as much as myself. I want my knuckles to fucking bleed. The swear words come to me, as they always seemed to have emerged when things go wrong. This is really wrong. I dig deep into my arsenal. All of the bad words I've ever heard on the playground. Every bad word ever uttered by my filthy brothers . It pours out of me. I can see Drew, my older brother, giving me that look, like hey dumb ass. Alfie is no better, a fucking carbon copy. That's what they always called me. "Dumb ass." "Queer," I say. I give it right back to them. They are right, though, because now I am a real dumb ass, and how will I ever explain this to anyone? The swear words bust out of me. It doesn't bother Mother that much because she has heard it so many times before, but not like this, never like this. This is something new. I am angry at all the fuckers of the world, God included. They have all screwed me over. Held me back to be the laughing stock of the town. Well, I'll fix them all. Yes, I will. I'll fix the fuckers. It is a bad, bad time for me. My rage boils over onto the stinking earth. I will bang my head until my worthless brain bursts. I am the dumb fuck of the world.

We pull into the driveway of the stone house. It is a warm spring day in May. The lilacs are in bloom. Who would ever know or recognize the wrath and misery spewing forth. One of them is standing back behind Dad. I can't be sure if it is Drew or Alfie, because whoever it is, they aren't wearing glasses. That always makes it difficult, even for me, the dumb ass brother to determine. I think it is Drew, but it could be Alfie. I can see his beady little black eyes, laughing out loud. I'll kill you, I scream at him. Mom and Dad don't know who I'm talking to, but "it" does. "It" busts into a full-fledged grin, as if to say, hey dumb ass, I told you so. You're a fucking loser, always will be. But I'll fix him. I'll fix em all. Just you wait.

Held Up

Islammed the door so hard the windows shuttered and the starlings took flight. One day Jeno and I would joke about this, but there was nothing funny about it on the day it happened. Years later, after we had passed through all of uncertainties of falling in love and marrying, and as we held each other within the pink walls of our farmhouse bedroom, we would remember back to that providential day. She would take me into her cool hands beneath the cool sheets and coax the truth out of me, beginning slowly.

"It was your mother's fault," she said. "She should have never let them hold you back. That has caused all of the damage."

"If they hadn't held me back, then I wouldn't have held you up."

She gave me a rare laugh. "And we wouldn't be here."

"All things are connected."

She squeezed me a little too much. "Ooooh, yes master."

"And leave my mother out of this."

She stopped. "Okay. Let's start over. I'll leave your mother out of this."

"Fine."

She began again, this time cupping me with her one open hand.

"God, I was only six-years-old then."

"And I was nine."

"Barely a child."

"But old beyond your years."

"I was out playing with my brothers. I was so proud of myself."

I said, "You had your hair done up in pigtails.

She said, "And don't forget my braces."

"Yes, and braces."

"I looked up suddenly when I heard the door slam."

I said, "I stormed out of my house, the windows shaking, my knuckles bleeding and bruised."

"The toy shovel dropped unexpectedly from my hand."

It was so strange, thirty years later, to be lying there in bed and recreating this incident from our childhood, but we were both convinced that it was meant to happen. The dark clouds of that day had joined us. We would say all of this and relive the event, while the portrait of Eli hung on the wall. In the first blush of our marriage, I had insisted that it be put there. Jeno had reluctantly agreed. I wanted Eli there to oversee everything, even in our most private chambers, the laying out of things with the apple blossoms just outside the window, and so on. But there were other reasons.

Eli had requested this picture done when he had only one week to live. He still looked remarkably good, though thin and wizened well beyond his twenty-some years. The blond hair hung down in thin strands. He combed it straight back on the sides. The eyes seemed always to be looking at you, full of love and kindness. Jeno had been there with him on the night he died.

The phone had gone off late one night. A co-worker calling from a hospital in Corpus Christi, reporting him sick and missing from work. First she tried calling him. She let the phone ring over and over for days. Finally he answered.

"I'm fine, really." His voice sounded convincing but Jeno had felt the tingly spots on her arms when she talked to him.

She was having trouble hearing him, yet the connection was good. I drove all night so she could catch a morning flight out of Detroit. She went down there and rescued him from that drab apartment where his "friends" had abandoned him. Later that same day she hauled him out of that filthy dive and drove him back to Michigan.

He wanted to go home, but he was too weak to get in or get out of the car. Instead, she took him directly to the hospital, where for three days and nights she joined the struggle. She fought off the death angel at that bout.

"Get out!" she had screamed, making swatting motions in the air. And then to him, "Eli, I want you to listen to me. You've got to stay awake. Do you hear me! Don't close your eyes. Don't go yet!"

Later, Eli would tell how she looked that day. How he saw her looking down at him from the hospital bed, only it was like he was at the bottom of a well and she was at the top, her face in the circle.

The priest arrived and anointed him, but it was Jeno who kept him alive, willed him to live for another fifteen months.

Jeno continued to work me . "Come on, " she said. "I want you to remember."

I was reluctant. "Okay," I said. "Okay."

I rocked the house with my slam. The windows shook. I walked out into the afternoon. I heard Mother behind me so I ran to get ahead of her. Sympathy was the last thing I needed, nor reprimand. I walked down into the field with its matted grass beaten down by the November rain and cold, looking for something live to shoot—a bird, a cat, a dog—it didn't matter, since Drew had managed to escape. I'm not entirely alone. My cousin Nichols had decided to tag along. I had almost forgotten about him. Nichols was there that day. His step-daddy was my uncle Hank, my mother's brother. Uncle Hank was visiting that day and brought Nichols along with him for the ride. My dear ol' uncle had dropped by to see his sister, I guess. He was there when I stormed past, sitting at the foot of Dad's chair, talking about something, I guess. I didn't pay much attention. I snatched my Daisy BB gun, a lever action with a full load. I just wanted out, and out I got.

I cocked the gun into action. I was not exactly crazy about Nichols being here, but he had sense enough to keep his mouth shut. I stood there, midway across the field, the dead, gray grass matted to the earth, and the innocent songbird in the V of my sights, my finger resting on the trigger, ready to kill.

My finger was on the trigger, ready to shoot, and ready to kill. I saw its little gray and white head, and the little black-dot eyes looking this way and that; and I thought to myself, this is just like killing myself. Then suddenly the clouds parted in a most dramatic way, like when Mother used to watch "The Guiding Light" on TV. The light poured down upon me, a beam from above. It was one of those rare moments when the dismal weather gave itself one last heave toward Indian summer, a brief release of raw sunshine. I put the gun down and looked off in the distance. There were three of them, Jeno and her brother, Martin, and of course Eli. I saw her and I know that at that moment she saw me too. It was at that particular moment that our paths crossed. I decided to spare the birds.

"Aw, what'd ya do that for?" Nichols said, after I put the gun down. "You had 'em."

I looked at him, the poor pathetic little fucker with the butch-cut hair and the gray sweatshirt pulled hopelessly over the pear-shaped body.

"Maybe I should shoot you instead," I said and pointed the gun at his head and laughed.

He began to tremble and sob. "Aw, don't do that, Bird." I let him tag along as I approached the others. By this time, Martin and Eli had also noticed my approach. I sauntered up to them, she with her pigtails and braces, and her brothers with their flattops, square faces, and black-dot eyes. It was a bold, awful, and unexplainable moment.

I cocked the gun and pointed it at her. "I want you to undress." It was then that I tasted it right along with her, that same peculiar swelling of the throat and awful taste of lead that Gregory Peck must have felt when he pursued "The Bravados." Like I said before, movies can make a difference. I had seen the previews just the other night. That's what I was, a bravado.

Then Jeno turned to me and said, "Is that why you did it? Because of a movie?"

"I don't know. There was probably more to it than that, but it had to have something to do with it, ya think?"

One thing was certain, though. I had screwed myself good that morning. I tried for damage control, but there was no going back. You cannot change history, and history had been created. "Not really," I quickly said to them. "Only kidding." How often would it be like that for me—"not really, only kidding"— crossing the river Styx midway, and then trying to reverse my course. Not this time.

The two of them, Martin and Jeno, stood up, quickly brushing the pink sand from their hands and knees. Only Eli remained, still sitting.

"We will be right back," Martin said. The two little dark raisins for eyes had become exclamation points. Both children put their shovels into their gaily painted buckets and took off.

I yelled after them, "Look, I'm really sorry. I didn't mean it." The other feeling was coming over me, the antidote of niceness. I felt the catch between the two worlds, the nice and the ugly. Forever I would know them, until I grew tired of it all.

"We'll be right back," Martin called back to me. "We just have to go home for a minute." As If I should believe them. Already they were shrinking into the future and the past. They would be gone if it weren't for Eli, who was still sitting there on the ground looking at me. He was in no hurry to leave, not yet anyway.

"I'm sorry!" I yelled. My words echoed back to me from the brick walls of the nearby schoolyard. It was too late for me. I was condemned. Eli knew it, as he looked up at me.

Martin came back and took his brother's hand and forced him up, brushing the pink sand off his bib overalls. "We'll be right back," he said again. This time they all joined hands and as they ran away. There were three of them, yet they seemed as one.

"I didn't mean it! Honest I didn't!" They disappeared around the corner of the old school. "I'm sorry. I am truly very sorry for all that I have done."

I was alone. Even Nichols had fled the scene. I stood alone beneath the maples, their bare limbs empty of leaves.

"Eli," I whispered. "Eli, you understood, didn't you. You didn't condemn."

"You poor, poor thing," Jeno said to me. "You have always been so nice to everyone ever since—too nice." We had our eyes closed in a perfect two-part harmony and I didn't feel much like talking anymore. Thunder was in the air and lightning filled the room, only to quickly disappear.

"Most of the time."

She rolled over on top of me and bathed my wounds.

It was finished.

Sargo

That particular Halloween me and Jinx decided to sneak over the Sargo Fence, a wrought iron, spike-tipped structure that ran along the backside of Grannie Grumble's place. Now Jinx was a real chicken about doing this, and I had my own private reasons for being afraid; but mine were different than his. Jinx was afraid of the dark, plain and simple. I wasn't going to tell him or anyone else about my reasons, though I bet it was buried somewhere in the back of Jinx's mind. It had to be after that embarrassing incident, the one we never spoke about, outside the gym last spring, when everyone was inside playing monkey ball on the basketball court and we were standing outside alone for those few moments. It was one of those things you would carry inside forever and never forget.

We called the fence the Sargo Fence because Sargo was the inscription that was on it in several places. We thought it might have been an old fence maker's name, stamped on along the supporting bars, but then I also saw the same name painted over two or three times on the front gable of the house, way up high in the center peak. I wouldn't have seen it then, either, if I hadn't climbed one of the maples along Grannie's house during a game of hide and seek. Somebody said Sargo was Grannie's maiden name or one of her earlier names from a previous marriage. You couldn't be sure of anything in a town like Blackwood. Gossip was a way of life.

Climbing over the fence was my idea, actually. We were playing Capture the Flag and the fence marked the boundary of a large lot where the action was taking place. We had sneaked across enemy lines. The others were behind us now laughing and carrying on. Their footsteps were heavy on the earth. The honeysuckle and ivy stood out in the moonlight against the wrought, dry and purple, and Jinx had his face between the bars. He had shiny black hair and a winning smile, like one of those game show hosts, and the moon made the part a straight blue line.

I said to Jinx, "Let's go. Nobody would ever find us over there."

"It's not about finding us, it's about finding the flag."

"Come on, I dare ya."

"No, I double dare you," he sassed back at me.

I punched him playfully on the arm. He was son of the preacher man, Reverend Terry, a Methodist man. He needed a little roughing up.

"You're scared, aren't you? You little punk, you're scared. I can see it in your eyes."

Jinx was a scaredy-cat. We both knew that. I had made him pee his pants more than once in the dark alleyways.

Then I said to him, "What's the big deal? This ain't Minnie Ha-Ha's place."

Minnie-Ha-Ha's place was actually Minnie Wells' place, across the street from Grannie's. She was an Indian woman, least that was what Grannie said. Grannie told us all this stuff about her, that she was a bootlegger and that she poisoned cats. She didn't come right out and say she was a witch, but me and Jinx could put two and two together. So we smoked her out last summer. She could have been a witch, judging by her house, big as it was with those gabled rooftops and open courtyards that weren't so open anymore with all of the overgrown grass and bushes, since husband Buddy had passed away. But when we peeked through the window all we saw was Minnie surrounded by her fifteen or so cats, and she was playing the violin all alone in the center of the room and crying. Minnie wasn't a witch and she certainly wasn't a bootlegger. Minnie was just old and heart-broken. There wasn't anything wrong with Minnie other than the usual human condition. I had cut her lawn on more than one occasion, and she always came out and gave me a cool glass of lemonade and paid me a dollar and a half, when all the others would only give a dollar.

I boosted Jinx first, pushing him over from behind with my head and shoulders. It was at the top where the wrought bars came to a sharp point that got him in trouble, catching his shirt and scraping his side enough so to leave red stripes on him. He started to cry and whimper, and I hissed at him, "Don't start none of that now, you little girl, or the others will hear and get the flag for sure." What else could you expect from a preacher's son? I tried to free up his shirt, but it ended up tearing free from the weight of him hanging and I heard him drop off on the other side with a soft thud.

There was nothing to be scared of. This was Grannie Grumble's place. She always gave us kids cookies and milk on our way to and from school. She was a sweet little old lady with her Jimmie Durante nose and button eyes. Grannie was all right. She sometimes talked a little nonsense about the signs in the sky and the end of the world, and she was strict about liquor and drinking of any kind. I must admit, though, I had never had seen this backside of her place with its tall grass and apple trees with the moon peeking through the clouds.

We stood shoulder deep in wet grass in the middle of what appeared to be an apple field. We could no longer see or hear the others. The long field was completely blocked by the dense covering of the fence. We could hear the others with their high pitched giggles and their hurried footsteps as they pursued their make believe captors on the other side, but they seemed far away. We were completely sealed off from them. The old oak tree squeaked and groaned a little in the breeze.

"Let's leave the flag right here," Jinx whispered. "They will never find it."

Grannie's house was only a short distance. It was tall with gabled peaks silhouetted in the night above. The moonlight poured down through the maples and willows.

"Not so fast, " I said. "We didn't come all this way for nothing."

"I want to go home," Jinx said.

I was trying to get the picture of where I was. This was the second house from the corner on the way to school. I couldn't get a sense of the boundaries. The soft blue landscape went on and on. The only boundary was the immense dominance of the house.

"Let's look around a bit."

I steadied Jinx's arm.

"Come on."

"Why are we whispering?" Jinx asked.

That didn't deserve an answer. I doubled up to hit his arm again, this time real hard, but held back at the last minute.

We began creeping along the wrought iron toward the house, which loomed up in the moonlight .

I counted my steps. At seventy-seven the foliage and overgrowth became thicker. My hands began to itch. At ninety there was a wall of thorns . "Let me see your jackknife." I said .

"Let's go home," Jinx began to whimper a little.

"Come on. Let me have the knife."

The thorns grew on finger size vines, which were stringy and tough to cut. A thick oozy fluid ran from the punctured ones and got on my hands. I smelled my hands. Nothing. Slowly, I produced a tunnel sized hole.

We slipped through and now stood ankle deep in fallen leaves in what appeared to be a large, spacious backyard. The moon hung in the sky, wide open. There were a few small buildings, leftovers of what had probably been a stable. To my right stood the remains of a tennis court, distinguishable now only by the iron poles, which at one time held the net.

Jinx started to pull away from my grip.

"Just a minute." I pulled him closer. "Look at that over next to the house. Right below the window. On the ground. You see that?"

"What about it? It's just the moonlight."

"It's more than moonlight."

Along the bottom of the house, running in a line about six feet long, a soft blue-green light shone, more of a glow really.

"Are you sure? I never saw moonlight like that before."

"I don't know," Jinx said, "but I've had enough of this place. I'm getting out of here."

I pulled him in tighter. I crushed him. "Not now."

I inched forward. We moved along the wall, our back up against it, and the old peeling paint was rough and scratchy against my cheek. Up ahead, the house made a sharp ninety degree turn to the right. If my calculations were correct, we stood next to the kitchen area.

A dim light suddenly went on inside the kitchen. We flattened ourselves up against the wall. Jinx was about to start crying. I put one hand over his mouth pulling his face against my throat.

"Shhh. Don't you cry now." I brushed the hair back up out of his eyes. It was an unusual sort of light because it did not stay on for more than a minute, and it had a wobbly sort of texture to it, as if someone had struck a match, or lit a candle.

We were standing in the blue-green light that he had seen a minute earlier. I knelt down. They were tiny plants of some sort, blossoming in the moonlight.

The same dim, flickering light came on within the recesses of the kitchen.

This time I was ready. I pressed my body flat along the side of the house and inched up to the window and peered in.

What I saw only lasted a few seconds. There stood Grannie by her wood stove feeding the coals of a long stemmed corn cob pipe, the old fashioned kind that they used in story books. In those few seconds I saw how she attended to the pipe, taking short quick puffs, and how the red eye of the coal glowed like some sort of jewel; and Grannie's hair. How long it was, hanging straight down to her mid-back. Always in the public's eye she kept it pinned up in a bun; but now her teeth were out and her mouth caved in about the pipe's stem, and I saw how big and protruding her nose seemed. How small and intense her eyes were, as they fixed in on the red coal, which now was the only thing that could be seen as the match died out—and once again the darkness surrounded everything.

"Jinx, you're not going to believe this. Grannie Grumble is smoking."

"No way.

I still had him in my grip, but he tried to break away to get his own look, but he lost his footing and fell down into the glowing grass.

"Get up. Get up!" I pulled him to his feet and pressed him against the wall.

"I want to go home," he started saying, louder and louder. Then he started coughing. "I stink," he said. I smelled his shirt, where he had fallen in the plants. It had a strong skunky odor to it, except it wasn't a skunk smell exactly, more of an old, funky mothball smell. Strong too.

Now he really started sobbing. "Sssh," I kept telling him, but it didn't do any good. So I put my mouth over his, just like I had done before. I held my mouth on his and he stopped crying, but he was still breathing hard. We stayed like that for a minute, until he threw me aside. He was pointing at the window. Then we both saw it, her face pressed up against the window. They looked almost like doll eyes, made of buttons. The long-hanging hair, was mostly dark with some gray tones, and she was baring a large, toothless grin.

This time it was me who lost my balance, and I fell down into the strange glowing flowers. This time I smelled them, too—the stinky, rotten smell—and I felt it, too, all over my body.

"What's a matter?" Jinx hissed.

There was no time for answering. I was on my feet and running toward the little tunnel of thorns, crawling through with sharp points tearing at me and making me bleed. Then we were running through the tall grass, which was wet and heavy now from the evening dew. Then it was up and over the wrought iron. Jinx was having some trouble getting over. "It won't let go," he cried. He was kicking his leg as if trying to break free.

"It's o.k." I got out my knife and hacked at the vine until Jinx dropped like an eighty pound sack of potatoes on the earth.

That night, I lay awake on the second floor of the stone house. There were pictures on the wall of me and my family, and others of me playing baseball. There were all these pictures that I couldn't look at anymore and I knew I wouldn't get any sleep that night. In the morning I would put on my best face and eat breakfast with Mom and Dad and go off on my merry way to school and be the tough guy.

The moonlight poured in the room and then something occurred to me.

I sat upright in bed. "We forgot the flag."

The moonlight pressed against the curtains. I pulled them apart and let the blue light flood the room.

And then I saw it and the cramps hit my stomach. I pressed my face against the cold glass for a better look.

How could it be? There on his window sill was the flag.

Nature's Way

Barkley is leading me through the wet ferns, parting them neatly —just like his hair on the right side—and taking me to the woods. His shorts have taken the darker color of olive, from the dampness where the ferns have touched him, on the hips and between his thighs. We have left Mr. Wells, our scoutmaster, and all of the others behind. Barkley had insisted that I go with him and Mr. Wells said okay. Barkley pretty much gets his way with him and even gets to call him Chucky. Of course Barkley is almost an Eagle and gets certain privileges over the rest of us.

At the edge of the woods, he stops and ties his first sign to one of the trees. He uses a nylon rope and makes a perfect square knot, so as not to the hurt the tree. The sign is an arrow fashioned out of plywood with red letters neatly painted across the front of it that reads "Nature's Way (trail)." Then he drives a shorter stake into the ground with a sign on it that reads "Bracken Fern *(Pteridium aquilinum)*."

We are supposed to be working on our merit badges, him on botany and me on cooking. We will blaze a trail through the woods to Talley Lake, where I will cook lunch, but we also have other designs in mind. I still have the half pack of Winston's crushed up in my front pocket. They are a little kinked up but still smokable.

We march along in single file, moving in and around the trees. He carries a walking stick that he snatched up from a pile of makeshift tent poles before we left the campsite. Our busy footsteps make chuffing noises against the soft forest floor. A light rain taps against the canopy overhead. His tee shirt glows in the semidarkness, but not as much as the stump of his neck, rising up out of it, red and blood-swollen.

We make intermittent stops along the way, as Barkley is busy tagging sugar maples, hemlock, basswood, and white pine, as well as the forest floor, marking lilies and mayflowers.

He runs his hand along the carpet of yellow and purple. "Another two weeks and these will be gone." He steps over a log to mark the spot, when the hissing throttles me—like air stealing out of a tire. It stops me up, first in my chest and then spreads in opposite directions to everywhere. My stomach sends up a protest and I taste something acid in the back of my throat.

"Snakes alive!" he says, taking a step back so that I run into him.

Our eyes fasten to the head, two inches wide, flat, and rising in a perfect string a foot and a half from the ground, where the other half lies coiled.

I think it's a cobra, but Barkley assures me, "That ain't no cobra," and gives his cackle-laugh, his neck going a sudden cherry-neon color. He takes his walking stick and pokes at the snake. "That's a hognose. Give him another minute and he'll go limp." He gives out another cackle and his neck begins to glow.

"Do you get it?" he says. "He'll go limp."

I don't get it, not yet anyway. But he sure isn't lying either. When it comes to the woods, Barkley knows more than most. The snake has lost its attitude. It curls up on his back, just like he said it would, rolling itself up like pretzel dough, its tail twitching back and forth, showing its pale underside.

"No different than people. First it's king of the hill and now it's Mr. Downtrodden."

I don't know what downtrodden is, but I get the picture. He has snagged it with his walking stick and is holding it up in the air. It falls off the stick and lies motionless on the ground.

"And now it plays dead." He lifts one foot and puts the heel of his boot on its head, as if he's about to crush it.

"I will make you hate this snake, Birdie," he says to me.

Sometimes Barkley talks so weird.

"Leave it alone," I say to him. There is more than a little pleading in my voice.

He cackles and crows again, and then steps away.

"Yeah. I don't know about you, but I'm getting a little hungry."

"Let's have a smoke first," I say.

We move on until we're in a stand of tall birches right up next to the lake. I move my hand up and down the tender bark of one tree and feel the white powdery residue on my palm. Across the lake, the smoke from the others rises up and hangs in a long finger along the shore. The water is a smooth sheet of dark gray to match the sky, except for a million little circles radiating out from the rain, which won't quite go away. We decide to make our own smoke. I light mine first and Barkley caps his off the end of mine. We sit there for a while and just puff away. I feel that stale taste in my mouth that cigs always give me, and I think less about the food.

Barkley smokes his cigarette like the English do on those old worn out movies I sometimes see on TV. He holds it down low in the wedge of his forefinger and middle finger, and brings it up to his mouth with his fingers straight up, clamped over his lips and nose. He smokes like this in a careful way, letting the ash get very long, before he taps it off in the cup of his hand. He also likes to French-inhale, drawing the smoke up in two silky threads through his nose.

The rain has let up for now. Barkley pulls out his transistor radio from his shirt pocket. It's a beauty. On certain nights after taps had sounded at the campsite and we're supposed to be in our sleeping bags, he would invite me and my friends over to his tent to secretly listen to Dick Biondi on WLS. Now he squelches through the channels, but there is too much static for anything.

"I got a better idea, Birdie," he says. "Let's go for a swim."

I didn't bring my suit, I want to say, but I don't. "What about the meat?"

"What about it?"

"It might spoil. I don't want to get sick." They had told us all about that in the merit badge class. We have a simple meal plan. Hamburger, carrots, potatoes, and onions, all rolled up in foil and placed on the side of a low-burning fire. We should start gathering the wood.

He says, "Don't worry about your meat. I got your meat handled."

He stands up and peels his shirt and begins unlacing his boots, kicking one off, then the other. Me, I don't really feel like a swim. It's too cold and overcast, but I would never say this. Even at that young age, I am eager to please.

"Besides," he says, "the water will be warmer than the land."

But I'm not cold, I want to say. I'm not cold at all. Instead, I stand up and begin peeling down. The water does look kind of inviting, all silvery beneath the cloud cover, like liquid mercury.

Barkley is completely stripped and standing there waiting for me. I feel more than a little self-conscious. I am down to my underwear. We are the same age, twelve, and I have only a little fuzz on my balls, showing on either side. You have to be in the direct sunlight to see it.

His dick is man sized, bigger than my father's, hanging down red and swollen looking, same color as his neck. He has plenty of hair too—a whole crop of it, in fact, reddish blond colored, to match the hair on his head.

The time for exposure has come and I kick off my undies. My dick is a coiled spring sitting atop a taunt set of practically hairless twelve-year-old balls.

I look at Barkley, but he isn't paying any attention to me, thank goodness. A family of ducks, a mother followed by four little ones, swim by in single file.

I am ready to get this over with. We walk down to the edge of the water. He goes straight in without any hesitation, until the lake swallows him up, dick and all. Once he is in to his waist, he takes a careful dive forward, dividing the water smoothly, not submerging his head at first, until he swims a few strokes. He dips down beneath and disappears for a good twenty seconds—until he finally emerges, spouting water like a whale. Barkley crawls out for another twenty strokes or so, and rolls over on his back, spitting water up in a straight line. He waves at me and lets out a whoop. His voice echoes off the cove.

Me, I'm Mr. Chicken Shit. I tippy-toe around first, one toe in, and one toe out; first the ankles, then the knees, slowly inching up to the private parts, which I cannot stand to submerge slowly. Instead I dive forward, going fully beneath to the silty underworld, where everything is blurred and the muck scrapes against my chest and belly—as I move out to the deeper, darker sections, holding my breath until my head begins to pound.

I am the first one out of the water. My teeth are already chattering. I go to my pile of clothes and begin putting on my underwear. Meanwhile Barkley has emerged. I am surprised that he has half a hard on, his dick pointing at three o'clock.

He acts as if nothing has changed. The water has beaded up on his chest and steam pours off him. By this time I have my pants on. It wasn't easy getting them up over my wet ass.

Barkley, however, is in no apparent hurry to get dressed. He grabs a cigarette from the pack, which is still lying there on the ground, and lights up. Then he begins gathering kindling for a fire. He moves around in a carefree manner, like one of those people at a nudist colony, except that his dick seems to be getting bigger, like he's threatening to have a full fledged boner or something.

Pretty soon he has a fire snapping and hissing. I am content to let him do all the work, though it is my merit badge I'm supposed to be earning.

He spreads his tee shirt out on the ground and takes a seat next to me. "You know," he says, "we have a lot of fun out on the farm where I live. You should come out some time."

"Yah, I should," I say, but not really meaning it, but just saying it to go along with the conversation.

"We have a really good time out there."

"I bet you do." I am thinking about horses, cows, pigs, and haylofts in old barns with ropes tied to the rafters and endless tunnels beneath the bales of hay. I am thinking about hens and roosters in the barnyard and the smell of manure.

He looks at me. His neck and face are taking on color again. "You know we actually screw out there."

Now screwing is one topic I know about, though not firsthand. Not yet anyway. But I'm not about to let him know that, so I keep my game face.

So I say, "Oh yah, who's that?"

Now his face gets really red. "Each other."

"Each other?"

"Each other. You should try it some time. You wouldn't believe how good it feels."

"Try what?"

He drags on his smoke and French inhales. "Screwing. Or getting screwed."

Even though he is smoking, I catch a whiff of that same smell on his breath that I'd caught before. The same kind of smell I'd get from my brothers, the smell of bad air, if we had been closed up in a room too long, the smell of flu and stuffiness. He is leaning over close to me and I can see that he is diddling with his pecker, which has gone fully hard like a large cigar.

"Let's eat," I say.

"In a minute."

I'm afraid to look down at his hand, but I do anyway.

"You should try it, Birdie," he says. "I bet you'd like it. I bet you'd never forget it."

He reaches over and takes my hand and puts it on his prick, but I recoil. It is a reflex.

"I'm sorry," I say. My voice is a whisper.

"You'd better get that food in the fire," he says.

I do exactly as I am told.

Legends

The word was spreading fast. "Moose Conlin's back in town."

Cecil was the first person I saw standing there on Conway Bridge, so I told him before it became old news.

"Are you sure?"

"Sure, I'm sure."

Cecil let fly a straight, even shot of spit from between his two teeth, and sent it down into the black waters that came churning up from beneath the power plant. Even from where we stood on the outside, you could still hear the hum of those generators. If you looked in through the large windows, you could see those black belts turning and crossing each other in the infinity sign, and then disappearing back into their gray, circular housings.

"But it ain't even summer," Cecil said. "What's he doin' back?"

Moose was a summer resident. One of the few that was okay with us. Every June, he would come and visit his grandpa on the farm and stay through August.

"He lives here now," I told Cecil.

"He does? Well I'll be, and it ain't even summer."

All of my friends and everybody I knew, including my older brother C.P. respected Moose. Nobody gave him any lip. There was only one exception to the rule. Only Ginger Griff ever dared to speak in any way disparagingly about the Moose. I never told anybody what Ginger told me when he was good and drunk. He said he had found a weakness in Moose, and it had to do with water, and that is all I am going to say, for now. It never pays to badmouth a legend.

Cecil was only partly right about it not being summer, but that was another thing I was keeping quiet about. I sure wasn't going to be the one to correct him. He was one of those older boys that would knuckle you if you gave him any lip, though I was just as big as him. It was almost summer. Close enough to be considered the early beginnings. The mushroom season was over. Mother had picked the last of the whites last week. The mosquitoes were beginning to buzz, and I even heard a June bug clunk against the screen outside my window the night before.

"Moose has got a list of people to get things straight with, and word has it that Link's first on it," I said.

"Link's on the list?" I knew Cecil had the heard the story, but I acted dumb and let him play me.

Cecil pulled a Pall Mall from the shoulder of his rolled up tee shirt. "Must be from that last time Moose was here. Link hurt him real bad. Damn near blinded him. Almost scratched his eyes out and then he kicked him in the balls."

That story had become part of the legend. Moose was only in the eighth grade at the time. Link was a man, a full grown man, one of these guys where there wasn't a tee shirt in the world made large enough to cover him; yet he always wore them, exposing those rolls of fat around his mid section. He had these fleshy, cherry-red lips that he was always puckering, and licking, as though he were some kind of reptile, and these little beady eyes rolling around in his head. One time I saw him eat a dozen eggs at one sitting. He was drunk of course. No sober man would ever do that. He fried them up and poured ketchup all over the plate and ate them straight down. He was a dirty player, Link was.

"I just can't figure it," Cecil said. "What's Moose Conlin doin' back?"

"His whole family's back. His dad's working up at Cedar Meadows." Cedar Meadows was the new, plush resort complex, a work in progress, located up on the eastern hills overlooking all the lakes and Grand Bay. Everybody in town had heard about how Belle Llewellyn had taken over her own father's bank and financed the deal.

"There's supposed to be a big gatherin' tonight at The Sand Bar," I continued. "Somethin's supposed to be happenin'."

"I'll be there," Cecil said.

"Wish I could."

"Why can't ya?"

I wasn't about to tell him that I had a curfew. So I told him I had to help my dad with some work around the house, which was a flat out lie. I felt stupid after saying it, but there was nothing I could do about it now.

"Aw, that's too bad." Cecil was being real smart mouthed with me, but there was nothing I could do about that either. He was a legend too, but not of the caliber of Moose.

Cecil sent another straight line out; this one hitting dead center into one of those little black-eyed whirlpools.

I knew I had to be out at The Sand Bar, no matter what. If Moose was going to meet Link and set things straight, I wanted to witness it firsthand. But I had my work cut out for me. Being twelve is a terrible age. Too old to stay in and too young to go out. But I had my ways. I told Mother I had a Boy Scouts meeting down at Reverend Terry's house, and she let me out for a couple of hours.

I knew the only way to get there was the hard way. None of the big boys would lower themselves to pick me up for the cruise out there. My own brother, Alfie, was going, but there was no way he would give me a ride. So I hopped on my bike and started pedaling. It was a brand new bike Mom had just bought for me at the Gambles Hardware in Barcelona. It was a nice new Columbia, red and shiny. It was a six-mile ride to The Sand Bar, and I knew I had to pass the cemetery on my way out there. I still had a half hour of daylight. If I hurried I could make it past the graveyard before dark. I'd worry about the ride home later.

I had my reasons for not liking the graveyard, more than the obvious ones. They had just buried Grandpa a few years back. The memory was still fresh. Died with his fists clenched, watching ringside wrestling on a Friday night up at the stone house. After that, I wasn't real fond of cemeteries. That was the one place I didn't want to be.

There wasn't much traffic on the little country road, and whenever a car came from behind me, I was sure to get well off to the side and let it pass. Pretty soon I made it to the big hill overlooking Stone Lake. I kept on peddling, zooming down the long, winding curve, straight past the cemetery, not looking to either side of the road, but keeping my eyes straight ahead until I got to the narrow strip of road called Stone Lake Drive, where all the rich summer people lived, and the maples and pines hung low and thick on either side of the road.

I pumped away, slumped over the bars, knees working furiously. I wanted to make the two-mile section before any cars passed. By then the sun had settled, and darkness was claiming the air. It was a quiet night and I had a chance. I didn't look to either side, but I knew the woods were there watching and waiting. I had a couple of aunts and uncles from my mother's side who lived out here. Bought the land before the prices went sky high and then refused to sell. I could stop there, I thought, if anything went really wrong, if anything tried to get me. As I passed their homes, I saw that they were dark. I wondered why old people went to bed so early. All of that thinking got me through that dark stretch of highway. Pretty soon I was at the little light that hung suspended over the intersection that led to The Sand Bar. I stashed my bike down by the deserted beach and looked around. Not much happening. There were only a few cars parked outside, and I didn't recognize any of them.

Now The Sand Bar had always been pretty good to us locals. It wasn't that long ago that Olie, the owner, had been a hell raiser himself. So he had become pretty friendly with all of us and let us go out there and shoot pool on a table, as long as we were far enough removed from the bar to make everything legit. It was one of the places everyone went to if they got real bored on a school night.

I sat around next to the docks for a while, out of plain sight, but close enough to see anything. I was hoping that I hadn't come all this way for nothing, when all of a sudden about three cars pulled up, making the dust fly. I recognized them. They were local boys, Cecil, Earl, Floyd, Nick, and Alfie, and then out from behind the shadows stepped Moose. I hadn't seen him in three years and he looked even bigger than I'd imagined. He wore this white short-sleeved shirt with the sleeves rolled up and the tails out over his jeans. He was big and heavyset in the shoulders. His blond hair always had that just combed look, as if he had just splashed some water on and parted it. His face was blocky and square looking, with a trace of puffiness about the eyes. But it was his hands I'll never forget. They were large and heavy, with these chunky red knuckles. He was only sixteen but he could have passed for twenty-five.

I could hear them talking and laughing, as they stood around smoking and listening to WLS on the radio.

Just then I heard the screen door slam at The Sand Bar. I was expecting to see Link coming through those doors with his sloppy, shackled-down pants and big belly, but this was even better. Link couldn't compare to the legends I saw ambling out into the night air. It was Leo Draper, Roderick Joseph, and Jack Tanner. It was hard to believe that so many legends could step out of one place at one time. Leo was known up Kaskie-way. Roderick was known in Iron Town and Jack was from Smith Crick. Legends from three different towns. These boys had always been feuding over territory for as long as I could remember and it seemed strange to see them all together, talking and laughing as if they were the best of friends.

Then Moose came walking over. He made it look real casual. Alfie and the others followed along behind him. Tanner drove this real sweet sixty Chevy with chrome hubs that had spiders in the center. He was just opening up the door and the others were getting in. I could see the car hunker down as each one of those big bodies hit the seat. Jack happened to look up and saw Moose standing there. I don't think he knew him.

"You reckon you boys could have a little talk?" Moose said. Jack was a big one too, a long lean machine in a black tee shirt and slicked back red hair that he combed in a DA.

"Who the hell are you?"

Moose had a toothpick in his mouth and he looked back at the others smiled. They were standing off at a distance because they weren't exactly sure what was going to happen, and also, no doubt, because they were a little chicken. They knew about Jack Tanner, Leo Draper, and Roderick Joseph.

By this time the other two had piled out of the car, and that sixty Chevy had gotten a little taller from all of that released weight. Now they all stood there looking at the Moose, not quite believing what they saw.

Moose slowly unbuttoned his shirt and tossed it over to Cecil. My, he was a big one. More than anything, it was those shoulders and arms, and that gut that told the story. It wasn't a fat gut. It hung out there and complimented his chest, something like a gorilla's, or one of those Buddha statues. He doubled up one of those triple-decker fists, and began softly punching his other open palm, and rubbing the knuckles in. Then he said, "Which one a you wants it first?"

Every legend has his moments, when they say certain things that go down in history, and this was one of them. I could feel it.

There was a short silence, a gathering before the storm, and then before any of the three of them could think of anything to say, Moose was at the door where Jack Tanner stood, and I saw one of those triple-deckers fly. The whole thing was so fast. That's why he made such a name for himself on the football field too, because of the way he could move for such a big man. There's a sound that a watermelon makes when it is big and ripe and you break it open. That's the sound that Jack's jaw made when Moose hit it. Blood flew all over, and Jack hit the dirty parking lot floor, holding his face and rolling over and over, till he was right up next to me, where I hid in the bushes. He didn't get up right away.

Then Moose scrambled over the top of the car and he was after Leo Draper. It was just like in the movies, the way he did it. He leaped up on his belly, and then rolled over. That quick, and he was on the other side.

Now Leo was another matter. Nobody knew for sure how old he was. Some say he was in his twenties and others say older, like thirty or something. He was a big block of a man, husky, with blond hair he wore in a flat top. Big, dumb, and mean: That was Leo. He had been known to clean out whole bars on Saturday nights when the liquor had sufficiently gotten to him, but he was no match for this force of nature.

This was where Moose really got his trademark, because he bear-hugged old Leo. Speed was the key. Leo never had a chance to react. Moose threw him on the trunk, where another solid hit from the triple-decks to the kidneys sent him rolling on the ground. Then Moose was on him, rolling him over like a calf at the rodeo. He held him down by the nap of the neck, and began Charlie-horsing his thighs. I'll never forget the way he doubled up one of his fists, protruding the center knuckle out, and then delivering a series of blows, short, and in rapid successions, over and over, like a jackhammer. First one thigh, then the other. Back and forth. Pretty soon Leo began to beg him to stop, but Moose wouldn't stop until that full-grown man broke down and began bawling like a baby. That's the way he left him. All doubled up, unable to walk, and bawling.

So what about Roderick Joseph during all of this? Now here was another legend. He was known for his peg leg and his brute strength. An ironworker from over near Smelt River. A crazy man who drank beer and ate the glass bottle when he was finished.

Old Rod was nowhere to be seen. He began running as best he could on that peg leg. Moose looked around for him and saw him rounding the corner up the road a way, tap shoeing along. Moose broke out in a sprint after him. It was amazing to see that much speed. We watched him disappear around the corner, and in a few minutes he came back with old Roderick in a hammerlock up to the back of his head.

By this time the others were gathering themselves up, and Moose was still out of breath, coughing and hacking all this stuff up from his lungs, his chest heaving up and down, and the sweat standing out on his head. He could barely talk. "Now, if I catch any of yas back in this end of the county again, this will only be a samplin', ya understand?"

That's when Moose looked over and saw me hiding in the bushes and he winked at me, and I know he saw my brand new bike, lying there on its side with the neon lights beaming off all that chrome. He would later claim that bike for himself at will whenever he saw me and had a mind to. That was fine for now. Legends enjoyed certain rights over others. He was only four years older than me, but he could have been my father, or even my oldest brother. Four years had nothing to do with the vast spaces that lay between us.

I peddled home through the darkness. I pumped my hardest. I was two hours late but I didn't care. The wind stirred through the maples and I could hear the pines along Stone Lake Drive. A skunk crossed the road and I nearly hit it. I passed the graveyard without any concern. I would pay any price. I had no fears. "They never die," I told myself. "They live on and on." I had witnessed a part of history, and now I had my legends to protect me.

The Big House

This is no prison I'm talking about—not *that* big house—although it was connected to the penal system, since the owner, the honorable Judge Harry W. Bradford lived there along with his six sirenic daughters, of which Nora was one. No sir. This is the *other* big house—the big cheese, the numeral uno, the B-F'n-D, the biggest house in Blackwood. A Greek revivalist, it was, with columned porches and two story sash windows and dormers. The judge's six daughters came from two different marriages brought together by the three D's of courtship: death, desire, and divorce. And such fine daughters they were. All of the them taking after their respective mother in one manner or another. Although it was the middle daughter, Nora, who would wound my heart, and make me cry out in anguish for one of two times in my life.

Nora, with her bad allergies, dark temperament and long legs. Nora, who had appeared one day to sit in front of me in fourth grade—second time around, already showing the promise of a future beauty far beyond my grasp, or any of the other farm boys in that classroom on that particular fall day in 1958.

Mrs. Godfrey, our fourth grade teacher, a large, somewhat brusque, but affable woman, promptly introduced her to the class. "Class, we have a new member today. Her name is Nora...Nora..."

"Pembroke," the new girl answered with that same piercing smile that would later become the stamp of approval upon my heart.

Which was it that had drawn me to her first? Was it the fine, fashionable clothes she wore? The delicate gold chains around her narrow wrists? These set her apart, no doubt, and drew the scorn and attention of Betty, Lizzie, Nina, Gayle and Trish, the class queens. For we were a group of wild horses galloping the hillsides during recess until the bell would bring us in with flushed faces and beating hearts.

But dear Nora would not participate. Her allergies would not allow it. It was then that I began to discover my real attraction to her, as I saw her sitting alone beneath the cool shade of the maple, staring dreamily off into the distance while the rest of us galloped like ninnies up and down the side of the hill. I sensed her melancholy humor, the bad bile gathering upon the brain. I knew we were somehow connected, secret comrades in despair.

I can remember on certain days her leaving the classroom in tears, crushed by something, some inexplicable factor in her life that we were not privileged to know—triggered unexpectedly by who knows what. Maybe it was the harsh tone in the teacher's voice, or the way the clouds would suddenly cover the sun, or a jeering laugh by some thick-handed farm boy. We were a coarse, vulgar lot, and we sensed the growing form beneath her soft sweater, as could Lizzie, Nina, Gayle and Trish, who made it a point to treat Nora coldly.

She was taller than most of us, and her fine hair with its reddish highlights curled down in a sensuous S around her ear and milky throat. She had that kind of exquisitely white skin that would be perfectly punctuated at places with a tiny mole, not unsightly. Quite to the contrary, it was more a mark of beauty.

How I wanted to take her in my arms even then, and to hold her, stroke her hair and sooth her. "Now, Nora," I would have said. "Don't cry," holding her soft hair next to my ear until her broken breathing became steady and calm.

She had her bright days, days when her pent up spirit would break free and spill out onto the world, and her laughter would rack against her congested lungs, bringing up the bad bile and phlegm from her system. She would hold the handkerchief to her mouth. "Sorry," she would say.

"That's all right," I would tell her. Nothing she could have said or done would have spoiled the appearance of her smiling and lifting the dark veil that seemed to cling to her.

I knew for reasons that were yet unclear to me that I could never have her, so one Friday night, I decided to leave my mark for time eternal. It was during the heat of the basketball game that I pulled out my pocketknife at the balcony of the Community Hall and carved our initials into the wood forever—JD + NP

A little later on, we would become friends, though I would never be allowed into her inner most confidences. There were a few of us with the same nocturnal inclinations. Nora, myself, Jinx, and Walter. We would venture out in the evening and play ghost and capture the flag, or we would spy on people through their windows, knock and then run away.

Another great nocturnal pastime was searching for haunted houses. There were many that could qualify in Blackwood. Turn of the century, two story Victorians with widow's watches were still quite common. They had to be occupied, we believed, by old women.

I would always bring my grandma's Bible and we would take the oath. All of us would kneel in a solemn ceremonial. I would administer the oath to each. "Do you, Nora Pembroke, solemnly swear to tell the whole truth and nothing but the truth, so help you God?"

"I do."

Each would take it, and then Nora would administer it to me.

"You know," she would say, fixing me with that piercing look, "there really is such a thing as ghosts and witches."

"I know."

"But you don't really know."

"Yes I do."

"Someday I will take you out to my grandma's farm and show you, really show you."

I thought there was something a little frightening in the way she said that, the way I could only see half of her face in the passing shadows of the night, but I acted real brave so no one would know the difference.

Then one evening, it was just Nora and I. "Let's go to your place, John," she coaxed. Nora called me by my real name. I was never just a bird to her.

"To my place?"

"Yes. I want to see where you live. Haven't you ever spied on your parents?"

"No."

"I do it all the time."

"You do?"

"Of course. You ever read Dickens or Mark Twain?"

I began to feel real dumb. Nora was always reading books and talking about them. "No, I haven't," I admitted.

"You haven't? Children are born spies. Wait till you try it."

The stone house where I lived had always been my home and intimate friend. We went up the old school house and swung for a while in the dark.

Then we went over to the tubular fire escape that led down from the second story.

I stuck my head into the dark opening and said "hello." My voice was naturally amplified and echoed. "Want to climb up?"

She laughed. "No, I want to go over to your place."

"There's a way we climb up and get into the school. Want to give it a try?"

"No. Come on, let's stick to the plan."

I looked out across the field to where I knew the stone house was. "O.K." We headed out. Next thing I knew, we were out by the old chicken coop in front of my bedroom. My father had built the stone house back during the Depression. He had gathered the stone from the field. He had put two simple square windows in my bedroom, one over Alfie 's bed and one over mine, facing the south. They were the old fashioned kind on hinges that swung open, each glass being divided into four panes. I always thought they looked like two friendly eyes looking at me from the school. That's where I would see them, from the schoolrooms, smiling across at me to the north, waiting for me to come home.

As we approached, a light came on. It was Mother. We could see her through the open window doing something, folding a shirt, maybe, or darning a sock. The sound of her cough carried. Mother always had this cough. It wasn't a bad cough. It was just always with her.

Nora began to laugh uncontrollably. "What's the matter?" I whispered.

Then she began to sneeze and wheeze because the tall grass. "I've got to get out of here," she managed to say. She sounded bad, but she was still laughing.

"What's so funny?" I began to laugh along with her, though just a little. I thought maybe she was laughing at her own condition. It wasn't really funny.

She sneezed again, this time loudly. I saw Mother stop and look toward the window, out into the black night. Nora was really wheezing by now and still laughing.

We eventually got out of the field and back onto the street, beneath the light, where I could see her. "Are you okay?" I asked. She had stopped laughing and was bent over taking some serious breaths. Then she started laughing again.

"What's so funny?"

"It just your mother," she said. "She looked so funny. The way she dyes her hair and wears that rouge on both cheeks. It just cracks me up."

Then came the season of those fabulous summer nights and the wonderful parties. All of us farm boys gathered together in one of those long, spacious rooms of the big house. There was more room in that one place than my entire house. I looked at the chandelier on the ceiling, the various gilded paintings on the wall, depicting dimpled children in knee breeches and velvet, posing before the artist.

I thought about the stone house in a terribly self conscious way, with its low ceilings and small, dark rooms—the yellowed pine siding Dad had put up, the ducks on the wall—four of them in a row, simulating flight to the north. The picture of the covered wagon with the hostile Indians attacking, the team of horses frothing, the driver hunched forward releasing the reins, and the shotgun doing the impossible task of fending off the force that spotted the countryside with their wildly painted faces.

I looked around at the people sitting in the ornate, carved furniture, and realized that many of them I didn't know. Most were older than I and some had that slick, downstate look. One in particular was Richie Fury, a tall, lean fellow with dark hair that he combed straight back, and a narrow face and large eyes that reminded me of one of those finger paintings of Santa's reindeer I would see in the storefront windows every December. Everybody knew Richie. He always came up every summer with a shiny new car that his old man would buy for him, and he would cruise the streets. He was one of the few resorters that the farm boys didn't bother running out of town. If you were lucky, you would get an invitation from him to go out to his summer cottage on Blackwood Lake and swim and go boating for the day. But what was Richie doing at this party? He ran with a much older crowd.

Then I saw Nora. She had her hair pinned up in the back, with a few strands falling down, accentuating the graceful curve of her neck down to those bare shoulders. She looked so grown up. She was talking to someone else, apparently engaged in the conversation, smiling, shaking her head yes, and laughing a gay, carefree laugh.

I looked at her in a whole new way. I really didn't have a name for it. It could only have happened in a small town in Northern Michigan during the summer of 1962. I would try it again at other places throughout my life, but it would never work like it did back then.

This is how it went. You picked a person out in a crowd. She was beautiful. You took a good look to get that lasting impression, and then you ignored her. It was like a negative in your brain, and then you went on with what you were doing. Maybe you were at the snack table eating chips or drinking punch. Maybe you were carrying on a conversation with someone about the big baseball game. But all the while, you were looking at that negative in your brain. It was like static, crackling and popping off in the distance. You concentrated with all of your psychic forces. You hope against hope that by appearing to be engaged in something else, someone would get the clue that you were hawking.

Not very smart, unless you were at a party at the big house in the summer of 1962.

There was a pause, as a new forty-five dropped onto the pile, and then the perfect record, the Fleetwoods, "Mr. Blue." I could feel the negative; it was crackling and popping away, off in the corner, burning a hole in my brain. But I could feel the words coming to me. They were approaching in a casual walk across the hardwood floors, laying a soft hand on my arm.

"Having fun?"

"It's a great party, Nora," I said in my purest, shyest Northern Michigan farm boy voice.

"I'm bored to death. Come on let's dance."

The sap was rising. It was everywhere. It was in the soft embrace of her hand, the smell of her hair, the smooth transition of her neck to her bare shoulders, and the new, wonderful presence beneath the sundress pressing firmly against my chest. I was a tall, gangly kid with bad posture, and I had to make it even worse out there on the dance floor, or else she might feel it too.

"Stand up straight!" she said to me. "You're slouching."

"I can't help it," I said. "It's my back. I hurt it." Such is the nature of rising sap. It gives you pimples, causes your blood to gather, and makes you slouch, lest someone feel its prod.

She squeezed my hand and moved in a little closer. I let the words of the song run through me. Feet were shuffling against the floor.

The record was over. I was leaning over real bad, with my shirttail out.

"Are you all right?"

"I'll be all right. I just need a little fresh air."

I decided to put a little distance between myself and the others. I walked up the straight line of maples that lined the street. The big house became even more of a spectacle from a distance. The night sat all around it like a huge encapsulating black hat. Leaves hung still in the trees. The rest of the town had already rolled up the sidewalks. Over across the street, Bobby Jo Smith pulled down the shade on the only light in her snug house. I thought about my own curfew. It was always there no matter what I did.

The fresh air did me some good. I walked one time around the court, 'til I felt like I had things under control. I went out to the lone hemlock and stood beneath the umbrage of its cover. It was like a long skirt hanging down, and I stepped inside. I could hear the music playing and people talking and laughing. That's how I will always remember the big house, as being one of those unique small town characters who broke all of the rules by sleeping during the day and roaring at night.

I lurked and brooded. I hung out by the punch bowl and talked to uninteresting people about equally uninteresting topics. I did everything in my power to get another dance, but the opportunity never came. Nora was talking to Richie Fury. I could see him looking down at her. I read the look on his face, the large eyes looking appreciatively at her.

I had to make my move and quickly. Time was running out. Ten o'clock my mother had said, and she wasn't too crazy about me going to a party in the first place. I couldn't be late. It was like the losing moves in a chess game, an inevitable loss, but I played on.

Nora stood with her back to me. I knew Richie was about to ask her to dance. I tapped her on the shoulder. She turned to me. Her features seemed sharper than ever. The ridge of her nose would cut me. Her chin was a chisel.

"Would you like to dance?"

"Oh." She looked at Richie. "Richie, this is John Dee." I took his smooth, bony hand into my own. "We were just talking about miniature golf courses and pizza. Richie's father owned miniature golf courses and pizza parlors."

The record had already started playing. It was a perfect record, Gene Pitney's Town without Pity. "I was wondering if I could get another dance with you. I have to go after this one."

She looked at Richie once again, then we moved out on the dance floor. Someone turned all of the lights down. I could feel the sap already beginning to rise again. She let herself come real close to me again. I tried to stand up as straight as possible.

"You want to watch out for Richie Fury," I told her.

She brought her head back and looked at me. "What's that supposed to mean?"

"I mean, just what I said. Be careful. The guy's up on vacation. He doesn't care about..." I tried to stop, but it was no use. I'd come this far. Might as well finish it off. "He's only after one thing."

She stopped dancing and let go of my hands. We were standing there in the middle of the dance floor. "I don't believe you said that." A few of the other couples on the floor stopped their slow shuffle and looked at us. She took my hands and started dancing again, but this time she wasn't getting close. "He goes with my sister, you know. He's just trying to be nice. He's like a brother."

"I'm just trying to warn you," I said. I could feel the situation turning bad and I tried to steer it back on course. "I know you can take care of yourself."

"You're just like everyone else."

I didn't bother asking her what she meant by that. The song was almost over and by now, she was keeping me at arm's distance.

She left me there and walked back over to Richie. My time was up.

I walked home past the lonely cedars that lined the street. I had never heard the wind like that before, going through them, nor had the streetlights ever looked so pale and weak, shining down like that with the roads running off in a cross of darkness. These were the same cedars that in the past had forced me out into the street, beneath the streetlight, during those dark Friday nights after movies, when I had to walk home alone and the shadows were dancing and the visions from Invaders from Mars were still with me.

Now these cedars were my friends. My legs carried me along their shadows. The darkness was my ally. It covered me when I stopped. I didn't want anybody seeing me like this. I wondered if anyone could hear the high pitched wail—a long, sustained note of agony, like a dog's song—erupting uncontrollably from the open spot where the wound flowed freely. The summer air was quiet and noises carried. Probably just one of the huskies over at the Northrop place, they would think. They were always making these high-pitched sounds in the middle of the night too. But then there was the coughing and gagging to follow, the sudden choking off of the breath from the pain. There were broken sobs, which eventually descended to an even lower level of misery. I bent over with my hands on my knees, and took some deep breaths. So this is love, I thought. I grabbed a fistful of the branches for support. The sap stuck between my fingers and on my palms.

Later on at the stone house, when things had settled down, and I could hear the steady rhythm of dad's snoring, I sneaked back out into the night. It was the most daring moment of my young life, a transgression. Once outside, I ran across the field and took the back way, through the alley and along the maples—making sure to avoid the highway and any cars, 'til I was once again in view of The Big House.

It was all lit up and glowing, a great solitary lantern burning in the middle of the night. Everything was still. The columns of the porch cast long shadows out onto the lawn. The door where the party had been was still open. I stepped up onto the porch and looked in through the screen to the empty room. All of the food was still out on the tables. Now I was right up by the shrubbery along the windows. Each room appeared to be empty. Slowly I moved along 'til I came to an adjoining room on the end. The shades were partially drawn, and the lights were a little dimmer in there, but if I looked at just the right angle I could see in. There they were, just as I knew they would be. They were on the couch, Richie and Nora. He was leaning way over on her and kissing her in a way that was much different from the little kisses she had allowed me. I could see the back of his shiny hair turning back and forth as he bore in.

I started to feel that awful feeling again. It was threatening to overcome me. This time it was mixed with anger. I wanted to warn her. She was moving on into new and dangerous realms, leaving me and the others far behind.

I wanted to hurt Richie Fury. I wanted to wipe that smirk off his face forever. They were always coming up here and taking our land and our girls. They wanted it all. I looked at his shiny new Falcon sitting out there. I thought about really fixing him good.

But I headed for home. This time I walked boldly up the middle of the street and beneath the lights. I hit my chest and beat the pain back.

"Never again," I said aloud. "Never again."

But it would happen, at least once more.

Two Tracking

At 110, Goose lost his nerve and jumped in the backseat and started praying too. Shark was already back there and been there since 90. Me, I stayed up front. I wasn't much for praying, and I wasn't about to chicken out. I was going to stick it out. See what would happen next. Besides, I wanted to watch Blake bury the speedometer at 120. I wanted to see that red needle lie down and disappear beneath it all. I was so far past my curfew that I'd be dead anyway if I went home. I never thought much about dying. This was living, I kept telling myself. You can't beat a 283 for top-end. Blake had a T-bar floor shift, and we both had our Blue Ribbons between our legs. He was grinning and laughing out loud as the centerline raced beneath us like some kind of tickertape. The headlights couldn't keep up.

We came on Dead Man's Curve, and he slowed a little for the wrap around. Any other car would have rolled, but not Blake's. It was sweet and sat low to the ground. He had slicks on the back that gripped the road. I didn't have a doubt in my mind as we slung around the curve and shot straight down the flats past Deep Water Point, where Blake began zeroing in on another dangerous curve by Wilson Farms. This time Blake didn't show any signs of slowing down. He just kept laughing and sipping his Blue Ribbon. Blake was one of our main buyers, but there were conditions to the purchase: you had to drink it with him on the road and withstand his driving. I had to laugh, looking at him across from me. He looked like some kind of gargoyle behind the wheel, maybe the devil himself, with black hair slicked back into a D.A., and those high cheekbones and dark eyes.

I watched the speedometer climb toward 120 and beyond. I figured if he could stand it, I could too. But I also kept waiting for him to let up a little for curve, which was coming right up. Shark was in the back seat, and when I looked back he was down on his knees, too. "Slow this fucker down," he was saying, "I don't want to die." This made Blake laugh all the more, not a loud laugh, but more of a low, uneven one, coming out in short bursts like a laugh-gun. He kept pulling the trigger.

We were coming up on Wilson's corner and he had it buried again; I was thinking, he will never make this curve, but I'd be damned if I would say it aloud. So I chugged off my Blue and tossed it out the open window, letting the night air come rushing in like some kind of hell hole, then I sealed it back up and let what was to be be. We were overrunning the headlights faster than they could light the way, but I did see a cautionary arrow sign and then a cement silo. Maybe we would hit that and come to a wrenching halt, with us propelling on through the glass to whatever was next. I was ready. I fought back the urge to grip the dash, as if that would have helped anything. We came up on the corner and just as I expected, he couldn't make it. I didn't want to close my eyes, but I did. Some things you just can't will. I thought about my obituary. I wondered if I would be remembered for very long. I waited for what was next.

Next it was, the loud ping of gravel flying up. I had forgotten all about that gravel road being there. It was like the Lord Himself had laid that road for us to use. There I was, getting religious, just like all the rest, because when I opened my eyes, there it was, when it wasn't supposed to be. That's my definition of a miracle.

We hit that road flying. I felt the rear end go into a fishtail, but one thing about Blake, he knew how to handle that '61 Biscayne. The rear-end went this way and that. We were down to 90 and I thought for sure he would take it down lower, but Blake always fools you. He kept it right there and we shot down that gravel road late one night in July. I knew he would never make the next corner either. This time I wouldn't close my eyes, no matter what. I wanted to see the end for myself, the veering to the left, the sound of trees scraping against the side, the lurching to the side, and the roll. One after the other, my head crushing against the top and then the bottom—the sudden jumble, one, two, three, four times, coming to rest finally on top, the wheels spinning.

But miracle number two, it never happened. We were down to 70, but flying along a two-track now, out near Shank's Orchard, going straight until that run out, and we were in a field chasing some of Shank's cattle, going round and round. He had it downshifted now into second, then first, and started turning donuts, until he finally came to a stop.

I could hear Shark and Goose in the back bawling away like there was no tomorrow, but there was. Tomorrow was here. Me and Blake jumped out of the car. He climbed up on the hood and lay back beneath the stars and drank a new beer straight down.

"God, I feel so good," Blake said. "I think I'll drive by the big house."

"Not me," I said. I popped another brew and took a good pull off it and stretched out up on top, where I could get a good look at the Milky Way sprayed on across the sky.

I was ready, ready for what's next.

Third Stone

This was my summer. These were my woods. This was my circle of friends. They were imprinted immortally on my mind like Keats's Grecian Urn—so I thought. However, there were no unravish'd brides nor pipes and timbrels in this scene, but there was the squelch of somebody's transistor radio beaming in WLS from across the lake in Chicago; and yes, we did ravish a few: there were Claudia and Mary and Kathy and Poochy and Kay. We ravished each other. It was a mutual admiration society. We did have our fair share of mad pursuits, like the rematch of Nicky Calhoun and Big Foot. Nicky had won the first encounter—mostly because Biggie was too drunk to fight and Calhoun was quick like a cat with that left jab. We all got to watch it go down, sitting there around the fire out at Hitchcock Swamp and sipping Blue Ribbon. We watched the fight. That was what we did. Either that or the other thing, which began with the same letter but was more prone to luck than prowess. Sometimes we would just tell stories. Sometimes we did nothing at all. We would just listen to the fire spit and crack while the bullfrogs sang all around us.

Not everyone shared these romantic musings. Fringe derelicts—Can you believe it? That's what some mutha-fuckahz had the nerve to call us behind our backs—fringe derelicts. They wouldn't dare say that to my face because if they did, there would be an ass-whuppin party at Hitchcock Swamp and they would be the star attractions. I know the type. They come to the woods and drink our beer and flirt with our women, and then be two faced enough to go to some preppy party and brag about it. They would be the kind that would make these plans to someday go away and come back like they were the king shits and look down on us locals. They would try to buy up our land for dirt-cheap and then go into real estate and turn the profit by putting up a row of condominiums right down there by Stone Lake so you couldn't see the ducks swimming when you drove by.

Well, they knew better than to show up at this party tonight. This was a good party. It was the kind of party you loved to be at because it was right in the Sherriff's backyard, and it was in the sweet summertime. Better yet, it was right in his own house. And we all were there because of his son, Pidge. Pidge did what any of us would have done. We had this code of ethics about home parties. When the old folks were away, then we would play. Man! This was a good party.

Back then, we had nicknames for nearly everybody. I was the culprit of most. My mother had started the process, calling me Bird—not John, but Bird. So I, Bird, continued the legacy. I gave names to all the animals. I had a host of characters. There was Bird, that was me, Calhoun, Freud, Biggie, Patch, The Pigeon, Shark, Moose, Elk, Monk, Yule, Frog—just to name a few. I could go on and on. Even Jean Louise—Jeno, my true love, had a nickname. I was the namer of names. I pinned the labels on and they always stuck. Later on in life and at great expense and suffering, I would be told that this inclination evidenced a need in my character to compensate for my own feeling of inadequacy and was a further manifestation of my latent violent tendencies caused by an at times fucked up childhood. Perhaps. It is always easy to claim the victim.

Like I said. This party was at Pidge's house. Pidge, of course was short for The Pigeon, and this party had all the promises of being a grand party, one that few would ever forget. The Pigeon was the tall, gangly kid hosting this get-together. We called him The Pigeon because his father was the Sheriff of Pembroke County, and he had a way of providing us with certain privileged information, such as where and when the cop patrols were happening and who was under the radar and who wasn't. He never told us everything, but he gave us enough hints to keep the party going with little or no risk. For that reason, he was something like a stoolpigeon, only in reverse. Now his daddy had been kind enough to leave town for the weekend and head up to the U.P. to try his hand at trout fishing. That meant that this grand place was ours for taking, and take it we did.

We had reached crisis #1; we were about to run out of beer. The solution to that problem belonged to Big Foot or "Biggie," our provider. Biggie was a large, grisly bearded kid who lived out in the wilds of Hitchcock Swamp. Now mark you that a "provider" was not to be confused with a "buyer." The provider was the man with the connections. He knew the buyer and was able to procure the needed beverage for times of celebrations, such as these.

I had a circle of friends that would stay with me always, at least in my head, long after they were gone. Sometimes during the latter years, when some of us chose the thin exposures of college life, while for others it was a flak jacket in the Mekong Delta, these names began to have an equally thin literary quality to them. Sometimes I would have to leave that circle of friends, due to certain rules in the game of life, but always I would return. I was a loyalist at heart, and a faithful dualist; and when I did return from my journeys, I would always carry the original images as negatives in my head, and then compare the before and after. I guess that qualified me as a hopeless romantic, a term that only Freud would have understood during those days.

One journey we all hoped to avoid. Much depended on your number. When your number's up, your number's up, we always used to say. Mine was 183. Every month we would gather at the Selective Service for the grand drawing.

So, wouldn't you know it. This party at the Pidge's place was just starting to happen. It was beginning to build toward something, and now I had to go. This wasn't your average party either with Sherriff Harry out of town. No sir, you might say, we owned this town called Blackwood, especially since his only other deputy, Rabbit McMahn was comfortably drunk at the dispatch. But still, this wasn't without its risks, being right here in the Sheriff's house beneath the stars on a summer's night in Pembroke County and drinking underage beer. It was like it shouldn't nearly be over, but already it was threatening to be. This was my circle of friends. I hated to leave them, but I had good reason other than being out of beer, but I would be back. I wouldn't be gone too long. Always, I would be back.

It was damn nice of Sheriff Harry to go off to the U.P. for a weekend and leave us his house. It was even nicer of The Pigeon, to give us this invitation. Of course that was the way, the unspoken agreement among all of us: when your ol' man and ol' lady left town, you threw the doors open. The place was packed. The sheriff's place was more of a hunting lodge, really, all done up in knotty pine with the deer heads mounted everywhere and rainbow trout turning on the wall. He had vaulted ceilings and lofts all done up in shiny varnish, and here we were right inside the village limits. There were people hanging off the two stairways leading up to the lofts, and every chair was filled and the open floor space mostly taken up. We had managed to get some new pretty girls in from Ohio. Their daddies owned property on the lakes. They were summer partiers, and we were providing the party. I could see Freud, standing over there in the corner with two or three of them standing next to him, soaking up his b.s. He had just moved to town a few months ago and was making a big splash with his long blond hair. It was only because he was my cousin that spared him the hometown initiation, an old-fashioned Northern Michigan ass-whippin. I had to hand it to him, though. The chicks loved him. It was his gift of gab. I guess they thought he was some kind of intellectual or something.

But I had to go. And besides, I also got word that we were almost out of beer. We were on the tail end of two cases of Blue Ribbon and the stereo was blasting Wilson Pickett loud enough so you could hear the scratchy needle right along with the screaming and wailing. But I had to go. It was just my luck. I guess I couldn't complain too much. You might say I had been pretty lucky in other areas. I slipped my arm around Jeno and drew her close to me.

"What is it about you?" One of the girls said to me. Her name was Stevie. Can you imagine that? A girl with a boy's name. I mean Jeno was a nickname for Jean Louise, but this girl's real name was Stevie. She was a tall, large-mouthed girl who always had a way of zeroing in on me in the wrong direction. "You always have to go." Her long dark eyelashes were shaded with mascara, not trashy but more like Hollywood. She snapped her eyes at me and then at Jeno. Jeno was my reason for leaving. She was underage with a curfew, but I couldn't tell Big Mouth that. She would have been all over that. I just knew I had to go. I didn't want to go, but I had to. But I would be back.

Biggie was making his way for the door to get more beer. "Where you going to get some brews this time of the night?" I asked him. I knew a few things about this. I knew that Chief Pontiac was our number one buyer. He was an old Indian with a long gray ponytail halfway down his back. We would pick him up hitch hiking. If he was in the right mood, he'd buy us some beer, and we slip him a few extra bucks so he could get himself a bottle of wine. But I heard Chief was laying low, especially after buying this load for us. "How you gonna do it?" I asked him again. "Chief ain't around. He's gone fishing."

Biggie gave that hacky cough of his and pulled out a Camel and lit up. "Don't you worry about that," he said. He scratched his beard. "I got my own sources."

"Don't tell me you're going over to Chucky Wells? You will have to pay a pretty big price for beer over there." I winked at Freud and the others because this was an inside joke. "You ain't pretty enough to get Chucky to buy you beer." Chucky Wells: that was another story.

I saw one of Biggie's triple-decker fists double up, but there was a twinkle in his eye, too. At one time or another, we had all been over to Chucky Wells.

"Well you better hurry," I said, "wherever you're going or this party is over."

Outside the air was sweet and warm with summertime, and me and Jeno could hear the frogs singing over in Sexton Pond. I fired up my Mustang. Jeno was in beside me, and I dialed up WLS on the radio. Jeno didn't do beer, but I did have a bottle of Cherry Jubilee that Chief had gotten last minute for me from the backdoor of Smitty's. She popped a mint in her pretty little mouth and snuggled over next to me. I still had my beer right where I liked it, between my legs, and we started the cruise home. Things were a piece of cake, knowing that the sheriff was out of town.

I lit up a smoke and said to her, "Maybe you better not get out tonight. Your dad might be getting wise."

She shrugged her shoulders. "If that's what you want." I wasn't sure what I wanted. The usual routine was she would go inside and wait for a half hour and then tiptoe back out and meet me. Then we would be gone till yonder light streaked the horizon with rosy fingers, or something like that. But tonight I had other thoughts on my mind.

So we drove on for a while to give me a chance to finish off my beer and smoke my smoke. I decided to drive on out toward Fertile Valley. I liked the drive. The trees hung over the road and every now and then a June bug would splat against the windshield. Had to be careful about deer though. Sometimes at night they would just run right out at you and smash your car up good. I had enough dings and dents in the Mustang already, so I drove real slow and sipped my beer. I rolled the window down and let the radio play. Pretty soon our favorite song came on the radio.

We still had a half hour to kill, so I pulled off next to Shank's orchard, down a little two-track between the pines, where no cops would ever think of bothering us. I cut the engine and drank off my beer. We just sat there for a little while and I rolled down the window and let the wind speak through the pines.

Jeno didn't say much. She never did. I could see her sitting there in the dim green of the dash lights, her profile, the hair coming down straight and beautiful, falling down toward her waist, her large eyes. There was always plenty going on the inside with her. Nobody ever knew what she was thinking, unless she felt like sharing. I pulled her over and smelt her perfume and soap, always clean and light, never overdone. Sometimes I just liked to sit there and look at her. That's exactly what I did. I drank off the rest of my beer and looked at her in green light of the dash, shining up on her, making her hair and face seem even prettier.

By the time I got back, The Pigeon's place had pretty much died down. There was one couple hanging around, making out in the corner. They saw me and headed off to one of the bedrooms. The music was still playing, but the needle was stuck on Little Surfer Girl, *in my woody, in my woody, in my woody.* Over and over it went. I walked through the rooms looking for some action. Nothing. Where the hell was Freud? The stereo was set up in one of the bedrooms and I stepped in not knowing what I might find.

There he was, Big Foot, in all of his glory. He was in the master bedroom sitting at one of those rough-cut cedar tables that the sheriff seemed to have a particular liking to, and he was passed out. His big meathead was turned sideways and there was still an open beer in his big paw. That wasn't the half of it. Right next to him was at least ten cases of beer stacked up and a whole wad of bills, tens, twenties, hundreds. There must have been a couple of thousand spilled out over the floor. I knew what he'd done all right. He'd gone and robbed Skeeter's Bait Shop. That was what he'd done. And now there he sat passed out in the sheriff's own home. I walked over and lifted the needle off the record and a dead silence fell over things. He was just lucky the house was empty. I don't know where everyone had gone.

I tried waking him up. First I gave him a little jiggle, which didn't produce much. Then I moved up to a good shake. His eyes opened up and his eyeballs seemed to swim around in his head. Then he sat up and drank off the rest of his beer.

"Christ, Biggie, what'd you do?" He opened another beer and then said, "I told you I would get more beer."

"And that's not all," I said, picking up some of the cash that lay strewn about the hardwood floors.

"Nicky Calhoun will be in town tomorrow, and I'm going to invite him out to Hitchcock and then I'm going to kick his ass." It was the rematch everyone was talking about.

"Come on man, don't give me that." I tried to help him up to his feet. "We got to get you out of here. The Pigeon is cool, but I don't think he would go for you bringing back your loot to his ol' man's house, you crazy fuck. You robbed Skeeter's, didn't you."

I managed to get him up on his feet and out of the house. We loaded what beer we could in my trunk and the rest went in the backseat. I drove him out to Hitchcock and I was feeling plenty nervous, no cops or not. That little Mustang was loaded down. When we got to Hitchcock, we went down the same old two track with all of the ferns on both sides.

Hitchcock was a special place. The air always smelled like mint. You could always hear the Pembroke River running at night. Out there the cops couldn't touch you. You could get as drunk and loud as you wanted. We would build a fire and do what happened naturally when young boys and girls got together on warm summer nights, that is to say, we would usually end up loving, but sometimes it could go the other way. All is fair in love and war. Alcohol, young men and young women can be an awful potent combination.

So I helped him stash the booze. I was an accomplice. I liked the sound of that word. I worked at a feverish pace unloading one case after the other beneath the ferns and covered it up with an old rain tarp so it wouldn't get skunky. Biggie rolled up a bunch of the money and put it in a jar and asked me to hold it for him.

"Why you want me to hold your money?" I said. He told me it would be just for a couple of days because if his brother Tanner heard about it, he would rob Biggie for sure, or maybe beat the shit out of him. The Hitchcock Clan was an awful clan. So I said okay, although I wasn't wild about holding stolen money because I knew the cops would be out looking to solve this caper. "Hold it just for tonight," he said. "Then bring it out tomorrow."

I drove home and buried the money out in the garden beneath the dark soil and the crabapple tree. By that time it was getting late. I heard the courthouse bell sound the half hour between four and five. I would be lucky to get two hours sleep before work in the morning. It would be a long day, but then it would also be good long night. Nicky Calhoun was coming to town and that always meant some kind of surprise. I hadn't seen him in quite some time.

I crawled into bed and listened to the courthouse bell strike five. It was already starting to turn toward morning. Darkness was thinning out, and the lonesome dove was making its call.

A young man doesn't need much sleep. In the morning Mother was having her morning cup of instant Maxwell House and a smoke. She was sitting at the table, kind of hunched over, closing her eyes as the thread of smoke ran straight up to the low tiled ceiling. I had twenty minutes to make the twelve-mile drive to Iron Town, where I worked at the factory, stamping out bomb casings for Vietnam. I didn't mind making the casings, just as long as I didn't have to be anywhere around them when the B-52s dropped them on the rice paddies.

"You're kind of burning the candle at both ends," she said, still keeping her eyes closed. Her vision was already getting bad in those days.

"I'll be all right," I said. "I'll get me a nap after work."

"You read that letter yet?"

"Not yet, but I will. I'll read it tomorrow, so just lay off, will ya?"

I packed a quick lunch and left her sitting there. I'll read the fucking letter was what I wanted to say, but didn't, this time. I hauled ass across the back roads. I knew them well, every bend and flap. I knew just when to floor it coming over the hill at Hinkley's junkyard and then held the pedal down across the flat with the mist rising off the highway, till I reached Blueberry Hill on the other side. There was nothing but the smell of cedar and morning dew in the air. I lit a smoke for breakfast on the way, and it had a stale cheesy taste going down in the morning, but I felt the nicotine buzz and knew I could make it through this day and any other that might be thrown at me, so long as I could get back to the comfort of my circle.

And I did. Another busy day at the factory and a one-hour nap. I was ready to go out. Tonight's get-together would be at Hitchcock. I felt better about that. I waited until Mother went to get Pops his six pack, and I wondered, maybe she was going to Skeeter's and she would hear all about the robbery. I walked over to the garden and dug up the jar. It still had the wad of twenties and tens in it, almost half full. Nobody had bothered to count it. I could have easily slipped a couple of twenties into my wallet and nobody would have known the difference, but I wasn't one for stealing. I wasn't any goody-goody boy either, and I sure as hell wasn't a snitch. I carried the jar back and put it on the rider's side bucket seat. I would have a lot of explaining to do if Sheriff Harry or anybody else for that matter stopped me. I jumped in and started up and backed out and slipped the jar beneath my seat. It was another summer night, the sky full of stars, the air thick and sweet with promise. I swung by and picked up Jeno. She was at her customary spot, at the foot of the hill below her house.

I drove on out to Hitchcock looking forward to seeing my ol' buddy Nicky Calhoun. We had plenty of beer stacked up high beneath a cedar tree, and some of it sitting down in The Pembroke River, where it would stay good and cold.

Every night was a different cast of players, with certain ones being the main ones. I guess what I'm trying to say is that it was like a play with the leading players being me, Biggie, Freud , and Calhoun. Biggie had his own way with words and he called us The Unholy Four.

By the time me and Jeno arrived the fire had already been started. I could smell the smoke as soon as I parked. We had a special place to park where the phone lines ran across a section of swamp and everything was cleared out. You had to look real hard to know there were cars there. No cops to worry about. The road just kept dwindling away from paved, to gravel, to two-track. Two-track was always best with me.

Calhoun hadn't arrived yet, but most of the others were there. We could see their faces around the fire. Jeno disappeared into the shadows and I went up front, where things were already beginning to happen. One of the true legends of Pembroke County was there, the Watson Twins: Vern and Cal. Long and rangy looking, they were a feared pair of bad-asses. Vern was messing with Cupid, but not in a serious way. Cupid was one of the gophers from Chums Corner who was just along for the ride. He had a chubby belly on him and a head full of curly hair that was slicked back in D.A. Vern was setting him up because he was an easy hit. They stood a little to the front of the fire, where everybody could see them.

"One thing you always got to be watching is the right," Vern said. He had a Pabst in his right hand and he set it down and began rotating his right fist in a little circle. "It's the one that'll get ya." All eyes were watching, and then lightning quick his left flashed out and smacked Cupid in the left jaw.

It wasn't a hard blow, but Cupid backed up a couple of steps and lost his balance and nearly fell in the fire.

Biggie came up beside me and asked, "You get yourself a beer?"

I had almost forgotten about that. "Oh yeah," I said, and walked over to the creek and pulled one out of the cold waters. It got that way at Hitchcock sometimes. You would forget what you were there for. We were getting a good crowd that night. I thought I spotted the same little honeys from last night, but I couldn't be sure. They were, of course, standing with Freud on the other side of the fire.

After the Watson Brothers' show, we were all getting ready for the next event. These things were not planned. They just sort of happened. The Patch was just getting ready to recite The Fall. This was vintage poetry that came directly from the bowels of Jackson Prison, recited by The Patch, who had been an inmate at Jackson not so long ago.

The Patch had reached legend status at Hitchcock . Only certain people had that status. He'd been in and out of prison for various felonies, usually a culmination of broken paroles and probations issued by lenient judges in hopes that he would reform and quit stealing and robbing, and he had for the most part done this. He had reformed himself as much as was humanly possible for The Patch, which meant he was being good enough to stay out of prison.

He stepped up to the fire and everything settled down a little. I went over and found Jeno. She was hiding in the shadows. Biggie had moved over next to her to make sure she was okay. She was only sixteen and this was a pretty rough crowd, but everybody knew better than to mess with my girl, I thought. I stood over next to her and slipped my arm around her to reassure her.

We could see the firelight shining up in The Patch's face. He was wearing his patch. Nobody knew for sure how he got blinded in one eye. Somebody said he got shot by a paper wad in school, but I figured he never went to school long enough for that. Couldn't be sure. His hair was thin and long and starting to push back a little, making his forehead protrude out like a smooth bluff. He had dark eyes that had "crazy" spelled all over them. He was one of my closest buddies. Next to Calhoun, he was the closest.

Speaking of Calhoun, I felt a heavy hand on my shoulder. I looked over my shoulder and saw those small eyes, full of mischief and contempt. He had arrived.

"Come on. I got something for you."

I had just opened my beer and it was still good and cold. I took a swig. "I want to hear The Patch."

"You can hear that any time."

The Patch was just launching into the invocation to his signature prison song, "The Fall." He had taken his teeth out so his face caved in, and the five-o'clock shadow, which was really a 24-7 shadow gave him a crazy look like some kind of perverted clown. "If you play the game, you gotta stand the pain. Cause it takes a steady grind." The Fall was beginning. I didn't feel like leaving just yet, but I was glad to see Calhoun. He had been off to college down in Big River and only came back home on occasion. Now was one of them.

Now Jeno didn't exactly like Calhoun. She didn't give me any trouble about most of my friends, and I've got to admit, I had some low-downs, all right, but that was the kind of people I preferred, the low-downs, because they knew what the score was and didn't play no games. I knew Calhoun had tried hitting on Jeno more than once, but she wouldn't have anything to do with him because she thought he was more than a low-down. She thought that Calhoun didn't have a soul, and that he would do anything to anybody. She didn't trust him. I knew what she said was true, but that was always what drew me to my friends, the fact they was all more or less dangerous, not in the big time sense, but in the small time Michigan hick town sense.

"Come on. Come with me." Calhoun was insistent. He had Freud with him, standing off in the distance.

"What you got?" I said, figuring maybe that he had a bottle of whiskey or something. I looked at my cousin. Sometimes he was a real pain in the ass. "What's Freud going to do? Give us a lecture?"

"You'll see."

"I can only stay for a minute."

"Follow me."

Pretty soon we were heading back down the trail toward the cars, and the fire was back over my shoulder.

We got back to the cars and we loaded into my Mustang. "Let me sit on the driver's side," Calhoun said. "I need the dash lights." I wasn't one for arguing, so I took shotgun and let him sit behind the wheel. Freud piled in the back with his bevy of chicks following along. He was right behind Calhoun. "Hey move your seat up, will ya?" Calhoun ignored him.

"I'm serious. I can't move back here."

"You're not supposed to move, Freud," I said to him. "You're just along for the ride, remember?" I turned my attention to Calhoun. "So what's up, man?" I said. "You got some hard stuff or what?" I expected to see him busting out the Styrofoam cups or something.

I heard Freud give off a little snicker in the backseat like he knew something I didn't. "Indubitably," said one of the girls in the backseat and she laughed. Her name was Ava. I could see her face in the dim green of things. She was blond and had low, half open eyes.

"In-what?" I said.

Then the other one chimed in. Her name was Karen or something like that. "Don't mind her. She's a bookworm." I couldn't see her very well either, but I could hear her chomping on a wad of gum. I knew Freud had his sights set on the blond. She was more his type, but this other one was up for grabs.

I thought Calhoun would be busting out the bottle by now, but instead he was all hunched over with a plastic bag. The others in the backseat seemed to know what was going on, but I didn't have a clue.

"Calhoun, whatcha doing?" I said in a half smurky way. Calhoun was the only one I knew who was maybe just as big a smart mouth as me.

"Bird food," he said. He had big nimble hands that were busy twisting up cigarettes.

"What, did you bring us out here to smoke, a cigarette?" I said. I was beginning to get the idea though, what was up. It was funny how he had everybody's attention. All of us sitting there huddled up inside, watching him do whatever he was doing.

He was neat and tidy. He carefully brushed off his hands and scraped together the remains and put them back in the bag. Then he carefully rolled the bag up and put it away. Now he had two of the neatest looking cigarettes. They looked like they came straight out of the pack. I had brought a half a beer with me and I drank it off and tossed the empty out the window.

Calhoun held the smoke up so everybody could see it. Then he said to me, "This one's for you, Bird. You'll never be the same."

"Turn on the radio," Freud said. "Put it on WBZ, Boston."

"WBZ?" I said.

"Come on, just try it, and move the seat up, will ya?" Calhoun handed one of the smokes to the group in the backseat and he lit the other one up.

"How do you adjust this seat?" He asked.

"Reach down beneath it. Adjust the lever." He fiddled with it for a minute and then slid it up a few inches to get Freud off his back.

"This one's for you and me." He took a drag and handed it to me. "Just drag on it and hold it in for minute."

"I know how to smoke, Calhoun," I said.

"Like this," Ava said, and she leaned forward and took a drag and made this dragging noise that sounded something like an air hose through her front teeth. Then she spoke all squeaky. "Let the cannabis do its work."

Cannabis, I was thinking. What the fuck is cannabis and who does this chick think she is? But I followed suit and filled up my lungs and held it in, feeling the smoke build up pressure. Calhoun had the radio going by then and was squeak-squishing through the channels. And I thought to myself, squeak-squishing, what kind of word is that, then I let the smoke out and felt a cough coming on.

"That's it," Freud said. "Right there. Jimi Hendrix."

Jimi who, I wanted to say, but by then there was no holding back. The cough had a mind of its own and it racked me. I could hear the others in back seat laughing. I could hear Freud smirking away too, and I had half-a-mind to slap him up a little, but he was my cousin on my mother's side, so I let it slide. There was this strange music like we were on a space ship or something with all kinds of dials and signals going off. It didn't seem like mean laughter that I was hearing, but it was laughter all the same. I was going to show them that I was no sissy though, and this time I took a long drag and watched the coal on the end of the cigarette glow red. I knew everybody was watching so I made damn sure I held it in this time.

"Take it easy," Ava said. "This isn't a chugging contest." She leaned up closer, so her face was at my ear. "That's the second stone."

"What's the second stone?"

She took another hit off the smoke and blew it into my mouth. "All that liquor and that violence—that fringe derelict stuff." She blew more smoke into me, this time into my nose. "I think you're ready to move on. Besides, this is much better for you."

I coughed hard, so hard that I saw a string of gold colored stars race across my closed eyes. They were the kind of stars my teacher used to put on my papers in third grade, the year before I flunked. "Oh yeah. Then what's the first stone?"

"You already know, don't you." She ran her fingers through the back of my hair. "You poor thing. She broke your heart, didn't she."

"Don't I know you from somewhere? I feel like I've known you all my life."

"You have."

Then the words came to me through the speakers and I heard her softly reciting them in unison.

> *Oh strange beautiful grass of green*
> *With your majestic silken scenes*
> *Your mysterious mountains*
> *I wish to see closer*
> *May I land my kinky machine*

"Wow, did you hear that?" she said.

"I heard it." I took another drag and let the smoke out slow and easy. "What the fuck," I said. "I can't understand what he's saying."

Then Freud said, "You got to buy the album and play it on 78 to get it."

"What?" I said.

"Listen to that guitar," Freud was saying.

> *Although your world wonders me*
> *With your majestic superior cackling hen*
> *Your people I do not understand*

"Well Bird, what do you think," Calhoun said. He had that shit-eating grin. "You're awfully quiet."

"Hey don't mess with him," Ava said. "He's crossing over."

"Crossing over," I said. "You make it sound like we're on a river."

"We are," she said. She handed her smoke to me, but kept it in her hand and put it to my mouth. "Think of it as crossing a river." I dragged on her cigarette. "Don't feel like you have to rush it."

I felt like I might be getting something from it this time. It was like the smoke went outside of my lungs and crept into my body from the inside. She pushed the hair back up out of my eyes. "You're such a little hood, aren't you."

"He's from the animus side of the family," Freud said.

I had half a notion to slap him up alongside the head for that, but suddenly I didn't give a shit. It was like we were all in this little car, but we were miles apart, or something like that. Then the other one, the one they called Karen, started laughing. The others started in laughing, too.

"What's so funny?" I said.

"It's all right," she said. "Don't feel bad. You've just lost your virginity." She wagged her finger at me like my mother sometimes did. "It was bound to happen sooner or later."

Then I started laughing too. I don't really know why. I guess it was because of all the crazy-ass talking going on or something. I knew I'd never felt like this before. That was for sure. Alone, yet together.

> So to you I wish to put an end
> And you'll never hear surf music again

There was another really important question that I wanted to ask Ava, but the music was exploding and warping; and then the dome light suddenly came on. I found my way out of the car and looked for her, but she had disappeared into the darkness. Everybody else had to go, but I didn't feel like going anywhere. I was just getting to understand that guitar with it low, twisty-windy sound, bending and sliding along, and the drums popping in the background like corn going off.

We walked back to the party. I moved slowly behind the others. The Patch was on the last leg of The Fall. I found Jeno. Biggie was looking after her, just like I expected. "Well how was it?" Jeno said.

Before I could answer, Biggie shot me his what-the-fuck look. "You got my money?"

"But of course," I laughed.

"I could use it."

"Right now?"

"Right now."

We walked back to the car. I didn't mind going back because the smells and sights and sounds had suddenly become more pronounced. Too much noise and congestion up here. I needed something smoother.

Back at the car, the dim little light of the Mustang put up a weak fight against the darkness.

I reached down beneath the seat and run my hand around. I never lose things. Then I got down on my hands and knees and looked. I pulled everything out one at a time, the screwdriver, the flashlight, and the old receipts. Then I put them back and took them out again, carefully this time. I looked again and again. I could have sworn I put it there beneath the seat. Where the hell could it have gone?

"I know it's here somewhere."

"What's that smell?" Biggie said. "And where the fuck is Nicky Calhoun?"

He walked away in that abrupt manner of the pissed off. The fight that everyone had been talking about was probably going to happen. This time I didn't follow. He left me alone in the seat with the starlight dancing.

I made my way home. I didn't drive fast, but instead let the Mustang idle its way at a slow trot through the two tracks and gravel roads, first to Jeno's, which took longer than usual and a whole bunch of smoothing out. Eventually I made it home. I pulled up in front of the stone house and tippy-toed in, but I knew no matter how quiet I was my mother would hear me. There was no fooling her.

"You're a dandy," I heard her say from the thinning darkness and behind the walls in the next room. "How do you ever expect to make it to work?"

I crawled into bed. I had my window open and listened to the lonesome dove singing in the dawn, and then it wasn't long before mother's feet hit the floor. She sat just outside my door in the little kitchen way with her eyes closed and had her morning smoke.

I closed my eyes, too, and let them rest. I felt a good sleep coming on—the heavy, droopy-eyed kind that could easily have gone all day. There would be no sleep, but that was okay. I was soon up and packing that spam between the two pieces of white bread with a thick coat of mustard. In no time at all I had that Mustang galloping down the highway heading toward the factory where I would make more bomb casings for the war that nobody cared about or wanted to think about.

Up over Blueberry Hill I slowed it to a trot and then a meandering walk with the sounds of Hendrix in my head stopping time and propelling me toward that third stone.

Goo-goo-gajoob

What is language without a face behind it? Well I'll tell you. It is the absence of presence; it is relaxation; it is no bullshit. This is why I feel best on an evening, such as this, when darkness covers everything and there can be no distractions, no static on the radio.

My headlights point down the gravel road and my knuckles grip the wheel at twelve o'clock to form a perfect V. I figure I might as well go to the party. I mean three years is a long time to be away from home. My number was up. So I thought, what the fuck. If Tricky Dick was going to end the war, I might as well have a piece of the action before it was over. My friends all thought I was crazy and that was all right with me. No college deferment. No joining The Coast Guard or Air Force. No sudden trips to Canada. The 9th Infantry Division, Mekong Delta it was, with my M-30 at my side. If Ho Che Minh wanted those rice paddies, he'd damn well better pack a big lunch.

But that is another story. I am home now, and my Camaro was waiting for me, but that was about all. I wrecked it before I left. Everybody thought it was totaled, and it probably was. But I sent money home over the long haul and made sure it was restored to its original shape. Now, just listen to that engine. It drones along patiently, tonight eating up the road, but always wanting more. I'm supposed to race Bird and his Mustang out by the airport one of these nights. It is always unofficial until it happens. That really won't be a race, but I will be kind enough to let him think so.

The gravel flies up and pings at the wheel-wells. Makes me worry about the new paint job. Just got it out of Joe's body shop. Redone in the original frost white with black pin stripes. Heat resonates from the hood and flows back. I check the gages. Things are cool. All systems are go. We are feeling it tonight. Fluids are flowing. I release the wheel and rest my palm on the eight ball on top of the floor shift. I punch it enough to make the back end fishtail and then take it back down to the go-slow drone.

I don't have any insurance yet. All the insurance I need is right here, hanging inside my nylon jacket. It's the real deal. I feel it there beneath my armpit, the bulge, loose and wanting to be ready. It will be. I drink off the last of my beer and toss it. There will be more of that where I'm going.

I think about the party. I remember the old parties . A bonfire in the middle of the swamp somewhere, all of us swatting mosquitoes, drinking beer and waiting for what's next. Some real characters would show up for those. Cal Hodges, Leo Myers, the Watson twins, just to name a few. I had my work cut out for me, going to those parties and having a name like Ginger. I'm no redhead. It was kind of like Johnny Cash's 'A Boy Name Sue,' except my dad didn't tag me with this name out of spite or for some kind of rite of passage. He was so drunk when I was born, he thought I was a girl and named me Ginger. The name stuck. I had to grow up the hard way, earning the respect that I deserved with such a name.

This party is a little different. Joe down at the body shop told me about it. "It's out at the old Katie place, Hookookachoo." I didn't tell him that he had mispronounced it. He wasn't alone.

The headlights shoot up a new stretch of road. Trees hang over the top and dangle down into the spray of the headlights. The two lanes of the two track are white, the center a rolling green. I turn off into an open field, the sky opens up and a gathering of taillights and reflections are at the far end. I cut the lights and my eyes quickly adjust. The field is there, a light covering beneath the darkness. The black outline of the woods is on either side. I wonder why there is no fire. The red coal of a cigarette approaches.

A hand goes to mouth and the red coal goes back down again. It begins to swing back and forth, until it is outside my window. I roll down the glass.

"You coming or going?" says an old familiar voice, but he made it real clear that he didn't want to be called that anymore. He wanted to go by his real name, Reese. Reese's Pieces is what I say. Some things never change. He was still smoking too many Camels and that hacky cough hung close to him.

He opens the door like a real valet and the dome light comes on. The black leather of the door is visible, but he is still outside the light, though I see white pants and sneakers.

"Where's the party?"

Already he is walking and I have to hurry to catch up. We move in single file with him in the lead. I can only see the white of his pants moving along through the field. There is urgency in his footsteps. Let him lead.

He stops several times to wait. I tell him to go ahead. "I'll make it," I say. "Believe me I will." The red coal of his cigarette falls like a star.

"You know Moose Conlin is looking for you?" he says.

"Moose Conlin?"

"He heard you were back in town."

I had nearly forgotten about Moose. There was that little matter down at the swimming hole the day before I left. I had heard all about him, but I knew something that most had never bothered to notice. In the water, he was a helpless child. This wasn't obvious to the casual observer. To the casual observer he crawled across the blue waters of our swimming hole with ease. He had big arms that reached out and pulled the lake toward him. On every fourth stroke he would turn his head sideways for air and swish his hair back. His face would only be visible for a few seconds but it was long enough to show this cocky smile on his face.

I made my discovery by accident. The old log raft stood on four water-soaked white legs above the blue, ruffled waters. One afternoon in the thick of things, I sprang off the diving board and pulled one foot up behind me into a "can opener" and cut the blue water. Little did I know that the Moose was right below me. The thick stump of his neck soon lodged right between my legs, knocking my balls halfway up to my throat. I soon realized that my moment of pain was nothing compared to his agony and terror. He twisted around and began flailing his arms, trying to pull me in. I saw him through this green underwater lens, his face blurred, his hair standing up wavy in the water. I kicked away, my feet pushing off the soft, squishy indent of his chest.

I came up for air twenty feet away, spewing water. I was fine, but the Moose was in trouble, not serious trouble, but enough so that he had an escort of swimmers around him. He wore that same kind of look that I would later see on others in the war when we were on night patrol and some poor unsuspecting bastard of a VC would trip up a Claymore a few feet away from us and blow the shit out of himself and a few others. It was like he was no longer fully a part of this world, but half-caught in the other, like a fish after they'd been on the floor of the boat. All the fight was out of them, but their gills kept working back and forth. Glassy-like. He had that look.

I submerged and swam low to the bottom where the water was coolest and the soft bottom rubbed against my underside. Down here was my domain, my kingdom. I did not come up for air until the beach had lodged against my chest and I had run out of the space. Still, I could have gone on further if I had wanted to.

"Ginger, you're back," a voice says to me all of sudden. It sounds like Shamas, my old childhood chum, but I can't be sure.

This is a new kind of party. No fires, no faces. Only voices in the dark and blankets spread out all over, some with candles on them.

"I've never been gone," I say to him.

"Always the wise guy," he says. "Weren't you drafted or something like that?"

"Or something like that."

"Come on. I'll show you the stage."

He takes my hand and leads me around and through the people, all of them sitting, nobody's standing other than myself and him. Voices murmur a peaceful drone that makes me think my own voice had carried across the entire gathering.

Somebody else says, "Hey Ginger, you're back," but it isn't exactly "Hey Ginger!" But hey Ginger, as if to say you've never really been gone and time moves on, but it stays the same. I can't really be sure who this voice is.

"I heard Moose Conlin is looking for you," the same voice says. Then somebody says something else, which I can't quite catch, and there is laughter.

"Yeah, well that's yesterday's news," I say back to him in a big, booming Blue Ribbon voice.

"Here's the stage," Shamas finally says. He lets go of my hand. The imprint of his hands remains. I rub it off on my pants. My shoes are damp from the wet grass.

The stage is an elevated platform, thrown together with scraps of wood. Shadows are moving all across it, people evidently setting up equipment. I turn to Shamas to ask him an important question, but he is gone. I am left standing there in the dark and I think about Moose again. He could be out there anywhere lurking. He must be really big now. Back then he was as big as me.

After our first incident in the water, I had begun to notice that he would leave as soon as I entered the swimming hole. He made it look casual enough, diving expertly off the raft, but always making it a point to swim to shore in that smooth powerful manner of his.

The days had dwindled down to a precious few. I had received my orders. Soon I would be leaving. I planned my attack. I knew my domain.

That day, my last before leaving, I slipped into the water from a great distance. The waters at the spillway moved in a dark current, the surface spotted with eddies as if magic fingers whirled just beneath the surface.

The raft was in the distance. I could make it in three tries, maybe two. The Moose's big figure stood at the top, bullying and pushing kids off.

I filled my lungs and quietly went down for the first time. I scissor-kicked and pulled myself along, passing the old underwater wall of the boardwalk, where the sawmill had flooded fifty years back. I moved with ease through the windows, the soft, gooey surface rubbing against my belly. Swimmers began to spot the surface above.

I swam upward and gently freed my lungs of air before surfacing. A startled girl said, "Hey," when she saw me, but quickly forgot my presence.

I floated along within striking distance. They were playing water tag. The top of the raft was slick and glistening. The Moose moved with his usual agility, as the one who was "it" climbed the ladder. Moose was on one side of the diving board. All of the others had scurried off. He placed both hands on the diving board, arms straight, as a sort of brace and divide. His gut hung over his blue trunks and his huge shoulders bowed. Then he moved to get a running jump but he slipped on his plant foot and went down with the edge of the raft busting his ribs and him hitting the water with a loud flop.

I went under and submerged to mid-level, 6-8 feet. He moved above in a broken pattern taking a few strokes and then going beneath the water and then back up, limping along toward the bottom, which would be within standing dept in a few feet.

I arched lower until I could feel the muddy bottom against my chest and I was directly beneath him. I shoved off with one foot and went soaring toward the top. I yanked his trunks down until they were around his knees and he couldn't move his legs. Then I spun him around on his back and locked my legs around his thick midsection and my arms around his neck and shoulders. I pulled him down. He kicked and thrashed. I raked my nails across his chest and rode him out until he calmed. I moved him gently through the water.

By that time I could hear the lifeguard's whistle blowing and I threw my hip into his back and hooked my arm around this throat. I towed him in. Others were soon there to help and together we beached him. He had spit up all over himself. Someone threw a towel over his lower half, but not before men, women and children had a good look at his drowned rat lying sideway on his hip.

He was still coughing and spitting when he suddenly threw everyone aside and went for me. He was in no shape to do much and the others easily held him back. He was puking up now all down the front of himself.

"You're fucking dead," he said to me, and he spit up more water and shit.

"I was only trying to help," I said. He went for me again and I pulled back just out of reach.

I had a bus to catch.

I shake myself out of the daydream. Cymbals are beginning to sizzle and snares rattle. Somebody has fired up a generator and soon there are red lights on the stage and sound of twanging guitars tuning up.

"It was never like this before," I say to no one in particular. I begin instinctively to move back out among the blankets. Candles have begun to spot the surface, small private lights, showing torsos, chins, and down turned faces. There are no distractions.

"You can sit here," says a voice to my right. It is a young voice, female with a kind of piping, melodic quality to it.

"Thanks," I say.

She is on a blanket, a baby's blanket, I can tell by the soft fuzzy balls on it. I rub my palms over it.

"What's your name?" I say.

"Lucy. Lucy Gentle."

I hide my skepticism. "Lucy Gentle. That's a nice name."

"No it's not. I can be a real bitch when I want to."

She is holding a small baby that is beginning to fuss and cry. My back softens, my shoulders slump. I stretch out a little on the blanket. A bass guitar is tuning up, playing a walking pattern off and on. Now and then a raspy guitar chord.

Lucy has quieted the baby. She continues to make a soft shushing sound while the baby now makes another sound in its throat, something akin to infant snorting or sucking, breast feeding, quiet contentment.

"Things have really changed," I say.

"You're from around here?"

"Use to be."

"You are lying on the future site of the 9th hole of The Dream," she says. "The incomparable golf course designed by none other than Roy Erskine himself. And up there behind those woods on top of the highest hill is where the lodge will be."

I eased back further and took the holster off, making sure to keep it within arm's reach.

"How'd you know that?"

"I just quit my job at The Coffee Cup," she says. "I heard all of the talk. This land is all going to be sold."

"Going to be sold?"

"You have been gone. You haven't heard all the talk about Belle Llewellyn taking over her Daddy's bank? The deal will be finalized tomorrow. That's why we're all here tonight. It's a going away party, I guess you could say."

She has stretched out on the blanket too, the baby now perfectly quiet and content at her breast.

"What's your baby's name?"

"Isabel."

"Isabel," I say, as if for emphasis. The baby comes off her mother's breast and looks toward me when she hears her name. She is a smart little girl. Then she turns back to her business.

"Why did you quit your job?" I say.

"I'm going to California."

"California?"

"San Francisco, California."

"What do you want to go way out there for?"

She pushes her hair back behind her shoulder. "You have been gone for a long time, haven't you."

A flashlight moves across the sea of blankets, beaming down on each, rolling bodies over—staring into each face, creating quite a ruckus. I know who it is without looking. A huge, hulking figure cuts away the night sky. It moves toward us, one by one.

Lucy pats the blanket with her free arm. I roll toward her. She smells of musk and patchouli. "Don't be afraid," she says, and covers me up.

Then I hear her don a Southern Belle's accent. "Land sakes, can't a mama even nurse her youngins anymore?"

She slips her other breast in my mouth. I drink her sweet, slightly bitter milk. Then she puts the covers over my head and gives me a squeeze until I grow painfully erect, just like back in seventh grade.

"There, there," she says . "You're just a child, too."

She puts one hand behind my head and holds me while the awful presence passes before us and away forever.

Then the music starts.

The Black Berries

Three a.m., the witching hour, and I am driving north out of The Motor City, a bag of cash at my side and a new 62 Vette, given to me at the close of the deal. I have the top down. I will make the five-hour drive up North to Blackwood in half-time, where at 10:00 a.m., I will announce the takeover of my father's bank.

My business card. It reads: Belle Llewellyn I Sell The North. That's my motto.

A woman stands on the corner of John R and Brush. Her red dress is slit up the side. A gust of wind comes up and exposes her dark underside.

That could be me.

"What is it about red?" Mother always used to say. "Men always like red. Your father was like that. The bastard."

In her latter days, she often spoke about Daddy like that, in the past tense, as if he were dead.

Daddy isn't dead, but Mother sure as hell is.

The sweep of my headlights passes, and the lady in red sees my flowing blond hair, my sweeping jaw line and dimpled chin. Our eyes meet. She tosses her head and gives me her best fuck you look. The radio plays and Billie Holiday sings, *God Bless the Child.*

The lawyers advised that I take my mother's maiden name, and I have. Belle Llewellyn. First name is my middle name, taken from Grandma.

The old first and last name have been clipped. Clara Stein. Ugh! Can you imagine? Clara Stein, Frankenstein. Something had to go. It sounds like I should be sixty pounds heavier and out in the field milking, the tinny sound of milk hitting the side of the pails. Tugs.

Besides, I have no boobs, and I am flat-chested; but I make up for it in other departments. There was some talk of me being a model. Back in sixth grade, my dance instructor, Mrs. O'Reilly actually suggested it. "You have it all," she told me one day, holding my chin in the palm of her hand. "Blond hair, athletic body, Kirk Douglas chin, and lots of smarts." I wasn't exactly sure what a Kirk Douglas chin was, but I could guess. I looked in the mirror one day and put my thumb in the little divide. I wasn't any model. I had a better way to make a buck, and it wasn't from other people's looks of admiration, although that would figure into the scheme of things. I didn't have to worry. Daddy nixed the idea. I'm glad. There are other ways to make money. I have the tools .

I'm no Clara either, but Belle is a name I can live with. Belle of the ball, Belle Starr, I can hear the bells ringing. People wonder where I got my looks. It sure wasn't from Daddy, though he is a handsome enough man. We're as different as red and blue. I would sometimes overhear his hunting buddies teasing him about me down at the barber shop or at the hardware, making not so subtle innuendos about old Cletus Shoemaker, who ran the dairy, getting special overtime from my mother for his deliveries.

Daddy had a good sense of humor about the whole thing, though they didn't dare push the envelope too far, since he had liens on every merchant's property in town. I guess he could afford to laugh at a stupid joke. What a contrast we made, him with his jet black hair and dark eyebrows, and me tall and blond with long legs and perfect posture. We had other big differences too. Differences that I would soon correct.

His side of the family were immigrant bankers and financers, all with a knack for thrift and money making; a gift that three generations of Presbyterianism, Lions Club, and Rotary were finally able to water down. It was a family inheritance that I wanted to reclaim.

Mother was a druid, a Celt, fair complexioned like me, but in a different way: fragile and reddish with freckles. Maybe that was what did her in—her constitution, that and the usual—Daddy's drinking and his taste for younger women.

I used to hear them fighting. All of Daddy's charm and wit would disappear when he'd been drinking. His voice became warbly and whiny like a bad yodeler in a country band. Don't think I haven't heard about you, too, he would say. You've managed to attract quite a little bit of gossip yourself around town with your little poetic escapades.

Poetic escapades? What was that supposed to mean? Even then I found it amusing that Daddy would suddenly take the moral high ground. Mother died, I've been told, clutching a poem to her chest. I never read the contents. I just know I hate poetry too.

Now it is poetry that stands in my way to closing this deal. One maverick poet who refuses to sell his land, but this will take care of that. I pick up the bag of money and smell the bills. Nothing like the smell of money. Nothing can resist it, not even poetry.

The town that Daddy referred to is Blackwood, "A Little Touch of Wales," as the advertising calls it, nestled away in Northern Lower Michigan: population, 730; topography, wooded, rolling hills, farmland, with abundant lakes and waterways. A forgotten little community in the remote wilds, a place that I plan to put on the map, starred with dollar signs.

While Daddy mismanaged his bank, Mother fled to her easels and brushes, poor soul. Someone should have informed her, business and art make strange bedfellows. She frittered away each day painting landscapes. Autumn leaves and sunsets over Stone Lake. I would have none of that. Her painting actually brought in a lot of extra money. Money that she didn't need and never really claimed. At least Daddy knew what he wanted and in a manner of speaking, he went after it. That was why when I moved into the summer home and Daddy was living with his latest floozy—a new hire, some poor teller with a firm ass and big tits—that is why the first thing that had to go was Mother's paintings. All of them donated to local museums and art shops, except one, a little known project that she made me promise to keep. A log cabin at the end of a little ravine backed up next to a meadow. A trail led up to it, cutting through a patch of blackberries . A man stood in front working a garden. Deer were on the premises. For some reason this was special. Not surprisingly, this picture was entitled, The Blackberries. I boxed it up and put it in storage.

There were other changes too. I had the stone fireplaces replaced with smoked bronze plating. Blinds were installed on all of the windows so I didn't have the lake and all of its splendors and magnificent sunsets and coral-colored chasms staring at me, unless it was on my terms, when I wanted it.

It was out with all of the old driftwood. Mother had this thing about collecting it and putting it around the living quarters in old vases, which were also filed with God-knows-what—dried flowers and weeds of all kinds. If it had a blossom, mother loved it. She would always have someone stop the car alongside the highway so she could go gather something growing, a flower or a pet apple. The bird baths and the Greco-Roman statues were out too. I gave some serious thought to keeping Athena, but in the final analysis, she had to go too. Out with the past. Bury it. Move on. Get up with it, I say!

I replaced them with wrought iron works, streamline figures, neither men nor women, all with bodies strong and angular. I bought them up in Chirk at the art fair from a little farm girl named Jesse. They were a steal. I almost felt a twinge of guilt. She was more than happy when I rolled the bills up tightly and placed them into her strong hands with all of their nicks and bruises and unpainted nails.

I had no intention of getting such a late start tonight out of Detroit, Gross Point actually, home of the rich and beautiful. But when business calls, business calls. God, I've never seen so many uptight people in my life. Take Henry for instance. Who would ever know that he's the CEO of Detroit National? At home he's a wimp and a lush. First of all, I had to sit around while he and his buddies from the NYSE got tight on scotch. I mean, come on! I knew what was on their minds. Me, I'm not a drinker. I sat around and watched them get soused. They thought their stodgy Victorian homes and in-house maids and cooks would impress me. I even met their wives, at least Henry and his local gangs'. The boys from New York City came alone. They know a good time when they hear one, even if it is in Detroit. But getting back to the wives, I've never seen a sadder, more pathetic bunch. Pampered, spoiled, but with no direction. They wore the look of alcohol and boredom. Henry's wife, Estella, was no exception. She wandered up to me during the pre-dinner cocktail party, which was really just an extension of the whole day.

"Tell me, dear, how is it that you manage to keep so thin?"

I was drinking my usual, ice water and lemons. I had especially chosen a light, peach-colored summer dress, done in silk with straps and low cut, not that I had anything in that department to show off anyway. But I made up for it in other departments. The dress was short, just above the knees. I could have gone higher, but I wanted to give just enough away so that the boys from New York would get the picture. They did.

"It pretty simple, Mrs. Morris. I run five miles a day and I play a lot of tennis."

She rolled her eyes up in her head. "Oh, that sounds so exhausting." She was wearing one of those expensive Cassini strapless dresses with a bow on top, where the boobs were, inspired, no doubt, by Jackie Kennedy. This was no house of Democrats. Besides, it did not compliment her flabby arms.

She unexpectedly took me by the arm and led me out into the courtyard.

"Don't be gone long with her Estella," Henry said from behind us. "I've got big business with that lady up North." He raised his glass when he said "Up North," as did the other little group standing there with him. They made quite the spectacle, the group of them standing there on the marbled floor with the winding banister behind them and large chandeliers hanging overhead. Up North had become our future advertising slogan for marketing and developing Northern Michigan. That was one thing that we did manage to accomplish over the past few days, we had a slogan and the contracts were signed.

"Henry tells me that you've managed to get hold of a great deal of land," she said.

I was surprised that he allowed her to know so much about his business. I decided to let that one sit for a while. I would answer her in due time. We were out by the pool and beyond that was the tennis court, clay no less. I steered the conversation in another direction.

"Do you play?" I gestured toward the court.

"Oh heavens no. That came with the property. Henry used it a little at first, but he soon lost interest."

"It's a shame to see it go to waste."

She took a seat next to me on a little wrought iron bench, painted white and meant more for ornamentation than comfort. I could tell she was a former fifties child, Bobbie socks and saddle shoes that had gone matronly. She still wore her hair parted on the side and swept across on top with little curtain bangs falling part way down her full forehead. Her eyes always seem to be looking someplace else when she talked to me, and she had this habit of chewing on her lower lip in a crooked way. I suppose she was still considered young, at least by Henry's standards. She had to be at least twenty years his junior. But from what I already knew of Henry, he was getting ready to trade her in on a newer model. I wondered if she was his second or third. We were in an arbor, thick and lush with all kinds of flowers and bushes, none of which had ever been touched by her precious jeweled hand.

"I purchased all of the hill country, woods, and lake frontage I could get my hands on. Three thousand acres and counting."

She seemed lost in thought and looked at me as if puzzled.

"The land," I said. "Northern Michigan."

An idea seemed to come across her blank little head. "Who would want to live up there in the middle of nowhere with all of those inner-bred barbarians?"

I couldn't contain my smile. "You would, in a beautiful getaway home located in pristine forests with streams at your doorsteps."

It was the same pitch I had given earlier to "the boys" after they'd come off the golf course. I had had my photos and contracts out. All I needed was the go-ahead, and of course, the cash.

What a steal. Over three thousand acres at fifty bucks an acre. A million-five that promised to increase in value fifty times over in the next five years. That was the kind of banking that Daddy never heard of.

Estella leaned toward me, her face placid as a doll's. "It's good to see a woman finally get the upper hand on Henry." We both heard the nervous sound of his footsteps approaching. She put her hand over the top of mine. It was cold and icy, but in her eyes was something else. If ever I could have trusted a woman, it might have been this one.

"Don't underestimate him."

"And what are you two doing?" he said. "Conniving a scheme?" He had his hands on his hips in fake admonishment.

"Oh no," Estella said. "Belle was just telling me that she loved gardening, weren't you?"

His smile went smirky sideways. "That will be the day. The only kind of gardening Belle likes is the green leafy kind with the seal of the treasury on it, Jacksonian lettuce, right Belle?" He took Estella by the hand and pulled her to her feet. "Let's eat. I'm starved."

Daddy always said that more deals were made on a golf course than in any office or corporate room. Maybe so. He was an avid golfer with perfect form. He looked the part, tall and lean and always dressed in black, like Gary Player, to compliment his own dark hair. When he teed off his driver would quiver through the air and hit the ball with a resounding thwack that sent it cruising out in a straight line that soon gained altitude and nearly disappeared from sight. I know because at an early age he forced me to be his caddy. I was an only child, my tomboyish figure the closest thing to an heir apparent, but not close enough. He tried to teach me, but I purposely played the klutz. I hated golf. It was such an old fart's game. All finesse but no power. Your opponent was always three hundred yards behind you teeing off while you were busy chipping or putting. I also hated the way all the old farts always wore their shorts up too high, as they were trying to hold something up.

Now building golf courses was another matter. I had no problem with that. One thing I understood at an early age was that there was money to be made on other's desires. The econ books called it supply and demand, but I called it something else, and I'm surprised Daddy didn't get it, being the letch he was. There was the thrill of it all, the sheer exhilaration of the deal, of wanting and getting. Some call it greed, but that is an oversimplification. Others called it freedom, but that isn't it either.

I thought he would have been open to the idea of installing some quality 18-hole golf courses using the cheap land that was available. But on this one he sounded more like my mother.

"I financed those farms out there," he said. "You think I'm going to turn my back on them now?"

"Nobody's asking you to turn your back, Daddy. Most of them I talked to are ready to sell. They're tired of farming."

I was driving the cart for him. In those days he always made it a point to go out and shoot a nine before going to work.

"You tell that to Larry McMurden. You tell him he ought to sell off his cherries or let his alp alpha go to seed." He was teeing off on his favorite hole, number five, the only one that offered any view. The golf course, itself, was unimaginative and ran parallel to the highway for the most part. It was financed by Daddy in a deal struck from Forest Weber's barber chair on main street. He often touted this story at our house. Blackwood was a one-of-a-kind town. One hardware, one drug store, one theatre, one grocery store. That was how the locals liked it and Daddy wasn't in any hurry to change things. I had different ideas though, ideas of my own.

Like I said, I'm not all that fond of golf. Earlier, Henry and the others had gone out to do their good-ol'-boy-thing. I let them get a little soused and tell their jokes and read the stock page of The Sunday News. Me, after I finished my run, I did some laps in the pool and finished off the morning with some sit-ups and push-ups. I took a quick shower. The water ran down my flat chest and slick belly. I slapped it. This was where my six-pack was. I was ready for this afternoon's meeting.

We all gathered for gin and tonics out by the pool. A canopy had been set up. There was a new face among them. Henry wasted no time in making the introduction. This is Wilson, from New York, he told me. Wilson looked at me with his big watery eyes and gave me a polite handshake. This was somewhat of a surprise to me. Nobody had said anything about a newcomer joining us. He was the only sober one in the bunch. His blond hair was clipped short, but there was a turf of curls there ready to sprout like cork screws if given half a chance, though I didn't see much of one, judging by his tight-ass appearance. He was the only one in shirt and tie, despite the August heat.

Henry continued, "Wilson is from the specialist firm of Duer and Law. He flew all the way out here just to join the fun."

There was no joking with this guy. He had already turned his attention back to the maps and aerial photographs I had supplied. He had them spread out on a table. "Wilson works 24-7 don't you Wilson. That's why I like him on my team."

He wore a pair of half-lens reading glasses that was perched on the end of his nose and gave him a more mature look, but still couldn't hide a youthful face. It was the first time I'd felt older than someone in a business meeting.

"Now Miss Llewellyn," he said.

"You can call me Belle," I told him, even though I couldn't imagine that name coming out of his mouth.

He was pointing at one section of the map. "There is one gridline here that hasn't been sold, is that correct?" He leaned down a little closer for a better look. "Apparently it's right at the center of the development. It will be surrounded. And it says the owner's name is Chase Letty." He leaned a little closer to the document. "Resident poet?"

"That's right. He's been the only one so far to hold out, but I expect that to change."

"Do you?" This was the first time that he managed to look at me.

"He's an old man and I hear his health could be an issue," I said. I of course made this up spur of the moment. I hadn't seen Chase Letty since high school, when he'd occasionally speak at an assembly. He was considered a bit of an odd ball, except for the usual English teacher crowd.

"Charming in a way, don't you think?" he said. "Quaint. Recluse poet in the middle of a huge development. We could have him as a novelty of sorts at the ninth hole."

Henry and the others hadn't been paying too much attention up to this point, but now they got a good laugh out of this.

"He will sell. I guarantee it."

"You guarantee it?" Wilson said.

Everyone else was already starting to lounge around in the chases. A couple of attendants were setting up a small buffet. Only Henry was sticking around. He seemed a little more in the swing of things, gin-soaked with his damp black and white hair slicked back, a dark pair of oversized Oli Goldsmith shades, flip-flops, swim trunks, Hawaiian shirt, drink in one hand. He was the least of my worries, but this little pinhead was beginning to aggravate me.

"We had Wilson fly out for this meeting," Henry said. "Good to get off that floor, isn't it, Wilson. Wilson is a specialist. You know what that means?" I shook my head. "It means he's right in the middle of all that shouting and pushing. I don't know how he does it. There must be money in it somehow, though."

Wilson continued to give me the cool distant treatment. "It's an auction," he said. "No different than any other auction, just a little larger in scale. The person with the most money wins. My job is to make sure things run smoothly."

"That's right, my boy," Henry said. "I'll drink to that," and he finished off his gin and tonic and ordered another. "Wilson's group is doing the same thing in 'how many states is it, Wilson?'"

He turned his attention back to the map. "Among other things we're in the real estate/entertainment sector. We are currently developing master plans for Vermont, Upstate New York, Michigan, Wisconsin, Minnesota, Colorado, Utah, Idaho, Montana, and California."

Henry said, "Wilson was real impressed with your proposal, Belle, weren't you Wilson?"

"It had a certain merit and plausibility, but we can't build a resort complex around a renegade poet, Miss Llewellyn. I'm afraid it's going to have to be all or nothing."

"I told you," I said, "he will sell. I haven't a doubt." I was getting tired of all this talk. I decided to let my body do the talking. I was wearing a tee shirt over my bikini. I peeled down and dove in, letting the silky water ripple over me.

When I stepped out, Henry handed me a towel. "Take care of the poet, Belle. If he's a man, he can't resist you. He wiped off my back with a soft, spongy circular motion.

"No problem," I said.

Poor old lop-eared Henry. They say that carpet covers a multitude of sins. Well I say, money does too. A fat wallet and deep pockets can make stars of us all. I knew that leaving his place couldn't be as easy as packing my bags with the deal in my pocket. Henry had plans of his own, some last minute details. Men always do. But I had a few of my own.

I was staying in the guest apartment out next to the pool. I could tell that Estella did the interior decorating. Everything was accented in baby blue, same shade as the Casssini she wore at dinner; same color as the Mercedes in the garage. A skylight was dumping the last of the daylight down on a little wrap-around bar and a kitchen. I was packed and was busy applying a little make up when I saw his reflection in the bathroom mirror. He had a drink in one hand and a paper bag in another. He raised the drink to me in the mirror.

"Here's to the future and your continued success."

I snapped my make up case shut and turned to him. "Here's to the North." I didn't have a drink but I toasted anyway. There was just enough light left in the room to see the white of his shirt open against the gray curls of his chest. I walked toward him and he stepped back out of the way just in time to let me pass. I caught the smoky whiff of scotch on his breath. "What's in the bag?"

He set it on the bar and opened the end so I could see in. "A little persuader for your recluse poet." I could see bills stacked neatly inside. "Something to make him forget his pride and prejudice. Ten grand. That should do it, don't you think?"

"Cash is king," I said.

"Give him whatever you think it will take and keep the rest for yourself."

I slipped up on the bar, kicked off my shoes and crossed my legs. He had a briefcase that he snapped open. "There's one more thing."

"And what's that?" I said, not trying to hide the amusement in my voice.

He took a set of car keys and held them up. "A little something to help you get home with. Compliments of our friends at GM. He took out a pen and held it up for me to see. "You only need one more signature to make this a go."

"I figured as much." I pulled my dress up and slipped off my panties.

He stepped forward, pen in hand, but I put my foot up gently against his furry chest and shook my head no. Then he dropped to his knees .

There are a few things that cash can't fix in this world, a bad marriage or set of ears that stick out like door handles. They had to be good for something. I latched hold of them.

"That's the idea," I said.

II

The mystery of this universe of love is beyond me. Dumb words like these sometimes come to me just before sleep, lying here in the middle of mother's studio. This is the room where we found her, curled up like a sleeping child in the wicker over there by the portal, with that silly poem pressed to her chest. I thought she'd overslept, until I caught the smell of vomit in the air.

Six a.m. There is no time for sleep. The air is always coolest here. It is the only room not in pine but in plaster and the floor in large ceramic tile. I wait for daylight and the activity of a new day. It is not long in coming. The room slowly fills with light. I rarely come here. I'm not sure why. It is the only section of the cottage that I haven't changed. Not yet anyway. White plaster walls with portal windows. It's like looking out the side of a yacht or something. I don't know what she had in mind with that design, but this was her room, her sanctuary.

She loved wicker. Her baskets are still all around the floor. I haven't done a thing with them. Of course, they're empty now, but she used to keep them filled with all sorts of junk—flowers, cattails, and her magazines. Her easels are still here and the lone chair she sat in while painting, high backed with the interwoven leather supporting the back.

And those silly bags of pine cones are still around the fireplace. She used to pay me five cents each for gathering them when I was a kid. Ingenious me, I subcontracted the job out to the neighbor boys from Ohio, Jesse and Martin. Poor dumb saps. I would pay them two cents each and earn a profit of three cents or sixty percent on my investment. My first business venture.

Mother would paint the cones and make little figurines out of them. During the Christmas season, she gave them away as tree ornaments. I hated those dumb things. I wanted a toy truck, the big gravel hauling variety like I saw bringing the dirt in, when Daddy built this place. Or better yet, a cement truck, churning and turning the cool gray mud that came slopping out the chute.

I didn't particularly like dolls either. The dolls that mother gave me sat alone and unattended in my room. I always turned them toward the wall so I wouldn't have to see the dumb looks they wore. There was one, a Raggedy Ann; that was worst of all. She had orange pumpkin-colored hair and a blue and white dress.

Whatever happened to Raggedy Ann? She asked me, shortly after it came up missing. Raggedy was as stupid as Mother's pinecones. Both had nothing to do with nothing. They served no purpose.

I never told her what I did. How one day I became so sick and tired of her dumb stare that I tore her orange legs and head off and buried them in a box beneath the big hemlock tree in the backyard. The same tree where we all used to gather for Christmas carols.

I opt for a morning swim before visiting Daddy. The water is clear and still this morning, the color of robin's eggs. The wet grass and gritty sand make my toes itch. A mother and her three ducklings paddle away from me in single file. This will be better than my morning shower. A wake up call before battle, reveille.

I dive effortlessly, my body dividing the water with no splash. I swim out a quarter mile or so to where water goes cold. I dive down and swim toward coldness, until its pressure surrounds me and my ears ache. That is not all that surrounds me. My body wants to kick and thrash, to fight its way toward precious air and life, but I forbid it. The pressure builds in my lungs and spreads, pushing out from inside my head. My nipples harden.

Only then do I go back up and break the surface without a ripple. I ease the air out of my lungs and control my breathing. The sun is breaking over the thick line of beach trees and spruce. I roll over on my back swim toward shore. My boyish breasts break the surface. Something dark and powerful moves just beneath the water, a shadow between my legs. I do not stop swimming until my back lodges against the sand. I spread myself. The new waves of morning lap me. Now I am ready for the day and you, Daddy.

Mother thought Blackwood was quaint, with its tree-lined main street, hardware, drugstore, and local service stations. I have another name for it. I saw a picture in Daddy's photo album taken in 1942. Take away the old Ford coup parked in front of the variety store, and it could have been today, August 3, twenty years later.

The bank hasn't changed much either since my great-grandfather founded it back 1880's. It is still in the original location, Grandpa's home, Chicago-style red brick, touched up and refurbished over the years. I'm sure Grandpa had no intention of founding a landmark. It was a matter of necessity. The gazebo does add a certain nostalgic charm. The porch had to be torn down a few years ago. I'm surprised Daddy found it in him to replace it with a flowered walkway. His longtime attorney and childhood friend, Jack Milford, advised him to do so because of the increased liability from the rotten timbers. The windows are the originals, recessed multi-paned things with cute little cap blocks running all in a row around the sill and casings.

Ruth looks up from the desk and greets me when I enter. She is Daddy's first line of defense, the model of efficiency and loyalty, his secretary for the past thirty-some odd years. I might consider keeping her around, if she can give a little, learn to bend with the times, as the good ol' boys would say. There is built in radar in those dark eyes. I like that. They measure you. She has the type of square face that can be both den mother and she-bitch. She stands as I approach.

"That's all right, Ruth. No need to buzz him."

"I believe he's on the phone," she says.

Protecting him already from the inevitable. I walk on past her. She does need to do something with her hair though, clipped short like that and so steely gray. A little color wouldn't hurt. I can see Daddy through his office window. Another Monday morning, he sips his coffee and talks on the phone. He sits on a stool outside his office window, his legs crossed, and the gray socks stretching up his calf from his black wing tips. Outside his window, a large squirrel that is gray mixed with silver moves along the lawn, its tail wavering behind. He continues to sip his coffee and talk into the phone, smiling all the while. Daddy doesn't know the meaning of the word stress. He turns and waves at me through the window and beckons me in. He is on his best behavior, full of wit and charm, a handsome man that looks much younger than his sixty years.

"How's my girl?" He gives me a wide grin with those perfect teeth. I let myself be hugged and he gives me a peck on the cheek. "Come on in." He looks fresh and clean, as if he'd just stepped out of the shower. He always looks this way any time of the day. His face is tan and tight against his jaw, his dark hair thick and combed back. He looks as if he belongs on the tennis court, though he has never played. His good looks and charm have always been his best line of defense and attack.

His desk is neat and clear of debris. He acts as if he is welcoming me back after a long trip away. The prodigal daughter. That's the way it has always been, even when all of us were living together beneath one roof. I seldom saw him, and when I did he always made you feel this way, as if ten years had passed and we are getting together for one grand reunion.

"I've been meaning to stop out and see you." He refills his cup from a little 4-cup maker and adds his customary dash of cream and lump of sugar. Three mistresses and three years later, and he still insists on wearing his wedding ring. A form of denial, I guess.

"Sit down." He beckons me toward one of the big, easy club chairs around his desk. Daddy tries to make everything comfortable.

I take the seat and he moves over and sits on the corner of the desk, sipping his coffee. He is dressed impeccably as usual, the coat fitting his trim, square shoulders, his dark tie falling just beneath his belt buckle.

"I have some time available today," he says. "Why don't we take a little drive up the lake and have lunch at Marcos?"

I snap open the attaché.

He continues, "Or we could drive the boat across the lake and have something at The Pier."

I pull the papers out and hand them to him. The top one says from The Law Offices of Rothy and Green. Henry brought in one of his big guns for this. Daddy sets the papers down on his desk without looking at them. "Or if you want, we could just take a ride up to Shank's Orchard and pick some sweet cherries."

"Cherry season is over," I say. "Besides, Shank doesn't own his orchard anymore."

"Or we could go out to Sanchek's and go horseback riding. You always used to like that when you were a girl."

"You hate horseback riding," I say. "Besides, Sanchek's don't have the riding stables anymore."

He laughs and drinks off the rest of his coffee before putting it down next to the papers on his desk. The spoon rattles in the cup.

"You always were a funny girl. You used to say the funniest things sometimes. Embarrass your mother half to death. You remember that time you told old Brent Decker he should quit selling alp alpha and start selling snow mobiles? You were only five years old. My, my, you talked big and grown-up for your age. It was like you didn't have a childhood."

Ruth is off to the cashier's window helping Minnie Wells, and Marv Chapman is bringing in his weekend deposit from the bar. He looks in the window at us and nods. He still has that thin, unassuming body posture that totally belies his shrewd little insides.

I take a pen out and hand it to him. He takes it and looks at it in his hand, turning it end for end.

"Or we could just drive out to the cottage. I could make some coffee and we could go and sit by the water."

"Sign the papers, Daddy. Make it easy on yourself and everyone."

He looks down at the papers, as if he has forgotten something. Maybe he has. "What is this? You need a loan or something?" He turns the page and glances at the second page. "Is this a promissory note?"

"This isn't any promissory note. These are papers asking...these are papers demanding that you step down as CEO of the bank."

He looks at me and the faraway quality in his eyes seems to clear for a moment. The look of the kind, loving father disappears. "What is this?" He laughs again and stops short. His voice takes a level quality with a slight tremble beneath. "Don't even try."

"It's too late, Daddy. It's over. I'm the major stockholder in this place and I want you to step down. You can remain on in some kind of supervisory role for a while, if you want, or you can retire. I've made sure that you got plenty of money to go along with what you already have. You will be well taken care of."

He begins paging through the papers. I can see the rage building in him. I prepare myself for anything, but just when he is about to boil over, he calms himself.

"What? Is this your way of getting back at me for your mother?"

"Leave her out of this."

"That's what it is, isn't it. You never forgave me for leaving. You never. . ." He rings for Ruth.

"Show the little brat out, Ruth." He turns his back on me and looks out the window behind his desk. The C&O passenger train has just pulled in from Grand Bay and is loading up for its final run to Trowbridge, Ferndale, Chirk and Talbot. Charlie Lamb is cruising around on his riding lawn mower and Jim Parks has just pulled into the parking lot.

I turn to Ruth. "You no longer take orders from him." I have known Ruth all of my life. She speaks to me now in that same paternal voice of the ages. "He's your father!"

At the counter, Minnie Wells is still waiting with more questions. She has shrunk over the years and walks with a cane to compensate for her bad hip. She recognizes me when I walk out.

"Good morning, Mrs. Wells," I say.

"I am having trouble figuring this checking account out," she says. I turn to Ruth. "Well, Mrs. Dickson will be happy to help you out, wont' you."

Daddy remains at the window. His shoulders are slumped, but he quickly corrects himself and throws his shoulders back to his usual erect self.

He needs a few hours to gather his fight. I will grant him that. Ruth has gone into his office and stands next to him. I walk out and leave both of them standing there.

The morning sun is well up. It's going to be a beautiful day.

I make my way along county road C620, following a map, stopping from time to time, locating the gridlines. The road is gravel with thick vegetation on both sides. The air is thick with the smell of cedar and swamp. A group of teenage boys drive by in a red Mustang. They make catcalls and wave their open beer cans at me.

According to the map, the road to Smith Crick should be about 150 feet from where I have parked. I have brought a change of clothes and make a quick switch in the front seat. Now I am into something more comfortable—running attire. I grab the bag of money and head out.

This much I know about Chase Letty. He is a bit of a recluse. He does emerge from time to time and give readings at schools and various assemblies. He also comes to town on a regular basis to get his mail and get an occasional haircut. He was a World War II vet and has kept his hair short military style, but the last I saw of him, he'd let his beard grow. It fell like a long gray tail down to the middle of his chest. Most people thought of him as a colorful oddball. You would have to be, to live in the woods without running water or electricity.

I begin following the trail. It feels like one that I've been on before, passing through a thick stand of trees then up a knoll into an open area and back into the woods. A sudden snorting sound to my right throttles me, then the heavy sound of running hooves and snapping brush, a white tail flashes up as the deer easily clears an old fence. This is prime acreage in the middle of undeveloped land. That hill up there will provide the ideal site for the getaway home.

The trail is smooth enough to suggest inhabitance. A breeze passes through the treetops. Whisper Meadows, that's what this subdivision will be called. The idea would be to clear just enough land to build homes surrounded by forests. A natural environment with all of the modern amenities. I start to jog. I always think best when I'm running. Things open up for me. Ideas flow. The trail passes down a slope of sumac, through a ravine, across an open sunny area and then back into deep woodlands again. My body is warmed up. It can't be much further. I should stop and cool down before I meet him, but I want to enjoy this moment a little further. I am envisioning chalets nestled in the woods with fairways in the distance.

Then I see an old makeshift sign nailed to a tree. SMITH CRICK. An arrow points to an open area ahead. The trail shows more use and goes into a two track. It runs through a large blackberry patch. Blackberry. I can envision the name imprinted on a piece of cedar attached to a gateway of stone. BLACKBERRY DRIVE. A paved road will run through this valley. The name of the subdivision will be Blackberry.

Something passes on the hillside to my right. Maybe it is the sun going behind a cloud. Patchy shadows form against the earth. One of them raises its head and looks at me. Our eyes meet. Hers are dark and small and suddenly fierce. They say, you bitch, get away from my children! The two cubs are closer, within fifty feet. I stop suddenly, but it is too late. I scare them, and they cry out for their mother. It is a funny, hoarse little cry.

I begin to sprint. The bag falls to the ground. I look back over my shoulder and see her behind me, stopping for a moment to sniff the bag and tear open the contents. A few of the bills cling ridiculously to her long, pointed snout, while the others begin to tumble away in the breeze. Some stick to the blackberry bushes. She snorts the bills and then looks at me as if her anger has suddenly magnified. She begins to move toward me in a slow, lumbering motion, and then faster, her black fur rippling against her haunches.

The cabin sits at the edge of the woods. Chase is standing out front watching. He makes a gesture with hands, palms down, pushing toward the ground. "Get down!" he shouts, and begins to move toward me.

I trip like one of those silly, weak girls in the horror movies when the monster is about to overtake them. Pain shoots up my right leg. The dirt sticks to my belly. I put my head in my arms and close my eyes. I will not cry. I will not scream out.

It's not the bear's body that reaches me first but another. The hot breath, thick with leaks. The dry beard against my neck. "Don't move," he grunts. He shields me with himself. The weight of him grinds into me. His arms are outstretched over my own, a human blanket. The shadow passes over us. The rage wilts to curiosity, the chesty cough, the damp nose, cold on the tip, between my legs, the scratchy tongue against my thigh, then gone. We lay there in unison, still, not moving, hardly breathing.

"Don't move." This time he whispers. "Be very still." His voice contradicts his presence over me. It is probably what a poet's voice should be like, a half whisper with something ordinary beneath it, yet with timbre. My heart is still racing. The spongy, gritty feel of moss presses against my face. His body isn't heavy. Secondary scents are there, something of pine and mint. The sun warms us. Our breathing returns to normal.

He lifts his head and carefully pushes off me. I let him help me to my feet.

"That's Rose," he finally says. "She won't hurt you. You just gave her a start. She's a little fidgety now that she has little ones."

"I've got to get my money." I realize how odd this must sound to him, being out here in the middle of the wilds, but he doesn't seem surprised. I can think of a million smartass retorts, but there are none.

"We can do that." He still speaks in a low voice that makes my own seem loud.

"It's not really my money." I decide against trying to explain. With him money wouldn't really matter, but it is money. I start out for the blackberry bushes but can only take a few steps before the pain hobbles me.

"Wait here." He walks off in his slow, leisurely manner and returns with a walking stick, a staff. I am able to move along if I lean on that and step gingerly. We start out, but I am hesitant to go back in the direction of the bear. The thought of the cash moves me.

"It's all right. Old Rose isn't going to bother us. She's a little crotchety in her old age." We walk down the trail. Several deer are feeding along the edge. One raises it head and twitches its large, leafy ears and goes back to munching. When this area is developed, a small area with deer might be nice. It would add a nice family touch. Most of the money is still there. Bills are spread out against the trail and others are caught in the thorns of the berries. I can feel the bear watching us from the woods. Resentment and jealousy are in her dark eyes. Chase busies himself with picking twenties from the bushes. He is unhurried in his movements, unfolding and straightening each bill carefully.

"I was just coming down to get a few berries for breakfast and gather some for Mel's Market," he says.

I have seen his berries before in town at Mel's and at the farmer's market. Chase's berries had their own special section, marked off from the other imported berries. The sign above them read, "Chase Letty's Blackberries." Blackberry bushes might be a nice touch too, except the thorns might be a nuisance, so scratchy and picky. I drop the stick and get on my hands and knees. I begin picking my own twenties. We gather up most of the money. I give him my bills. He has organized them neatly in even stacks, piled perpendicular to each other in crosses.

"I've got another bag you can use up at my place," he says, and we begin walking back up toward his cabin. How generous. The man is even going to replace my worn out, shredded up moneybag. "And we'd better take a look at that ankle."

I have almost forgotten about that, but the dull ache seems inspired by his words. It begins to throb. The crutches are shaky and we have a difficult time moving.

Finally he says, "If you will allow me," and he picks me up and carries me the remaining distance. His place is neat, compact, and spare. The logs have been hand hewn and notched, taken from the local timber and felled by axe and his labor. I have the sensation that I've seen this place before, though the notion is ridiculous. I've never been here before.

He carries me around back to where the axe is still stuck in a stump at 45 degrees. "We've got to get that elevated," he says, meaning my ankle. There is a row of neatly cut and stacked firewood. He sits me down and grabs a few sticks and props my foot up in the air. I hear water running from somewhere. It is a natural bubbly sound like a brook or a spring. I am not wrong.

"I don't have any ice, but I've got the next best thing." He strokes his beard for a minute, and then he says, "You're Fritz Stein's daughter, aren't you?"

I can only nod because the pain has suddenly escalated to the misery level.

"I knew your mother."

Even in my agony, this surprises me. Nobody ever knew my mother, not much anyway. It was always, "I know your dad." Daddy had liens on practically every piece of property in town.

"We graduated from high school together," he continues. Then I remember mother's painting, "The Blackberries."

He begins unlacing my shoe. "Here's what I want you to do. See that crick over there? Well that's Smith Crick and I suppose you already knew that and it had a lot to do with your visit today. Everybody knows about the fine Brookies that swim up and down the crick from one end to the other. But most don't know about this. He helped me up. Right behind it is the springhead. It's a hole about yea-big." And he forms a circle with his arms about the size of a basketball. "That water bubbles up from who-knows-where, somewhere far beneath us and it's only about 43 degrees on a warm day. I'm going to help you over to that spot and I want you to stick your foot in without giving it a second thought. We got to do this right away as soon as I get your shoe off or otherwise you will have all that swelling, okay?"

"Sure. Fine." At that point I would have done anything to stop the pain.

He helps me to the spring. I sit down and grip my calf, holding my bad foot up in the air. He finishes unlacing my shoe. His beard and hair have gone gray but his face is young, his skin smooth, wrinkle-free, the skin on his neck stretched tight.

"On the count of three, I want you to take the plunge, okay?"

"No need to count." I move on my own to the springhead, but lose my balance and partly fall in. My entire leg submerges in the dark water hole.

The pain becomes pure and then goes to liquid. It moves up my leg. The whole world begins to bubble. It is like a musical note that keeps moving farther up the scale until it reaches a point of pleasure, where the pain disappears and numbness moves out and slowly across.

He watches me intently. "It's better now, isn't it."

I cannot talk, nor do I want to. My eyes are closed and my body is relaxing. The water moves about my leg in little eddies, packets.

He continues to study my face. "There, the pain is gone, isn't it." I can only nod, as he helps me out and back to my sitting position with the leg elevated. He has some old rags and begins making shredding sounds as he tears them into strips. He wraps my ankle. His fingers are precise and nimble. He ties each strip into a small, compact knot. Soon there is a figure-8 wrap on my foot and the pressure is snug enough to reinforce my foot.

"That should hold you for a little while. Might not be a bad idea to see Doc Duffy when you get back and let him take a look."

A blue dipper hangs over a nearby branch. He dips it into the bubbling water and offers it to me. I am thirsty. The water has a slight aftertaste, something like mint, but not exactly. It takes three fills to satisfy me.

He finds a fresh bag, one that still has the imprint on it from Mel's. He puts the money in it and tapes the top shut.

It's just like in the movies. He walks over to the other side of his cabin and gives a whistle. The heavy sound of hooves approaches. A brown horse with a long white patch down the center of its face walks up to him and nuzzles against his open hand. A blanket hangs over some fence rail. He puts it on the horse's back. "This is Janey," he says. He carefully slips a bridle in. I had forgotten the stories about how he didn't drive a car, and all that.

I say, "Janey—Rosy, don't you have any male pets?"

He is busy brushing her mane. "Not really, I guess."

He helps me on the back of the horse and then climbs on. We begin at a slow, ambling pace. I stuff the money in front of my shorts. I am forced to hold on to him. I hook my thumbs into his belt loops. I try to keep my back upright and my distance. Today is not the right day to do business. Never try for a deal if you aren't a hundred percent, I always say. Right now I'm about fifty percent. But that will change with time. Time changes everything.

Horseback riding might be a good thing to add to the list of amenities: golfing, swimming, hiking; why not horseback riding? "Has anyone ever told you that you look like your mother?"

"My mother had freckles."

"Yes, she did."

I let it go at that. I really don't want to know anymore. The wide, solid back of the horse is beneath me, the ridge of its backbone running up the center. I study the back of Chase's head and his face when he turns sideways to speak. There is something almost familiar in that jaw line, beneath the beard, the way the chin stops short and clefs.

We are in the blackberries again and passing through the heavy bushes. He dismounts and gathers a small handful. They are large berries, nearly as big as my thumb. He hands me some. I accept the offer. Rule two: Never refuse the hospitality of a business client. I have to admit that the berries are sweet. I can see why they are in such demand at the market. It might be nice to develop the lots here in such a way that the berry patches remain as a novelty, although their thorns might create a problem. My legs are red and scratchy from them. Some people may object. That would be something that marketing could certainly determine.

Deer flies are beginning to buzz and dive-bomb our heads. He clicks his tongue and the next thing I know we are trotting in a three-beat cadence. The move is sudden and unexpected. I put my hands on his sides to steady myself. He is lean and firm and I make sure my grip suggests nothing more than necessity.

Then he kicks Janey's sides and releases the reins. We are going at a full gallop and I am forced to wrap my arms around him and hold on tight. He probably feels my small breasts against him. There is firmness to his back and solidity of substance. My hands are around his stomach, where there is no flab either. The horse is between my legs.

The ride is rollicking and rocking. It pounds me. I think that he will slow for the forest trail, but I am wrong. We rush into the darkness of the trees. The sunlight breaks in small patches and there is the smell of damp leaves and rotting. Branches are swiping at my face and I must duck down and against his should blade for protection.

He takes it up another notch and now we are in full gallop out and across an open field. I close my eyes and cling to him. The open sunlight hits against my face. My insides are shaken and I feel a side ache. I feel anger wanting to well up inside of me, but I am out of breath. It takes all of my concentration to keep from falling off. We go like that for a few minutes, wide open, without stop. His back is sweaty against me.

Then just as suddenly he slows to a trot and then to a slow walk again. A few minutes pass before I realize that I am still clinging to him. His belly is slick with sweat.

And then he stops.

"Here we are," he says in the same husky, piping voice.

I let go of him and he slips off the horse and then lifts me down. I find it remarkable that he still hasn't asked me why I was walking through the woods with a bag full of money. I find it even more remarkable that the peculiarity of this fact didn't occur to me until this moment.

He climbs back up on his horse. The sun is behind him so I can only see the flash of his teeth through his beard.

"Come back and see me again," he says.

I smooth my tee-shirt back down over my body.

I take a moment to regain control of my breathing before I speak.

"Believe me, I will."

Adagio

It was an unexpected accolade bestowed upon Minnie Wells, when one of her "poems" made the front page of the local weekly, The Blackwood Sentinel. Dr. Drew Burgess, President of the local writers organization—Professional Writers of Blackwood or PWB—heralded it as "a startling work of post-modern sensibilities, done with wit, charm, and playfulness." Few, if any, of the local community understood much of these words, nor did Minnie, since she could not read anymore. Minnie's words read as follows, printed exactly as they appeared on the crumpled piece of notebook paper that found its way to the editor's desk:

When the light the light of
The house when house light of
My light went out
Through the light of
The light out of my house
Is no light
When more out the light
Is no more
Darkness rains.

It was the final line, along with the "syntactical ruptures" as he termed it, that convinced Dr. Burgess that this was a poem of "surprising merit" and that Mrs. Wells was a poet of great promise.

Now Blackwood already had its resident poet, Chase Letty, a recluse in his own right, who lived alone up at the spring head of Smith Crick. But Dr. Burgess was no fan of Chase's poetry, though he dare not express that opinion publicly. Privately, he found the local poet's words provincial at best and highly indicative of his unabashedly bohemian nature. So he was more than happy to embrace Minnie, who, in his opinion, expressed the sensibilities of the modern age.

Minnie was no poet. She did play the violin, but she was no maestro of the word. This did not stop people from flocking to her house for interviews or feature stories and so on. Such a beautiful house it was, an English

Colonial with the slanted salt box roof, shrouded with trees and shade on all sides, and the signature white picket fence in front. Most of the interior was now draped in ghostly white sheets that had become layered with dust. Beneath these sheets and the vaulted ceiling above lay high-backed Windsor chairs of yew and elm and pedestal mahogany tables, all from a bygone era. Minnie had hired one of the local boys, John Dee, to come in and paint the walls of the west wing, where she now resided, an aquamarine blue. She found the color strangely soothing, which contrasted with the dark tones of the sheeted furniture. Donna, her homecare nurse, had gathered up other scraps of paper from the west wing and took them without Minnie's knowledge or permission to Dr. Burgess who became further convinced that this was a post-modernist version of Emily Dickinson in the making. The recluse poet who lived alone.

The truth of the matter, little known to Minnie, and unknown to all else, was that the poem was nothing more than a garbled note that she had attempted to send to her utility company, Power and Water of Blackwood or P&WB, complaining about a recent power outage at her house that occurred amidst a rather severe thunderstorm. In her haste, she had forgotten to include the ampersand, and the note instead found its way to Dr. Burgess office. The rest, as they say, was history, revisionist history.

More than its imagined poetic sensibilities, the note was indicative of a larger problem in Minnie's life, when her words were becoming increasingly harder to come by, and when they did come, they were out of order. The problem was not limited to language. Her whole world was going backward and every-which-way. Night had become day, and day night. Fortunately, man had not become woman, or woman man, not yet anyway.

So it was in the late afternoon and early evening, when the sun played against the willows at her front window and made dancing shadows across the glass, that she would arise and her day would begin. Today was no exception.

But the pain was a recent addition. There were all the others, when you got to be this age and sat up in bed and put your feet to floor the first thing every day, waiting for everything to fall in place. Not this one, though; this one cleaved her heart with an unexpected pain and pleasure, and yes, though she hated to admit it, with guilt. She sat there upright in her rocking chair and with one hand stroked her lamp. It was the only thing that brought some relief. Something about the front and back petting motion with her hand against the smooth porcelain, as if the lamp could have been one of her fifteen cats, relaxed her. So there she sat knocking her knees together, waiting for this long, terrible, delicious moment to pass, and pass it did, with her stroking her hand up and down the porcelain base of the lamp that was beside her. The lamp was rather plain in design and was a gift from someone who had purchased it in the housewares department at Mel's Market. She hardly ever used it. There was something else to it. This lamp and all of this stroking business reminded her of something.

Every day it came at the same time—afternoon to most, but morning to her—as if she had done the unthinkable. What was it? If only she could remember. If only she could hold the thought. But it slipped away. She was a dark, vertical line against the pearly light of the room. She tried and tried to remember. The willow outside her window gave her a shadowy clue. It began to shake its stringy locks and do a slow, graceful dance. "The evening breeze caressed the trees tenderly." She could sing, too, a crooning voice laden with sadness and longing. She clamped a hand over her lips and pinched off the giggle. Ginger, her calico cat, looked up. A shudder passed between them.

Last week they had sent her off in an ambulance when this happened. The youngest Dee boy, what was his name? "Bird" they called him. He had found her sitting on the front porch, clutching her chest and rocking back and forth. He was there to collect for The Grand Bay Courier. Off he went like the jack rabbit he was, to call Willie Harper, the town marshal, who in turn called Spike, and the next you knew, they were out in front of her house with their lights flashing and all of the neighbors coming out and standing in the street.

"Minnie Wells, what have you got yourself into now?" old Willie Carper said, as they were about to load her up on the gurney. So much for sympathy. The little brat.

They carried her out to the ambulance with all of the sirens whooping and whining, which brought every neighbor out onto their front porch, ready to enjoy the Friday free show. Old Della Dewey was right in the middle of it all, ready to spread more gossip and lies about her.

"Let them talk." She cleared her throat and began to rock. The three or four cats sitting around her began to keep time with their tails.

"Vicious lies."

Already she had half of the neighborhood convinced that she was poisoning their cats. She would never hurt anything, especially a cat, since she had fifteen of her own all over spread out in every dark shadow and alcove of her property. Della created enough of a stir so that they sent Willie Harper over one morning. Oh, just the sight of him made her so mad. She had to choke the off the choler that rose up in her. The little brat! He was no different than when she had taught him forty years ago in Sunday school, still dumb as a mud fence, with his big gut and toting a pistol and shiny badge. Stop it! Stop it! Buddy was like that near his end, too; bitter and angry about everything and so distrustful. She took a deep breath and let him lead her off into the tangles of her property where he found a bowl filled with green fluid. "Know what this is?" he said to her.

"Haven't a clue." He smelt it and then tried to hold it up to her nose.

"It's antifreeze. Cats love it. It smells sweet and when they drink it they crawl off and die a horrible death." That did it. Patience be damned. She ordered him off her property.

She didn't care what they thought. Not anymore. She had stopped caring a long time ago. She couldn't stop laughing when they carried her out to Spike's ambulance. That was the first time she had wet her pants from the pleasure of it all. She really had little control over anything anymore. "It's just gas," Doc Duffy had told her, the old fart. Since when did gas feel like this? If this is gas, give me more. And more she got. Sometimes it came over her and nearly throttled her and made her legs wobble. She would sometimes have to stop and whistle, blowing steam off like a tea kettle.

Enough daylight remained to give the blinds a soothing pearl color. She paused in her rocking and looked at the sheet music that was strewn about the floor all around her. Her violin case lay open with the Stradivarius inside. The sheet music awaited, Bach's Brandenburg Concerto #3 in G. The members of the local string ensemble had invited her to join them on the court house lawn (Was it tomorrow?) for the annual hospital fiesta, a fund raiser. That was what they called it, a fiesta, even though the only Hispanics in the area were the wandering nomads that descended upon the area every cherry season for a few weeks at most, and then evaporated just as quickly into thin air. Call it what you will, she had been invited and now she must get ready. It was a fund raiser for the old folk's home, the one place she hoped to avoid, the end of the road for old people; and Minnie was getting old, not terrible old, but old enough. Close to eighty. She had lost count of the years since Buddy passed away. Her body had been good to her. That wasn't the problem. She had the thin, long-boned physique of a tennis player. Once, long ago, she had played and played well. Then something happened, the usual; the years, the decades, all slipped by and the family and the children—all of that. But her body remained, faithful to her, retaining much of its streamline suppleness. Her flesh still clung to her, no doughy parts. Her skin stretched tightly to her high cheekbones and her high silver hair looked elegant, pinned up to her head with a few loose strands falling down. She had an exotic combination of Ottawa and French in her blood. Minnie-Ha-Ha was what the neighbors secretly called her, except it was no secret to her.

She picked up one of the sheets and squinted at it. How was she supposed to practice with all of the plunking and chunking of the clocks in her home? Buddy had taken up so many queer hobbies near the end, raising bees and bicycling all over town during the wee-small hours of the morning, before the sun was up; and clock making was the last one. He got it into his head to make these clocks, and make them he did, spending twelve or fourteen hours a day in his workshop, tinkering and painting away. Then he put them up all over this section of the house, just after he sectioned off the north wing for her living quarters and sealing the rest off. It was a huge house, two-storied with a basement and multiple rooms, dining areas and foyers. He hung these clocks up on every wall, six or eight of them. He knew death was coming and he worked feverishly, transferring accounts into her name and arranging for the people down at the Methodist Church to come and look after her. Donna from the Methodist Auxiliary would be coming tomorrow, and she promised herself that this time she would insist that she take down these clocks and donate them to charity or give them away to whomever. They must be silenced.

She was growing to hate them.

It had worked well for a while, her living alone like this in her own section of the house with people dropping by to look after her, and the monthly checks deposited into her accounts. But it always seemed as though someone was knocking at her door. People could not leave her alone. First it was her grandson, Charles, as he now preferred to be called, rather than Chucky, which was what everyone had always called him since childhood; the little draft-dodger. She would honor his request. Everyone deserved to be called by the name they respected, so Charles it was, from here on out. He showed up and came marching in her door without bothering to knock and practically demanded a place to stay. She finally caved in to the pressure and gave him the south wing of the house, but just for the summer months. Try as she may, she could not like that child. Guilt dully panged her tired old heart. She took a breath. He was, after all, her only grandson, born to their one and only son, Charles, whom they lost in WWII. This left Chucky—that is, Charles—to be raised by his mother, who had her own torn life between three other husbands plus divorces and domestic violence. Life was so tangled and sordid at times. A year had passed, and he was still there. He was taking some photography classes over at the college in Grand Bay and working nights at the new lodge that had just been built by some down-stater. It wasn't long after he arrived that she began to hear the cars pulling up along the outside gate at all hours of the night. They thought she was asleep, but these were her new waking hours. She too had become a creature of the night. Her hearing had improved over the years, and she could hear the cold jingle-jangle of beer bottles being transported or the punctured *sssop* of beer cans. Her olfactory senses were keen, too. Did they think she was born yesterday? She recognized the musky scent of reefer floating through the still night air. She knew it well. Her brother, Marcel, had been a jazz musician in the forties, a clarinet player, and he often came home reeking of it. She could hear him carrying on in the courtyard, and all of those teenage boys coming over. Wearing his hair long like that and keeping that five o'clock shadow. He was a mix of Ottawa and French, too, which gave an exotic Mediterranean look. Who did he think he was kidding?

Funny how things turned, how they faded away like the television set at night, when it went to the test pattern, and the grainy static sound filled the air; then just that quickly fade back to pictures and sounds. A movement through the door to her left turned Minnie's head, doll-like. The bustling figure moved about picking up and straightening up.

"I loved your playing," it said. "You must be getting ready for tomorrow." The noisy buzzing of gears, the chains she pulled moving the weights of the clocks upward, rewinding; one-by-one she moved to and adjusted, and then to the blinds. A stab of light hit her eyes.

"And how did you get in here?" she said to the girlish figure with the rabbit and red-chapped lips.

"You let me in, Mrs. Wells. This is Donna."

You little liar, she wanted to say, but did not, censoring herself from the delicious temptation of anger, biting her knuckles instead.

"Oh, yes, Donna, of course."

"And you really shouldn't bite your knuckles anymore," she said, as she began busy-beeing about.

"Don't touch that," she said, meaning the sheet music she was about to touch. She arranged the stacks anyway.

A patch of light covered her bare feet. It came through the gunnery windows, up on high, which Donna just de-blinded, pulling the ropes up and down, until the slats were as horizontal as salutes. She marveled at the warmth and wiggled her toes and became dismayed at the dirty, thread-bare carpeting. She bent over and turned her hands in the light, as if it were warm water pouring out.

"Isn't life grand, Donna?"

"It can be. Yes it can." She disappeared into the bathroom, leaving the door slightly ajar, from where the steady roar of water filling the tub could be heard; and then came the fade, again, the water drizzling down her blades. "They're going to love you at the concert, tomorrow." Donna's long fingers worked the lather into her hair. "But the Adagio, why the Adagio? All of that pomp. This wasn't court music." The warm water poured down her head, across her throat. Bach, with his preoccupation with threes. Three violins, three violas, and three cellos. Concerto III. This was court music. And the second, movement, the Adagio, an odd seven second interlude that led into the third movement. Such solemn tones with its broken triads. This was court music, not meant for a summer outing.

Then fade again, and now this, standing at Mel's, the housewares, stroking the lamps, the smooth porcelains, while Donna busied herself in the other aisles, fulfilling the list. Yet she remembered how her white silk top made the perfect contrast to the dark tweed pants, and the lavender scarf floating in the breeze. Ducking beneath the roof, she had slid into the leathered front seat and watched the world slide by and by, until here she was.

Her eyes fell shut, and just as quickly opened again, as the image passed. The red shirt drawn taunt across the shoulders, the slow easy walk, the long ponytail, grown gray with the years, falling down to the middle of his back. She swayed back and forth, still stroking the lamp. So that was it, the stroking! The smooth electric skin across the flat stomach. How could she forget that? The fine pain in her chest, now she understood it, too. She stepped forward, but there was nothing there. Nothing between the floor and her knee. No pressure. No weight. It was like an amputee.

She went sideways against the lamps, spilling several against the hard floor, and making a terrible, shrill, shattering sound that filled the store. Then there was the whole matter of her chest, it was splitting. People moved in from all sides. A store clerk in a white apron, a young housewife with her toddler in a shopping cart, and of course, Donna from behind.

But she was getting her legs back by then. The clerk took one of her arms. "Are you all right, ma'am?" She hated it when people called her that. He was a young kid with curly brown hair set atop a face that was battling teenage acne. What did he know about anything! She pulled her arm free with such force and determination that he lost his balance and fell back against the dinner plates, creating another loud mess.

But she was gone by then, and her mind was clear and working. It was one of those rare moments of lucidity, like clouds parting. She took advantage and moved swiftly toward the front entry, walking with great intent and purpose, past the checkout and out onto the street. Her eyes ran the distance of the street, right and then left. Nothing. She slumped back toward the doors, when a crow raucously scolded her, atop a street light. She turned and saw him crossing the street at the far end, near the Smith Crick Tavern. He was probably going in for a morning beer. That would be his style. He moved in that signature manner, as if everything was loose and swinging.

She called his name. Someone tugged at her arm. "Denis who, dear?" "Why Denis Pontiac, who do you think?"

She crossed the street, her eyes fastened on the broad back and the long ponytail. She knew that back. It had been in front of her that night in the canoe, with her in the middle, and Papa at the back, drunk. He skillfully maneuvered the dark waters, while she held the torch. Night fishing, Papa with the spear in his hand, but too drunk to accurately aim and throw. Onward, they went, nonetheless.

She didn't care how stupid it was or how juvenile it might appear. She was a school girl again. She would call his name.

"Denis, Denis."

Everything was beginning to break free now, huge chunks of it floating up to the surface. A horn blared at her and forced her back up onto the sidewalk, next to Florham's Furniture, where she moved along with her left hand tracing her path along the window and the wall and the window. Her father was John Baptise, a merchant from the Detroit area before he packed up all of his belongings and moved north to Blackwood in hopes of capitalizing on the lumber boom of the 1880s.

At the post office, she stepped onto the street and brought another car to a screeching halt. She didn't care. She crossed over to the Colby Hardware. In the fall of 1889, he met and soon married a cousin to the great Ottawa Chief, Pontiac.

"Denis, Denis!" What had happened to her voice? It was a mere whisper.

They had three children, two in wedlock and one out. It was the first they had hidden away with relatives, for fear of the scandal. Here she had to stop. The pain was buckling her. She was the third, but who was the first?

"Please God, not that. Anything but that."

They lay next to the campfire embers, inside the teepee, with the night stars above them through the opening in the top. It was like a blue eye into eternity. She stroked his ivory smoothness, running her palm up and down this thigh, up to the curve of his buttocks, palm first, then the back of her hand, stroking, stroking, stroking.

She moved between two cars, parked. He stood at the point of a circle of men, at twelve o'clock, high noon. His words made them smile and laugh. His hands were sheathed in the back pockets of his blue jeans. She was close enough to see his thumbs extending out on either side. He wore a large knife, sheathed on his hip. His voice carried. It was not a loud voice, but it carried. It cut the air like a pure knife, it resonated.

"But when she did this," and he made a curvy sweeping motion with his hands, "I started to laugh." Then all of the others laughed too.

She was still carrying her long-strapped black purse. She dug into its content and produced a Wrigley's gum wrapper. On the backside she wrote something, a word that came to her, and then folded it up and threw it on sidewalk, where she believed he could see it. It was a clear, still day. She had already forgotten the word she wrote, but she did it anyway.

Then she turned and began walking away. She scolded herself. "You foolish girl. Your mind is playing tricks on you."

A little gathering awaited her at Mel's. This time she looked both ways before crossing. Her heels sounded firmly against the pavement.

"What's all the fuss? Can't a girl be a girl if she wants to be?" She pulled out a hanky and dabbed at her eyes where the mascara had gone dark and purple down her cheeks, and then she blew her nose.

Her evening, that afternoon, passed without an inch of sleep. Her body formed an S beneath the sheets, the pillow cinched between her legs. The pain, the God-awful, delicious, guilty pain had returned. It was a stake driven through her heart. It flayed her. The bitter, sour, smell of urine clouded her. She cinched the pillow up tighter. The headboard was cherry, framed in brass parts, up against gold and black colored paper, more suited for Christmas than décor. A hand emerged and found the cool of the bedpost and began stroking and caressing. She slipped into sleep, not deeply, but just far enough beneath the waters that pieces of memory broke free and drifted to the surface.

She was in the middle of the canoe and someone was behind her and in front. Was it Papa behind her? Yes, it might have been. He was too drunk to throw the spear. They had no business carrying four in the canoe that night. Three was plenty. She had jumped in last minute. It was past midnight and here she was, a 13-year-old watching the foolish behavior of three drunken men. Well, only Papa could technically be called a man. The others were her cousins; at least that is what she called them, though their exact relationship to her was not clear. If only she could remember. Papa had married Mama and there had somehow been other children in the mix. Eugene stood at the front the canoe holding a lantern out over the dark waters. That left Denis in front. Yes, the broad back, sweat-stained between the blades, tee-shirt white and glowing in the moonlight. He was the youngest next to her. Sixteen was it or seventeen? Even then he held his liquor better than the others. The mason jar of Papa's blackberry wine passed between them, always excluding her, not that she wanted any, anyway.

Papa was too drunk to handle the team that night, so they loaded him into the back and Denis came up front and took the reins. He had an easy natural touch and clicked his tongue and made soft tones, which put the horses on remote control. They stepped along and began the trip home.

Eugene was in the back, passed out with Papa. That left the two of them up front. Sleep came over her like web of gauze. She never slept well, but this was enough that she leaned her head against his shoulders. That was when she first caught his scent, a dark, smoky, earthen scent. It seemed to be coming out of his skin. It would linger everywhere, on her fingers, in her clothes, and in her sheets.

"Come on cousin, I'll see you home." Cousin was a term that meant a lot of different things on different levels to Indians.

"Is that what I am? Am I your cousin?"

He pulled out his pocket watch to check the time. She was taken by the picture on the inside cover. She had seen the same picture numerous times in old family albums. She recognized the long hair and birthmark on the left check, just in front of the ear.

"Who's that?"

"That's our mother, who do you think?"

Her eyes fell open. This was not sleep, but a mere imposter, though her room had become silver and opaque. Her schedule was off again. Instead of ten to six, today it was something else. The room was stuffy, bringing her to an upright position, and then out.

She slipped on her robe and moved outside for air. A nearly-full moon filled the courtyard with that blue, haunting light of dreams. But this was no dream. She pinched her arm hard until the red welts rose. Proof enough, for now. There was enough light to make things look elegant, almost : the tangle of things became her enchanted garden. Once though, this had been the site of the most high, the murmur of conversations, the pure note of crystal touching—the toast; Buddy had gathered the most influential. Bernie Gordman's jazz band played; Bernie's reedy clarinet was piping. And Buddy had this thing about fountains, Romanesque-style. Of course he had Minerva, but also Cupid and Venus. They had all been stilled with time and now were overgrown with moss and chipped from the wind and winter and everything else time had to offer. She found her favorite spot on a bench, where a pool of moonlight found her and encircled her, while six or eight of her cats gathered around her.

At half-past eleven, Chucky and his noisy crew arrived, amidst glass packs, screeching tires, and a.m. radio jamming. Chucky was driving a rag-top green GTO with an all leather interior. They sat there for a bit, with their car doors slamming and the dust rising (Buddy had always meant to get that shoulder paved). Pretty soon they all moved in through the white picket gate. His was getting to be a younger crowd all the time, really not that much past puberty, it seemed. The moon was passing in and out of the clouds, and they did not see her sitting next to the cedars and crab apples, where gin and caviar used to be the order.

Rain was in the air. Heat lightning flared up along the North horizon, out on Lake Michigan, she supposed, beyond Burry Port, out where water surrounded all, and land was nowhere in sight. She remembered those days, sailing with Buddy, standing at the mast, wind in her hair. That too would be gone in a few minutes. Everything was a moment's delight. Everything was. Chucky and a few others decided to stay outside, while the rest made themselves at home and moved into his personal living quarters. One of the group, a heavy-set kid in shirttails (Why did they insist on wearing them out instead of tucked in?) sat down on a folding chair and immediately collapsed it. Everyone got a big laugh out of this. The moon broke free again from behind the clouds, and she got a firsthand look at Chucky's face. He was a handsome devil, a mix of French and Indian, with his square mould, five-o'clock shadow and that glassy, disconnected look that could go off in any direction.

"So what happened then, Goose?" one of them asked. They had nicknames for everybody.

The one they called Goose said, "The one guy's collar was crooked and so was his tie." This caused more laughter among the group. "So when I gave him the address, I could see the veins popping out on his neck." Everyone laughed again.

She thought she recognized him, this one they called "Goose." It could have been Morley Gibson's boy, Roy. She couldn't be sure. He was a good looking kid, eyes the blue of deep water and that thick auburn hair. He was wearing it long, like all of the young men seemed to be doing as of late. It really wasn't that bad, the hair, quite pretty actually, with its red highlights.

Some of her cats drifted into their circle. She recognized Bridget, her white angora, long and feline and sensuous. Another one, Rusty, lagged along behind. Fluffy, the big black and white one, also appeared. Bridget rubbed up against someone's leg, and Chucky stamped his foot and hissed, which sent them scurrying.

"I hate cats," he said. "They make me sneeze."

"Only a sick mind could hate a cat."

"What's that?" Someone had her arm and was guiding her through a throng of people. They surrounded her.

"I said, I said my cat is sick."

"Oh that's too bad my dear. Do you want me to send someone from the animal shelter over?"

"Well no, not exactly. It depends on if events allow. You know how things go. They just pass along."

A bright sun hung in a blue sky overhead. Collectively they moved her along past the tennis courts, toward the gazebo, where the crowd was larger. All of this activity—the contacts, the bump of elbows, and the touch of a hand against her arm—it made her dizzy. One hand, though, was firm at her elbow.

"You're doing just fine," Donna said.

All of these people, they came up and grilled her as if they had known her all of her life. "They will probably need to decide one way or another," a lady said to her. She had snow-white hair pinned up in a bun.

"Yes they will," she replied.

This made the lady and the others around her laugh. "You dear-dear-dear thing," Snow-white said. "You are absolutely precious."

At the gazebo, the other musicians were setting up and nervously tuning their instruments. Hers was the third seat in the front row. She climbed the step in a slow, mechanical fashion.

"Mrs. Wells! We've heard so much about you and thank you for the cookies." It was a young girl sitting behind her. She wore braces and kept her hair in pigtails.

"Oh you are so welcome, my dear."

"And do you remember our promise?"

"Why of course I do."

"Marsha and I will be over to deliver it in a few days."

Things were beginning to come to a focus, the tuning died down. It was a perfect summer evening, the stillness of the old swimming hole, green from the reflection of the trees, now broken by a pair of swans gliding across the water. The space around the gazebo was quickly filling. People were spreading blankets and lawn chairs out. She had her instrument out and tuned. She was ready.

The Allegro began. This was pageantry; this was spectacle. Those three notes: G, F, and D. Not intended for a summer night in Michigan, yet the audience had gathered, the young, the adults, and the elders. More groups of three, including the players: three violas, three violins, and three cellos. Harmony, harmony, harmony: the nine muses, blah, blah, blah. A procession should be passing. Louis XIV and his court. G, F, and D, everything in threes, harmony, balance, and purpose—everything that was lacking in this brief morning of her life, that was occurring just before its end. Tears began to spill.

Then came the Adagio, those two notes and that queer interlude that was over before you knew it. It was at this precise moment that something prompted her to look up and she saw him emerging from the dark cedars. His huge frame stood out against the others at the edge of the crowd. Then just as quickly, he disappeared back behind from where he had come. And it was also at this moment, that she let go of the neck of her instrument, and with her free hand, clutched her breast.

Maybe she had only imagined him there. Nothing was certain anymore. But this pain in her heart. That was undeniable. Therein lay the proof.

Her instrument lay in her lap. The bow slipped from her hand. Ruth Bagby, the conductor, shot her a series of puzzled looks. The third movement, The Allegro, had begun. Behind the sheet music were the cedars, harkening in the shadows, where he once stood. She put her instrument back in the case and snapped it shut. She gathered herself up and wandered down the steps toward the image that once had been before her. The crowds parted. She moved trancelike past the barbeque pit and beyond the wall of cedars, until she was at the spillway, where dark currents and pungent smells made teenagers do forbidden things.

The music should have been behind her. It was not. Instead, it was all around her, everywhere at once. The tones richer, deeper, more distinct. She took off her shoes. The grass wedged her toes, damp and scratchy. The wall of the spillway was gray with time, a patchwork of green moss, squishy against her fingertips. Someone had set fishing lines along the wall. The poles were lined up one after the other over the waters. A curl of smoke rose from behind a tangle of wild vines and brush. She followed the trail toward the smoke. She stooped and pulled up a handful of wet grass and rubbed it into her palms until they were green and then spanked them clean, just to be sure. Then she climbed the wall, just like one of the kids would do and began walking it. The dark water passed in spinning eddies and bass idled underneath in the shadows.

From this vantage point, she could see him in the tangles. She let go of the violin case and clutched her heart. The case fell and now floated along the currents toward the power plant. She nearly fell and almost decided to let herself go along with it, to let the dark waters claim her. She was tired of all this, but decided to dream on. So she went to him, to this shadow from her past. It was his hair that was unmistakable, just as it had been the other day, still thick and the color of storm clouds, swept back on both sides with a single braid in the back that extended to his belt buckle.

He glanced up at her as though she had never been gone. He was slicing cucumbers with the same large buck knife he wore on his belt buckle, while something cooked over an open flame, fish of some kind, sizzling and sputtering in an old cast iron pan. She stepped forward and then staggered sideways, but then recovered. His campsite was neat, almost tidy, his bedding neatly folded, everything in place.

He unfolded a piece of paper from his pocket and handed it to her. "Kuda." Is that what you want me to call you? She recognized the Wrigley's wrapper. It was her ancient Ottawa nickname, Little Bird. She never cared for it. She was not a little bird. She was a falcon.

"You sounded wonderful tonight. Why did you stop?"

"Why did I stop?" She thought for a moment and then half-smile-laughed. The sound of the strings floated over the water. "Oh that, let's just say I had a vision."

This time he laughed, too, a hearty, leg-slapping laugh. "Still the same old Kuda, a little bird with the tongue of a viper." He had a couple of old cherry lugs situated around the fire. He pulled one up for her. "Compliments of Pembroke Orchards."

"So you brought back the cherry harvest?"

"I didn't bring it. It brought me."

She laughed. "Aren't you the clever one. Always the satyr in the forest. It didn't bring you, you brought it." She laughed again. "And you didn't bring me, I brought you, remember that." An angry spot passed over her face.

"I came back to pick a few lugs and take care of some other business."

"Other business?" She laughed again. "Can a cherry float a pain in the heart?" She took his hand in hers. "Keep me in your focus."

"I've heard you've become quite the poet." He pulled one of the cherry lugs up next to hers and took a seat, up close, right next to her. He put one arm around her. She neatly lifted it off her shoulder.

"Don't let the hen-house into the foxes."

"Tell me your story, Kuda."

"Well," and she sat up straight and cleared her throat. "The night sky sucks away my light, away the light. The evening shadows come to me in the late afternoon of my morning. I watch them emerge from the woods and stretch across the field until they arrive safely at my door. My door is always open to strangers, though I do hate surprises. The purpose was to door the opening and seal the message. You see, not everyone has listens to ears. This pain, it shreds me. The pain is my yesterday, and yesterday is just another word for not today." And here she fixed him in her pale blue eyes. "And today, the pain is you, mister, mister."

He stopped her and brought more food to her mouth. "You mustn't talk. Not right now. Here, eat."

"Don't tell me what to do."

He brought one forkful after another into her mouth, until the cucumber juice ran down her chin and her tongue slathered out. He unscrewed a mason jar of homemade wine, gave her a drink to wash it down and pulled a clean linen napkin from his knapsack and wiped her face. Then he pulled out a small double-sided mirror, circular and mounted on a pin, so it could spin round and round. He spun it several times and put it up to her face. He took her chin in his large, soft hands.

"What's with this?" His dark finger was up against her face.

"Why so white?"

"Too much stormy weather."

He gently rubbed her face. "That's not all pale face. Isn't there a little make up involved?"

Still in the mirror, she touched her cheek.

"Must you betray me with a kiss?"

"You aren't hiding, are you Kuda?"

She pulled her face away from the reflection.

"You need to get out more often. Expose your better half."

He picked at her dinner with his own fork and gave her another bite. "How long has it been since you've had catfish?"

Once again the fish crumbled and things ran together. "I think you've missed your calling.

"Not really. I've cooked in more greasy spoons and fancy restaurants than I care to remember. I used to cook for your daddy down at The Whiteford before it went belly up. Remember?"

"I don't remember much of anything anymore."

"No wonder you're so skinny." He began eating some of his own, taking large bites and dipping a biscuit in the juices.

"Skinny Minnie."

"Tell me about my better half, Denis."

"There is no better half. You are one."

She stopped chewing for a moment. "Tell me about my mother."

"About your mother? I would like to save that for another time. How about your father? That's a better story. Much more interesting."

"If the father precedes the daughter, where does that leave you, oh Jerusalem?"

"Okay, let's do this." He set his plate down and slowly wiped his lips with the napkin.

"She looked a lot like you. Pretty. Same hair. Same face. I didn't know her that well. She used to babysit. Got married not much over sixteen, maybe earlier. Just a kid. A straight-A student. She loved mathematics and would always help us with our homework. She would have made a fine teacher—with her way of making learning fun. I don't remember her all that well. I will say this. She deserved a whole lot more than your father. I'll leave it at that."

He pulled her close to him. "Now listen to this."

He put his mouth to her ear and his tongue filled her cavity like calk from a gun; it crept along every contour, spiraling its way until it reached the center of her being, where the light was. There it stopped. "I will be your voice. I will be your memory." She let out a moan; and he began.

His story came first, the war in 1917, serving in Belgium, digging down in the trenches; followed by a decade of decadence, bootlegging his way to fortune in Chicago; then a turn for the worse in the 1930s, riding freight trains across America, writing songs, a lifestyle that seemed to fit him. There was the one shot he took at settling down in the 1940s. Working in Detroit at the factories, building tanks on the assembly lines. Then in the 1950s, it was the merchant marines, malaria at Cape Horn and typhoid in

Sydney. Then it was back to America for a stint in the movies as a stunt man next to John Wayne, Randolph Scott, and Gene Autry, getting paid for being a whooping Indian.

"And now I've come back home to be what I have always been, my one true talent."

"'And what's that?'"

"To be all Indian again, one hundred percent. And you know what?"

"'What?'"

"I want the same for you.

"Your father was John Baptise, a Frenchman from Detroit who moved north in hopes of capitalizing on the great lumber boom of the 1880s. He opened several unsuccessful stores before he finally managed to eke out a living as a cook specializing in French dishes and pastries at the new hotel, The Blackwood Inn that opened within walking distance of the Chesapeake and Ohio depot.

"In the fall of 1889, he met and soon married a sister to the great Ottawa Chief Pontiac, our mother, Florence, who bore him one daughter, who was born premature, and soon died."

She brought two fingers to his lips and pulled her ear away. "I have a question, if only I could remember. But I thought, thought I that a mother's body and my body, came from a body, a body gone."

He hushed her and brought her back to him, and then he reentered. "Patience. It was not long before he opened a gift shop. This is where you come in." He moved the tip around in a small circle and darted at the center.

"'Straight out of medical school at the U of M, Buddy was. Traveling way up north to Blackwood.

"'I first saw him at Papa's store. He stepped in out of the storm and doffed his fedora of the white winter's snow. It was the Christmas season. He wore a full length trench, gray tweed, a fine cut. A handsome figure, tall straight, but already with the round spectacles that would mark his failing eyes. I was sixteen, ten years his junior. He came over looking at the glass display of jewelry that my father, John Baptise had brought up from Detroit for the Christmas season.

"'Was it the Christmas Eve of 1907 or 1908 that he came into the store? I forget. I always forget. It was one of those severe winters when Stone Lake and the whole of Grand Bay had already frozen over. The air was already dimming toward evening and the scene could have come out a storybook with the gas lit streets, heavy snow falling down and people closing up shop for the evening. I had just put another piece of coal into the stove and adjusted the air on the flame until it was a solid blue, when he came stomping in, a tall man who practically had to stoop to get through the doorway.

"'Mother is always difficult.' We were going through the fine chinaware, some of the better merchandise that Papa had brought back from Detroit.

"'How about these?' For the first time I ventured to look at him, into the small portholes of his blue eyes. I brought up a crystal set of salt-and-pepper shakers with silver stoppers on top.

"'Very nice,' he said, 'but she's not really the domestic type.'

"'The domestic type?' The first trace of a growing arrogance and elitism. It was five minutes past closing time and if I didn't get upstairs soon with the cashbox, Papa would be down. I began giving him enormous discounts, quoting prices that I vowed later to make up out of my own pocket. Still he hedged and mulled. This was another trait of his personality that would unfold over the years, his inability to come to a quick, firm decision concerning money matters. Finally we settled on a silver cased deck of playing cards that I discovered last minute in a box beneath the counter. And for his father, I sold him a fountain pen set, a more expensive item that was gold-inlaid. He got them both for next to nothing."

He extracted himself, and with his white napkin, he wiped down her neck and jaw, until they were clean. Her eyes remained closed until she began to clear her throat back to consciousness.

She said, "I have a question, if only I could remember. Why do storm clouds always appear ..." He stopped her again. "Not now," he said.

She looked up at the clear blue sky. "I can't find my way home."

A tall man took her hand and they emerged out of the thick tangle. The still waters moved slowly toward the slap and whine of the generators. He stopped for a moment and extracted the soggy violin case from the grates where the weeds collected and the water disappeared. He put one finger beneath her chin and lifted her up.

"Why the long face?" he said. "We can probably find another."

"At the root of things a seed has been planted."

He slipped an arm around her and guided her out of the thick cedars onto the sidewalk. She paused and looked to the left, where a bridge separated her from a quaint little town with shops on both sides of the street. Other than an occasional car passing back and forth, the street was empty, as if it were the close of a day. An American Legion Hall was the nearest building with its glass-block windows and flags swaying in the air. She smiled.

"What a darling little town. Can we go visit? I would love to spend the day visiting the small shops. I bet I could find a lovely pair of earrings."

"Not right now," the tall man said to her. He took her hand. "But I promise. We will return."

The sidewalk moved beneath them. They were moving, but going nowhere. The scenery passed. Twilight in a small town. Two Indians treaded along. They were not hard to miss. The homes were all from the 40s and 50s. One by one, the lights came on. Two story Victorian cottages with gabled roofs and quaint front porches, except for this one: a three story with widow's watches and plenty of gingerbread, lit up like a lantern. A metal engraving above the front steps said 1903.

"What year is this?"

"1967."

"Are we walking uphill or down?"

"What's it feel like?"

"It looks like down, but it feels like up."

Across the street, the white of a steeple rose above the dim lights. She paused at the foot of the cement steps, looking up towards the heavens.

"It was right here, wasn't it?"

He said, "The things you *do* remember! Yes, it was right here."

The steeple came to a point, where a cross touched the starry night sky.

"I had no right to do that on your wedding day."

"On my wedding day?"

The church door had swung open to an explosion of light, a cement stairway, and a shower of rice. A beautiful June day, a wedding day with sunshine, green trees, puffs of white clouds, and blue skies. She clutched the white bouquet. A crowd had gathered beneath them. She tossed the bouquet. A sigh, then laughter, and then a ruckus. Faces turned as a broad set of shoulders parted the crowd and caught it midair.

He was drunk in the middle of the afternoon and tried to get into the ceremony, but her father intervened. A near spectacle until the town marshal Jess Holton arrived. It was spectacle on spectacle. His corny blue light flashing on the dash. Enough of that memory.

"That was a long time ago," she said.

"Fifty years. And look at you, still the princess."

"Don't you ever feel like you have to apologize to me again."

"I won't."

Streetlights passed. One turn led to another and then another. His arm ran down her back, his hand on her hip.

"What month is this?"

"July."

"What day?"

"Thursday."

"I can ask you anything, can't I?"

"Anything."

"And you won't laugh?"

"I won't laugh."

They turned another corner. It was summer time and she was among the night's lovers. She put her head on his shoulder.

"I feel so young again."

"Yes."

" I could go like this forever."

Too soon, a white picket fence appeared with a name printed on it. Cars were parked out front.

"But I can't. Where are we?"

He pointed to the black lettering on the fence, a strange configurations of markings on the front.

"What does it say?"

He pointed to each letter, "The Wells, Buddy and Minnie."

"Whose cars are these?"

"I don't know, but I like this one." He stood next to a forest green GTO convertible with a black leather interior. He walked around it once, checking out the whitewalls, the leather interior, and the way the night lights play off the chrome.

"I don't know why those kids insist on parking in front of my place. I have half a mind to call Willie Carper."

The spring on the gate squeaked open. The tall man beckoned her through its entry. Voices, murmurs of frequencies, drifted through the night air. The red coals of the cigarettes rose and fell. Laughter.

"Buddy must be entertaining tonight."

"I don't think so."

"We bought this place when we first got married. It's our home but it's also a boarding house."

Another car pulled up, teenagers, unloads. Three of them, all boys, pass. One of them, a gangly kid in a tee shirt stopped for a second.

"Chief, that you?"

"Get lost."

A shadow covered half of his face. He stood beneath a small outside light. The air was grainy. She began searching for something, through each pocket, one by one.

"Maybe not."

"Maybe not what?"

"Oh, I don't know. Stop asking all of these questions. Maybe, maybe, maybe. Isn't that the way it always is?" She grimaced.

Then a new voice entered.

"Grandma, what big teeth you have."

Shadows spun and blurred, a face blended into them; dark hair slicked back, coating of new growth beard, flash of smile.

"Surprise, surprise," she said.

He stepped closer, out of the shadows. He was the same height as the tall man, but much thinner. "Grandma, it's me, Chuck, your grandson."

Once again, she was looking for something, sorting through the geraniums in the big vase by the door.

"Lose something?" He handed something to her, an object, heavy like money of the old days, gold or silver. She brought it her lips and tasted the serrated edge, the metallic taste. "My key, but of course. I was just about to…"

Then the stranger looked at the other man. "Is everything okay?"

"Of course everything is okay," she said. "Why would it not be okay?"

He took the heavy object out of her hand and inserted it in the door, making it fall back and open. "Donna was here earlier looking for you," he said. "She said you wandered off again."

"What does that brat know about anything? I certainly did not wander off. Drifted, yes, but wandered, no." She reached up and stroked the tall man's face, where the skin was still smooth like fine leather. "Though it is not so bad to wander, is it dear? You've wandered all over the world haven't you. While me. Well my life has been pretty boring, until now. I found this leech gatherer in the woods. He is not a draft dodger. He fought bravely in the war, didn't you darling."

"Well you got one thing right," the other man said, the one who purported to be her grandson. "He's a leech."

This stranger who stood before her, the great impostor who called himself her grandson had lacked the common decency to wear socks. He wore expensive Bass Weejuns, but no socks, white silk pants, thin belt, and a short-sleeve shirt with an exotic tropical design.

"How did the concert go?"

"The concert? Oh yes—the concert. Well let's put it this way. I think I finally understand the Adagio."

He passed another look at the man who accompanied her, the tall, handsome, upright, man whose name now escaped her, but whose smile and bundle did not.

"I'm afraid I don't understand what that means," her intruder grandson said.

She dug around a little further for a stick of gum and slowly unwrapped it, then inserted it, but not before elbowing her gentleman escort, playfully.

"Hi, I'm Charlie," he said, extending his hand to him.

Now I know you. "Chucky," she said. "Call him Chucky. We all do." But who was this man that was with her? She decided to play the waiting game.

"Charlie Wells," he continued, his hand still outstretched.

"Denis Pontiac," the tall stranger said, and she could not hide her giggles, as everything came rushing back. Denis, her wild one!

Denis gave him a nod—more of a slight leveling of his eyes.

"I'm her grandson. I live in that end of the house. He pointed toward a long outline of peaks and dormers. "I look after Grandma, don't I Grandma."

"Denis is an old friend," she said. "Almost like a brother, to me."

"Almost ."

"He looks after me now, don't you."

The shadows covered one side of Chucky's face. "How nice, an old friend. Are you just passing through?"

"Out." Denis flashed his mischievous smile. "I live here. You might say I'm a local. My ancestors go back a ways."

"Oh, a longtime inhabitant."

"From the beginning."

Chucky leaned up against him. "I see."

"And beyond."

"A mystic, no less."

She turned to the door. Gray Boy had been rubbing up against her leg, purring, but then skittered off. A scraping noise behind her turned her back around. The two men were embraced. Chucky had the other firmly by the throat and pressed his face to him. The older one began to crumple and fold and finally stumbled against the petunias, knocking them to the floor, with himself falling on top of them.

"Stop it!" Her voice surprised her, so shrill and full of authority. Once she had been this way.

Chucky stepped back and his white teeth flashed a smile. "Just a little hug for an old friend."

"He's old enough to be your father. Treat him with respect."

Denis struggled to his feet. From beneath his belt something gleamed in the moonlight. Now it flashed, open and free, but she took his head in her hands and pressed it to her breast.

"How dare you! He is my guest." She held him and rocked him back and forth for a moment. Then she gave her final order. "By tomorrow, I want you"—but the little son of a bitching draft dodger had already vanished back into the shadows.

Denis was back on his feet by now and walking after him, but she pulled at his arm.

"Put that away. Let it go." She kissed him hard on the mouth in a way that surprised her. She pointed to the door. "Before I forget."

The door erased them.

So this was her sin. She could live with that. The stabilizing effect of a man. She was secure in time, for now, within her own four walls, the shades drawn, the doors locked, and the old familiar syncopation of the clocks weaving through the air—for the first time, they weren't annoying. Who could ask for anything more? Well, there was one other thing.

"First things first," she said. "We've got to get you out of these old smelly clothes. When is the last time you had a bath, Chief Pontiac?"

"Don't call me that. I could never walk in his shoes. I am only a distant cousin. Not even a shirttail."

"Oh yeah?"

Water tumbled into the tub. The first draw was the preliminary soak. One year of road dust and campfires would take some time. She turned her back while he undressed, but kept her eye on the mirror. Slowly, he settled in. The water rippled and received him. Suds slid over slick brown skin. She soaked the cloth and applied it to his neck first and then his back. The water made puddles beneath her grip. His back was a lean slope beneath the washcloth and his shoulders slumped across the blades. The warmth flowed, it trickled and oozed all the way down. Then she got to his ribs and felt him tensing. She washed around the tender spot, where the purple flared out. Then she moved down, until arriving at the vulnerable area, where she left him to his own designs. The bathroom tile was cool beneath her step, and then the furry, softness of the living room. She sat in her chair and reached for the lamp, but stopped. The room was dark. She turned the lamp on and then continued in the other rooms, one at a time, until everything was bright and rosy.

When she returned, the water was coal black. He stood, white towel wrapped around him, while she drained and scrubbed the tub clean. Then she drew another bath, this one rose scented. This time she did not turn away when he entered and began pouring pitchers of warm water over him. Next was the blue pearl of lotion in her palm. She slowly worked it into his scalp. His hair was still thick. She continued to work the lather, twisting and turning the thick ropy hair, the dust and grime loosening. She rinsed him a second time and then helped him from the tub.

His body was remarkably preserved, a body that has endured much. Despite her best efforts at cleansing him an odor remained, faint, but still there. It was like the old smell, only stronger, more graduated—the smell of dampness and rotting wood. The smell of decay.

"You silly, silly man." He was standing there before her, towel wrapped around him, a magnificent specimen.

She handed him a blue terrycloth robe, a leftover from her closet, Buddy's. Then she gathered his clothes and passed quickly through the doorway into the narrow hall, where she switched on the light. Her footsteps were short and precise. In the laundry room she separated the lights from the darks. His underwear was stained and his tee shirt soiled. She put everything together and ran it through a short cycle cold water wash. Then she ran everything through the drier and neatly folded them. When she returned she found him in the leather chair, just like a man. The TV was on but the channel was off the air, only a test pattern on the screen. His head hanged to one side and he snored loudly.

She placed the clothes on the table next to him and switched off the lamps. In the darkness she listened to him for a moment and then went into the kitchen. Her pantry was sparse. She blew the dust off everything. A few cans of chicken noodle soup, some crackers, and pancake mix. She settled for the pancakes.

Dust covered the mixing bowl. She wiped it clean, so the purple shined on the grape pattern and the green vines wrapped around, as if they were alive. She poured a mound of white powder in the center and then carefully added the water until the consistency was just right. She stood at the window by the sink. The yard was still full of darkness and the afterglow from the streetlight stretched across. She covered the bowl and put it in the refrigerator. The small freezer door above was coated with ice. She opened it and peered into the restricted insides. It was large enough only for her hand and a little more. The ice was abrasive and cold on her knuckles. The package was frozen rock hard. She pulled it out and placed it in the sink. The red letters of years old handwriting were still on the butcher paper: Sausage. Leftover from the Boy Scout pancake supper at the church one evening years ago. She peeled the paper and put the links into a pan and then ran warm water over them before leaving them to sit. The refrigerator door was still wide open. She took a deep breath and then went after the defrosting job.

She boiled some water and began. This was a widow's icebox; an old jar of mustard, some leftover Jell-O, and some celery. She emptied everything and took out the shelves. Then she wiped the inside down and chipped out the ice. She put everything back in order, categorizing the contents, condiments, dairy, meat, and produce. Done.

The bathroom was next. She went after the black ring in the tub with some Ajax. Then the sinks and porcelain. After that she mopped the floors and straightened her own room up, picking up the cloths and putting things away.

She tiptoed into the living room. He was still in the chair, undisturbed. She carefully removed the sheets from the furniture. The dust threatened to make her sneeze. She heaved several times but managed to hold it in. The old feather duster was still in the closet. Over the surfaces she went, lightly touching everything, the couch, the two rockers, the coffee table and the piano, which hadn't been played in at least eight years. A Steinway.

She rolled back the key cover. The stool was still in place. She held her hands over the middle C, and then touched one note, F. It was still in tune. The feathers swirled and danced over the keys and then she moved on to the blinds, where silvery lines of dawn were beginning to form. She wiped each slat and carefully pulled them up. Warm water and vinegar removed the blurry film. She wiped them clean. The street was vivid, the lone light above shining down, the pavement dark and glistening, the outline of Cap Shullee's garden taking shape, mop-haired corn, pin-neat rows of cabbage.

The book cabinet sat next to where he slept. It hadn't been opened for years. Dishes were on the top. Teacake porcelain and various bric-a-bracs. Pictures from days of old. Her own children lost to the war. Vinnie, Burl, and Charles, all mugging for the camera. Standing beneath the elms, next to Ford that Buddy had just bought--all of them in uniform, their chests thrust out, invulnerable, Vinnie saluting the camera, Burl with the dark serious look he always wore, and Charles reserve and serious. All of the sun was behind the trees, the green grass, a day of immortality. Only Charles to return before dying from kidney disease shortly thereafter. She wiped the gold-colored frames and polished the dishes, and one in particular that was engraved, "This Is Our Home."

She went to the cuckoo and pulled up the three weights and adjusted the house so it was level. Something fell to the floor, a key, stuffed back behind. She looked at it for a moment, a long skeleton key, most likely fitting the door beside it. She tried it, beneath the knob, and heard the lock disengage. A cool whiff of forgotten air greeted her from a mysterious passageway. She quickly closed the door, locked it, and put the key back.

In the center of the room, the white of her pajamas filled the spot, behind her, the blinds glowed toward the morning. Now the chair was empty, but leather still held his imprint.

One step and then another to the kitchen, where the griddle was black hot and sparkling, sitting atop blue fingers that conjure and hold. The first pancake formed a perfect circle, puckered with bubbles. Then there was a second and a third. The sausage slowly cooked in another, the lid loose on top of the skillet. Coffee perked. He appeared, sleepy-eyed, still wearing the robe. The first three had been flipped, a golden brown. She stacked them on the plate with some links on the side, a slab of butter and a small pitcher of maple syrup. Then she put it and the coffee on the table, the steam rising. He took a seat and dug in. He made short work of first stack, but could only get two-thirds through the second. She cleared his plate and once again he disappeared into the other room and returned wearing his clean jeans and blue cotton shirt.

She did the dishes, and he went into Buddy's tool shed. He returned with a long-handled pair of pliers, a crescent wrench, and a few other things. This time he went into the bathroom, and before long, the low, constant hiss and breathing of the leaky toilet—a noise that had become second nature to her place—disappeared. In its absence was the new silence, punctuated faintly with the rhythms of the clock.

He left after that, simply walking out without saying thank you or goodbye or anything. No words had been exchanged. But there was something in how he paused for a moment along the walkway and breathed in the air, taking in large breaths through his nose like the deer sometimes do in the morning, making his huge chest expand and then relax. It was the Indian way. He would be back.

She twisted the sheets. No lamp this time. Her hands formed a beatific vision around her face. She opened herself to things. The morning grew. The leaves took color, a dark reptilian green with gray in the spaces between. All ran through her from afar, she heard the footsteps—soft, padded sounds that only can come from deerskin. The S straightened. She collected herself. Then the brassy knock-tapping. She sat upright. Her feet touched the floor. She began to move. One step and then another and then another, till she was flying. Along the way, she grabbed her white summer robe and wrapped herself. The knocking went to knuckles, brown skin softer than any leather pulled over long fingers. She cracked the door a few inches to a slice of him;

his back to her, two fishing poles slung over one shoulder, and a paper sack in hand; all against a splash of blue. Wider now, the tee shirt and blue jeans from the night before, still looking freshly washed. He turned to her. This morning, a piece of leather tied around his neck. She opened wide. His hair was in two braids, each resting on his chest.

"Come on, Kuda," he said. "Let's you and me go down to the spillway and give those bass hell."

She took color. He pulled a red bandana out of the bag. "This will protect your precious head. And these—your eyes." The sunglasses were aviators, green. He slipped them on her. There was more. He pulled out some baggy blue jeans and a loose blue tee shirt.

He held the tee shirt up to her shoulders. Then she took over, pinning the shirt against her bony frame, so he could take a step back for the appraisal. It was long and loose, falling down to her thighs. Across the front in white letters it read, STONE LAKE 45th PARALLEL.

"That's more like it," he said, giving her an exaggerated wink.

She went into the bedroom to make the change. When she came out, he tied the bandana around her head and then slipped the shades on one last time.

"Now nobody will know you. You're old Chief's squaw as far as anybody is concerned." He pulled her out through the door into the warm sunlight. She giggled.

"I look like a hippie."

"Better than that."

He stood outside the neat row of pickets and opened the gate for her. Her hand was small but firm in his. Together, they strolled down the road, taking their own sweet time to get to wherever they might be going. Their figures became smaller and smaller, as they put more distance between them and the gateway. Pretty soon their talking blended into a low murmur, his being several octaves lower—while hers was high and carefree sounding, punctuated with an occasional laugh. They disappeared around the corner and moved down the narrow alleyway that ran next to Willie Kent's lot. Sunflowers leaned over the fence line.

"Where are we?" she whispered.

He squeezed her hand. "Don't worry."

"Okay."

They continued on, following narrow pathways, worn smooth and brown that took them through tall gardens, orchards, and waist-deep grass. At various points he would stop and gather a few things, until eventually his sack was full with cucumbers, corn, squash, and potatoes, before continuing on with long, steady strides. Soon they arrived at a certain vantage point, where the village of Blackwood lay below them. The belfry of the old orange courthouse rose above the maples, while in the distance, Pembroke River made a thin, blue line through meadows on the horizon.

They emerged out of a thicket and once again were on paved roads, but not for long, before he took a sharp left down a steep embankment that wound its way down to the river's edge. Though it was midmorning, the sun had not yet climbed above the steep embankment. This gave the water an Arcadian green quality, the green of chartreuse, reflecting the willows that hung over the embankment on either side. The water was smooth and clear and passed like a slow moving sheet of glass, the occasional dimples of current excepted. The scene was enough for Denis to fall down on the bankside and pull off his long buckskins.

"Come on Kuda, now it's time for me to return the favor. Take a bath Indian-style."

No sooner had these words escaped his mouth than he began to shed his clothes until he was naked. She still stood a few feet above him, clinging to a scrub maple, to secure her footing. He bent over and splashed water on his legs and torso. His lean body was slick and shiny. Then he stepped out and extended a hand to her. She was transfixed. He led her down to the water's edge and began undressing her. She stopped him, took his hand as it lifted her tee shirt off, and gently pushed it back, and then continued to remove everything including the loosening of the long braid that always kept her long hair in check. Her hair fell to her waist. Her body was lean, too; her breasts, though shrunken, were small and boyish looking, with nipples the color of raisins. Her pubic hairs were most amazing, the silvery white of frost on thistle.

She dove into the water, a clean graceful dive that neatly sliced the placid surface. Beneath the water, she scissors kicked and breaststroked, moving like a goddess phantom across the sandy bottom, her hair blooming and spreading out like an exotic plant. She longed to stay there forever, but she heard a voice that she somehow associated with her dead mother, a feminine voice that whispered to her in her native Ottawa: "Not yet, little bird."

She surfaced two-thirds across the channel and blew water out. Then he, too, dove in, and she met him at mid-stream, where they embraced and her limbs wrapped around him, squid-like, and together they floated along the still water, as the sun broke over the embankment and poured warm balm on the entire scene.

They got dressed and worked their way along river until they passed beneath the Conway Bridge, where the howl and drone of occasional traffic passed overhead. They inched along the shallows, pressing themselves up against the tall concrete embankment that held back the landscaping overhead and marked the boundaries between land and water. It was from there, up above, that the lads of the town would leisurely cast their lines down to the water, twenty feet below, and fish for the rock bass that frequented the mossy green shallows.

At the base of the plant the waters came roiling up mysteriously from beneath the plant. As a young man, Denis had been among the foolish and daring ones who had risked death by swimming beneath the plant, where the water spun the turbines to produce the electricity. He had also taken his place among the elite legends of Blackwood, by becoming the only person who had dared to dive from the bridge into the shallows and live to tell about it, with nothing but a thin cut down the center of the his head, the scar of which served as living proof of his foolish bravado in those tumultuous days of youth. It was here, nonetheless, on that particularly warm summer morning in 1967, when her heart thrilled so, not with pain, but the glow of life, that Minnie felt the mysterious return of the dark clouds of sorrow. Gone was the morning blush of the swim and the carefree thrill of love, gone just as quickly as it had come.

It was a short swim across to the embankment. He took her by the hand and pulled her in. The bubbling waters ran up and through her clothing; her shirt filled with it. She let him do the swimming, while she kicked her feet just enough to keep her head afloat. It was only a few seconds before they were on the other side. He helped her out of the water. The grass had been worn away to a dark path that was damp and slick.

"What's the matter? Are you tired? Do we need to take a rest?"

She could not answer. He sat her down on some dry grass that was up next to the warm concrete of the plant. She closed her eyes, but managed to keep one eye on him, as he gathered red worms into a glass jar, from the heaping pile of briny weeds and grass that accumulated there.

That done he helped her up the steep grade until they once again stood at the old familiar haunts of the spillway. She rubbed the side of her head, near the temple. "Wasn't it here that..."

"Yes it was here that we just met."

"When?"

"Why an eternity ago, called yesterday."

"Don't tease me. I just don't want to forget. I don't want to forget you."

He put his arm around her. "There's no way that will happen."

"But there is something. There is this one thing." She rubbed her head. "There's this thing."

"Don't worry. We will get to that, too."

"But what day is this?"

"I don't know. I think it's Saturday."

"But what's the year?"

He laughs at her. "What year would you like it to be?"

"I'm serious," she said, wiping her nose on her sleeve. "I can't tell if this is or if I'm dreaming. I hate it when this happens. I want it to be real."

He pulled his shirt up and showed her the black and blue marks around his ribs. "Somebody fixed these ribs last night. I wonder who?"

She flutter-laughed and wiped both of her eyes with the back of her hand. "Sometimes I just can't tell." She knelt down and began rubbing the grass with her palms. "This is the only way I can tell." She held her hands up to him. "When I wake up tomorrow these stains had better be there."

"Velcome to my castle." He made a sweeping gesture toward the campsite.

Blackened scents were in the air, a thread of smoke rose. He gathered up a few things, a few blankets that he rolled tightly, and some this-and-that's, which he threw into a paper bag. He got two more poles and they went back along the spillway where he set lines all in a row twenty feet apart.

A jingling sound, miniaturized. His hands dwarfed the bell. He sat on the wall and let the water run over his feet. He rang it again. "This is the dinner bell." He tied it with a surgeon's precision to the end of the first pole, and then all of the others on down the line. When he had finished the last one, he waved at her and wouldn't stop until she waved back. Only then did he begin to move toward her, walking with ease along the narrow wall, stepping over each pole that pointed outward at forty-five degrees, his image growing, the water steaming off his naked torso.

He spread the blankets out on the grass. She lay on her side, her head propped up with one arm, while he leaned over the wall and washed his hands and splashed water on his face and slicked his hair back. He sat down next to her and sliced up the fresh cucumbers that he borrowed from Claude Jensen's garden and put them on crackers.

He gave her one, with a dash of mayo and some black pepper sprinkled on top. He said, "We can go up to Mel's and get some cheese, if you want."

"Whatever you want."

He took two at a time in one bite. She nibbled the edge off one and then a little more. She asked, "Is this what you do every day?"

He finished slicing the cucs and placed them in a brine of vinegar and water, floating on the top of a shallow glass bowl. He sprinkled a light coating of pepper over them and handed her one, so thin that it was nearly transparent. She reached out to take it, but he signaled for her to open her mouth. She did so and he dropped it in.

"Oh my," she said. "That is good." She cleared her throat several times.

"It's pretty easy, once you get used to it. Doing nothing."

The blanket and soft earth molded to her back. She buckled her fingers behind her head. A few wisps of white clouds passed over.

"That's all I ever do," she said. "Nothing, but it's not like this."

"There's a difference between nothing to do and doing nothing."

He checked each line and then leaned over the water. Two swans floated by. They accepted his offering of crackers but not without a warning hiss. The river had gone blue in the center and green along the banks where the trees were. Now he was back, plopping down beside her, arms extended behind him, resting on palms, hands pointed backward, long, smooth fingers stretched out into the grass.

"And why the long face," he said.

"I wish I knew. I probably do know, but I can't..." and she pointed to her head. "I just know I get it whenever I have a good time with you. This feeling comes over me. Aren't we allowed to have a good time on this earth?" The question surprised her.

"Of course, you are. I told you I was going to tell you about your mother, remember?"

"Please do. Please do, please tell me."

"I want to take you some place, but let's do this first." He eased her down on the blanket. "I need to speak to you." And he did, this time in a new way, from a new angle. Her babble filled the air.

"Is this where you want to take me? Is this it?" She could not stop laughing. They crossed the bridge. He walked in front and practically had to pull her along. She walked with a noticeable limp on the right side and pressed one hand to her hip, but she felt no pain. They were on the outskirts of town. Joann Mosier, Billy Friend, and Cletus Shoemaker all passed in their cars. None of them knew. She had a large wad of toilet paper that she had taken from the public restrooms, that she used to wipe her runny nose.

She pushed the sunglasses up on her nose.

"I feel like I'm on Candid Camera, only I'm the camera."

They crossed the street. An Indian man and an Indian woman. Cars slowed for them. He turned down the alleyway to the back entrance to Smitty's. A red Mustang pulled up. It had noisy hotrod mufflers and the driver made a point to rev the engine loudly. There were three passengers, two in front and one in the back. The driver stepped out for a minute. He was a skinny kid with his shirtsleeves rolled up. Minnie recognized him, though he didn't see through her incognito. He was her old paperboy, John Dee's boy, "Bird"—the one who had called the ambulance. He was not one of Chucky's followers. The other one on the passenger's side also jumped out. He was shorter and wore his dirty blond hair over his ears and down his neck.

"Hey chief," Bird said. "Get us a case of Blue Ribbon, will ya?" He handed him a ten. "You can keep the change." They looked at her and she began to laugh all over again. The third kid managed to work his way out of the backseat and also joined the party. He was a gnarly looking kid with a beard and spike teeth. He let out a long, racking cough and lit up a Camel. "Looks like you been hitting it already, Chief," he wheezed.

He grabbed the ten and stuck it in his breast pocket. "I'll be out in a while."

"Don't be too long," Bird said. Then he said to kid with the dirty long hair, "Freud, you take the front, and Biggie you take the rear. I'll park this horse in the parking lot. When he comes out, one of you signal me. I'll just pull up, and we'll load the beer in the trunk."

He took her by the hand and they stepped into the dark world, the sweet and sour world of beer and cigarettes. There was the shattering sound of the pool game's break. Someone put a quarter in the jukebox and Roger Miller sang King of the Road.

"Where do those little punks get off calling you Chief?"

He shrugged. "I got the money, didn't I?"

"So don't talk to me about Indian pride."

He had no opportunity to reply. He had celebrity status. Everybody recognized him and wanted to buy him drinks. A man at the pool table paused before taking his shot. "Chief, how you doing man?" He took his eye off the ball and looked back at him as he took the shot. "Four ball in the corner." Down it went. His red hair was cut short and his face was pink and freckle-splotched. A cigarette hung out of the corner of his mouth. The name Frank was stitched over the right pocket of his blue shirt. The place was crowded and more people were coming in. The afternoon shifts from both factories were out.

They stood beneath a TV at the end of the bar, where a long line of faces watched the Tigers and the Yankees tied in the bottom of the eighth. Willie Horton was up to bat with runners on first and second.

He ordered two beers and gave her one. She took the empty barstool and pressed her thumb into her hip joint. The man next to her was disinterested in the game. Furrows of curly white hairs began high up on his shiny forehead and his eyes were too small for his face.

Then Denis said, "Smitty, this is Kuda. Kuda, Smitty. He owns this joint. Kuda here is my guiding light."

Smitty laughed. He spoke with a Canadian accent. "She is, is she? Well dat show don't come on for another hour." He looked at her and winked. She winked back.

"Oh, I get it," Denis said. He elbowed her gently but enough to spill her beer a little. "The Guiding Light. That's a soap opera." He made an animal noise that sounded like R-R-R-R. "Kuda here, she don't watch TV, do ya?"

Whistles and cheers erupted as Willie Horton banged a triple and drove in two runs.

"And how about those mink traps?" Smitty said. "You bring me any pelts yet?"

"Not yet, but they're coming."

Then he said to Minnie. "Does he give you the same line?" Then back to Denis, "You've been telling me dat for six months. You don't have to buy any fishing license or permits of any kind cause da state and da feds got a guilty conscience over stealing your land. You can go out any ol time you want and hunt and fish to your heart's content, yet you can't even get your old buddy Smitty a few measly mink pelts." He winked again at Minnie. This time she did not wink back.

He took her hand and moved toward the pool tables. Her limp had become worse. He pulled a chair out for her. "You're not used to all this walking, are you. I can get you a ride to your place."

She took several sips of beer. "I'll get us a ride, don't worry." Her glass was already nearly empty. Several more arrived at their table from Smitty. She finished it off and started on another. "I'll be okay. Just let me rest for a while." She leaned over and whispered in his ear, half-giggling. "Where did you say we were?"

The back of his forefinger against her cheek, he pushed a strand of hair back. "Don't worry about it."

Sunlight was the gold beyond the screen door, where the lilacs and parked cars were. Profiles sat along the bar in a straight line, looking into the mirror as they talked and smoked. A few occasionally turned to the person sitting next to them and made small gestures to emphasize a point, and then it was back to the mirror, followed by a long, slow drink. Men, all of them, gathering on a summer afternoon. Their numbers increased. She was the only woman. She reached up and found that her sunglasses were still on. She started to take them off, but then thought otherwise.

Denis took the ten dollar bill and got change, ones and quarters. He racked in the first quarter. The balls fell with a low rumble and fall. The first challenger approached and took the cue. A few ones were laid on the side table. The game began. He walked around the table, chalking his cue before taking each shot. There was laughter and conversation, but his eyes always remain fixed on the balls. He ran the table. Then came the second challenger and the third. A wad of bills grew in his breast pocket and hung out at the top, like cabbage. Four more glasses of beer appeared at her table. A six-point buck hung from the wall, its brown eyes frozen, as was a rainbow trout, caught in mid turn, and a bobcat curled on a branch and snarled, just above the jukebox.

A pyramidal light shade, labeled *Stroh's* in red letters, extended from the ceiling and hung over the pool table and swayed slightly from left to right, as if some tremor from beneath was making itself felt—it was not—and it cast its light on the green felt. He continued to circle the table, chalking his cue all the while. Then he leaned over the table, so far over that he cast one leg up for balance, before sinking the eight ball in the corner, and put enough English on things to bring the cue ball back to his awaiting hand.

That ten dollar bill was growing as he stood next to her while some new challengers from O-hi-0 stepped up and racked the balls. By now his eyes were more than a little glazed over and the room was getting louder by the minute, but not so much so that she couldn't hear his voice cut through it all, to her. "You ready to go back to those math lessons I was giving you?"

"Two plus one equals four?"

"Something like that."

He kept his eyes on her while he took his shots: four ball in the corner, seven in the side, two in the corner; he ran seven straight. Game over. Next.

"I think you're probably ready for this. I think you're thinking clear." He took a piece of paper out of his pocket and handed it to her.

"Put that some place where it won't get lost."

"I've got just the place." She folded it and put it down the front of her top. "The forget-me-nots place."

He looked at the next challenger, a man called Doc, a Lon Chaney look-alike, hair slicked back, dark eyes flat against his face. He drank off his beer before taking the winner's break. Explosion: the triangle spreads, eight ball in the corner. Another five in his pocket. They agreed to continue the game anyway.

This time he sank the nine ball to the corner one rail, while looking at her. "Will you remember all this?"

She reached up and pulled the matchstick out of his mouth and put it in her pocket.

"Now I will."

"Four in the corner. There were two babies born that day. Six in the side one rail. One over on the poor side of town in a vacant room at the back of the ice plant. Seven in the side, two off the kiss, no slop. That was the one he wanted to keep a secret, a lovely Indian maid named Assiginac or blackbird, a 14-year-old who worked for him and gave birth to her own baby. She mysteriously disappeared, but her baby did not. It was a simple matter of a switch." He hung the cue up took the last of his money up from the table and stuffed it in his shirt pocket. "That be you, my illegitimate bastardized half-sister. That be you." He let out a war-hoop, loud enough so everything came to a standstill. "That also means you are one hundred percent bona fide." He pulled her chin up toward him and kissed her full on the mouth. "There's no reason to be sad. I'm your brother, but only in spirit."

He put his cue back on the rack and took her toward the golden light. She could not stop laughing.

The red Mustang was still there, and the skinny kid came gangling up to them.

"Hey chief, where's the beer?"

He gave a long yawn and a stretch. "You're too young to drink."

"Very funny. Where's the beer, man?" The kid continued to walk alongside them.

They moved across a patch of lawn between the buildings toward Main Street. Willows hung over them and slithered shadows on the grass. She was lagging behind, her limp noticeably worse.

"At least give me back my ten bucks?" the skinny kid said.

The wad of bills was still sticking out of his shirt pocket. The skinny kid grabbed for his ten and the old wad of bills spilled to the grass, where the breeze began to blow them in separate directions. By this time the bearded kid had jumped out of the car, came running up and tackled Denis and scuffled with him for a minute on the ground, before the other skinny kid came up and pulled him off. Then both of them started scooping up the money, but by this time Minnie was there. She grabbed the one by his beard and pulled him off Denis. It was coarse, dry stuff.

"Goddamit," he screamed. Tears came to his eyes and he pulled himself free. He doubled his fists and she let go. He ran off toward the other. Denis was slow getting up. She tried to help, but he shrugged her off and ran after them for twenty yards or so, and then stopped and came back, leaning over, his hands on his knees and chest heaving for breath. The sun was behind him. He cut a dark figure against its radiance.

"I know who they are," he said.

She rubbed the bend in his back. "Of course you do."

"I'll catch up with them. I'll even the score. "

"Of course you will."

"And when I do," he said.

"And when you do, they'll be dead meat."

"Your damn right they will. They'll be sorry they ever messed with me."

"Of course they will."

"They took my money."

"Don't worry about that. We will take care of that."

They entered the street. She brushed the grass off his shirt. There was a swatch of grass stain across his right shoulder. She checked his face. His eye was swollen, the flesh going purple and soft.

"We need to get some ice on that."

"I'm fine."

She limped into the front entry of Smitty's and returned with a rag from the bar, filled with ice. She held it to his eye. She made him sit down on the bench. They remained there for a few minutes before crossing the street toward Mel's. They did not go far before she was forced to sit again. This time a different sign attracted her attention, and it wasn't Mel's. This sign was right above her: Thomas Chevrolet and Buick.

"I can get you a ride home," he said. The swelling around the eye had spread across the whole left side of his face.

"I have a better idea."

She got up and walked into the showroom. A young salesman wearing a nametag that said Barkley. She recognized him, the flush face and the shock of red hair standing up on his head.

"Good afternoon folks. How can I help you?"

"We want to buy a car."

He chuckled. "Well, you've come to right place. We're running our Fiesta Day weekend sale."

Denis took her hand to leave. He got as far as the doorway before she stopped him. "Come on," he whispered. "They will call the cops on us and throw us in the drunk tank."

She pulled her hands free of his. "Don't be silly."

She returned to the salesman. Denis stepped outside and stood next to the entryway, shifting from one foot to the other.

"We have some nice Chevrolets in."

"No, Buddy and I have always been particular to Buicks."

Barkley perked up suddenly and looked over at Denis. "I see."

Then she said a little louder, so Denis could hear, "We don't want any Pontiac. We want an Indian car." She gave a laugh, a laugh that she hadn't heard since childhood, sharp and musical. "An official Indian car. That's what we want."

"Yes Ma'am, right this way."

They stepped into another showroom. "We just got this one in. It's the new Electra 225. Just rolled in off the delivery truck this morning."

Denis had moved inside a little, but was still fidgeting back and forth, looking up at a calendar that showed a girl in a blue one-piece bathing suit.

The car was a champagne-colored two-door with dark leather interior and wide, white-walled tires. Barkley opened the door and pulled the front seat up.

"As you can see, there's plenty of room. You've got push button windows."

"I'll take it," she said.

He walked around and opened the trunk. "It's got a spacious trunk, and we don't take any short cuts on giving you a top notched spare tire. Nothing but the finest."

"I said, I'll take it."

Denis moved a little closer, but was still pacing back and forth like an expectant father.

"Hey, Pontiac, you got a driver's license?" she said. He nodded yes and stepped into the men's room.

The owner of the place, Lefty "Bill" Thomas, had been signaled out onto the floor by one of the secretaries. He was a tall, gangly, sandy-haired man in his fifties, one of those understated types that kept an eagle-eye on everything.

"Can I help you?" he said.

"No thanks, Barkley here is doing just fine," she said. She turned back to Barkley. "How much are you asking for it?"

He looked at Lefty. "Fifty-two-ninety-five, plus tax and license."

"You take cash?"

This time they were doing the laughing. "Sure, we'll take cash."

"Good. Draw up the papers. Put everything in his name." She pointed to Denis, who had just stepped out of the bathroom. "I've got to go across the street to the bank. I'll be right back with the money."

"The bank isn't open on Saturdays," said Lefty, hiking his pants up a notch.

She pulled off her sunglasses. "Oh yes it is, she says. I've known Fritz Stein for forty years."

"Fritz isn't the owner anymore. The current CEO is Belle, his daughter."

"All the more reason," she said. "I've heard all about that, too. I remember when that girl was in diapers and she should be ashamed of taking her father's bank over. I can deal with her too. You have those papers ready."

She looked at the clock, a quarter past four. "What time do you close?"

Lefty raised both hands like this was some kind of a stick-up. "Five o'clock."

"Come on," she said to Denis. They stepped outside. "Which way is it to the bank?"

He had this look on his face like he was suddenly sick to his stomach. "I'm telling you, they're closed."

"Don't act so downhearted. You know this isn't about me. It's about you." I don't care if they are closed. Just show me the way."

He led her through a series of twisting and dizzying turns, through alleyways, across lawns, and down sidewalks, until she stood at the doorway of the bank. It was one of those neat and tidy looking Victorian homes, groomed and refurbished over the years. Still the original building, formed out of Fritz's own house. He lived right there in the upstairs. Buddy and Fritz had been friends for years. Buddy was on the board.

There were a couple of cars parked out front. She gave several sharp knocks on the door, again and again, until someone finally answered. A stern looking woman with half-moon reading glasses appeared at the front door and pointed through the class at the closed sign. She continued to knock. Her reflection looked back at her in the glass: baggy pants, tennis shoes, and green aviator sunglasses. She began to laugh again, but continued to knock just as insistently.

Now it was Belle Llewellyn who stood at the door. "It's me, Minnie Wells." She unlocked the door and let her step through but motioned for Denis to stay outside.

And it was little wonder she gave Minnie the red carpet treatment. "You have $75,000 in your checking account and another $500,000 in CDs, and that doesn't include your land holdings. So yes, you can afford to buy a car."

Belle was a paper-thin blond with platinum hair coming down to her bony shoulders. Her tan skin was stretched tight around her eyes and her nose was thin and sharp. Everybody in Blackwood had grown accustomed to her ways. She had taken up serious running and exercise. In fact at this very moment, she was preparing for a run. She wore a bank tee shirt with a bank insignia across the front and some lightweight nylon shorts and pink running shoes. Her legs were tan and lean. There had even been some talk that she may be a lesbian, as she hadn't yet taken up with a man and here she was in her early thirties or approaching them. She was the executor of Buddy's will.

"Good," said Minnie, looking at the account sheet that Belle had put before her. "That helps me to understand things much better." She looked out the window for Denis, who wasn't in sight. "I want to draw out ten thousand dollars in cash."

"I could give you a cashier's check instead."

"No, I want cash. I want to show that Lefty Thomas that I mean business."

Belle smiled. She had a nice smile, square and neat, the smile of the exclusive and privileged, yet with something warmer always trying to break through.

Minnie looked at the clock. Ten minutes to five.

"We've got to hurry."

She started for the door and then stopped.

"No wait. I've got a better idea. Belle, you call that Lefty Thomas and tell him to get over here right this minute and bring that car along with him."

She sat down in one of the soft leather chairs in the lobby.

"Too much thinking and doing," she said. She put her feet up on the ottoman. "I think I'll go back to being daffy and confused."

She buttoned down the rider's side window and let the afternoon breeze sweep through her. Denis was a good driver. They were cruising somewhere outside of town, going somewhere. "Drive," she told him. "This is your car but take me for one ride. Get me out of town. Then you can do what you want."

The car rode like a cloud. The afternoon had gone hazy, the sun mellow and golden, trees and pastures passing alongside. Talbot Lake was in the distance, the sunlight flashing off its smooth waters.

"I don't believe in daylight's saving, Buddy always said, 'You can't fool Mother Nature.'"

"What's that?" Denis said. He had the car up to eighty now and the wind was roaring in. "You can fool what?"

"Nothing. I didn't say nothing."

The voice was Denis's, but the person behind the wheel was Buddy. She rubbed the leather dash and stuck her hand out the window. He slowed now to fifty.

"I don't want to go to Mellow Brook," she said. "Don't let them put me away." Mellow Brook was the old folk's home, the one she had played the fund raiser for. They called it assisted living, but it was an old folk's home, the end of the line.

The driver took her hand. "Don't you worry about that. Not as long as I am here."

"Sometimes I get so confused."

He looked so handsome and free, the wind in his hair. She dabbed at her eyes with a Kleenex and then blew her nose.

"One more thing," she said. "Don't get mad if I call you Buddy, and don't get mad if I call you Denis. I love you both."

He turned to her, the dark penetrating eye of the French, but with the piping, warble of Denis's voice. "It's all right. Just be whoever you want to be."

She smiled back at him. Buddy would never have said anything as romantic as that.

Seven or eight o'clock, (who knew for sure what time it was), they were back home. It was still daylight, but the air was creamy colored. He parked outside and had to help her to her apartment. Pools of gray-blue light filled the living room. He carried her into the bedroom and put her down. She staggered to the blinds to close off the light, but he stopped her, gently.

"It will be dark soon enough," he said. "Let's watch the last of the daylight. It's the best time of the day."

"I call it morning."

"Not anymore. "We got you straightened around on that. Now it's the night time."

"But I don't want you to see me. Not like this."

He put one finger to her lips and began undressing her. She tried to hold back the tears. It was approaching dusk. It was the type of light fit for God or a liquid apparition. But even this light cannot clothe her in splendor. One piece after another, gently, he discarded, until she lay naked before his gaze. The light poured over her once magnificent body, now shrunken.

"It's awful growing old," she said.

He silenced her again and then began kissing her, starting with each finger, first the tips, then the knuckle, and moving down to the palm. He pressed his soft lips to its center. Next was the wrist, and then one arm and another. He left nothing out, sliding down to the elbow, the inside first, where the old blue veins were, the scaly nub, bathing her like one of her cats would, licking slowly, contently, his eyes half-closed. He moved up her arms to where the flesh was loose. The long forgotten flame began to ignite itself, like a spark caught in the middle of a page that widened and worked its way outward, the circle getting larger, until all was consumed, curling and twisting, as he formed her and brought her to life. She reached up and stroked his hair, which hung straight down over her, like exotic vines, pooling on her stomach. Further down he went, across her stomach. Surely he was not going to. He was! This time he would tell a different story.

Now that he had her, he played her, made her babble. When he at last came down on top of her, cushioning the weight with his two hands and putting the side of his throat to her mouth and nose, she again smelled the odor, dank and powerful emanating out of him, so much so that she sprinkled him with perfume from her wedding day, vintage, yet even that could not take away the smell, the stain of death within him. She cried out, "Oh my wild one," and spoke to him in the ancient tongue of her ancestors, a language that he understood. And she could not control all that was rising up in her, and yes, finally overflowing in her, onto him, onto the sheets, onto everything.

"Not another. I don't want to lose another. Not fair. Not fair."

Days became hours and weeks days, when you're at this age. One season ran to another. Leaves filled with color only to fall.

Now he lived with her.

She tried to prepare exquisite meals for him; baked chicken lightly seasoned with garlic and lemon, served on a bed of rice pilaf, but she got the ingredients confused and forgot to check the oven. The kitchen would fill with smoke; the rice stuck to the bottom of the pan. So they began to eat his fish and game, hearty stews and seasoned jerky. He continued to run his trap lines and left early each morning. Chucky continued to live in the south wing, but no one ever saw him or heard him either.

The rides continued and became extended. Sometimes they would go on two or three day excursions. No sooner was she in the car than she forgot where they were. She completely abandoned herself to him. One time they drove to Talbot and found her mother's gravestone. Another time they drove as far north as the shrine at Saint Maelrhys and looked up several cousins. Then they ventured further to neighboring states in the far north to see more family. He talked of trips to North Dakota and Montana.

"Some day I will show you the ocean," he said.

The winter passed, a long hard winter, with high drifts and long storms. They made plans for the spring.

One morning over coffee he told her, "I will take you out to Spokane this spring and then on to Reno. I have cousins out there."

"I'm worried," she said. The mysterious odor seems stronger and in the mornings she found traces of blood in the toilet after he left.

"Don't worry about him. I'll take care of that. Grandson or not."

"Not that," she tried to say, but it was too late. He had already pushed away from the table. Like most men, he did not listen well once his mind was made up.

March was making its last gasp, and the winter's storms were pounding them. She stood at the window and let the weak morning light in. The scrape of his shovel sounded against the ice and cement. The path had been cleared to the road, but instead he went the other way, past the kitchen, toward the other wing of the house. She saw them talking. Little pockets of steam rose up with words. Chucky wore a dark scarf thrown over his fur collar and mirrored sunglasses. He had a winter tan from skiing and a stubbly growth of beard.

Then one morning he announced, over elk sausage and biscuits, "We will have him out by spring." The dinner table had become their place of conference.

"Have who out?" she said.

He laughed. "Why, Chucky, you forgetful old fool."

"Chucky?"

March passed and the Chinook winds began to blow. The smelt were running. He would leave, sometimes for days at a time, and sometimes only for a few hours. The weather was full of promise, though flakes still drifted down from the gray skies.

"Soon," he said, stomping the snow off his boots as he entered.

"Soon," she said back to him.

He took off his coat and hung it over the doorknob. "Soon he will be gone." He blew into his hands to warm them and then rubbed them briskly together.

"Soon he will be gone," she said, emphasizing the *soon*.

He held up two rabbits by the hind legs. "Dinner," he said.

"Dinner?"

He took the game into the kitchen and she heard the sharp, rhythmic sound of his knife on the chop block, and then the faster, staccato sound of the vegetables. The rich, wholesome aroma of the stew drifted out to meet her. He brought papers out for her to sign and handed her a pen.

"Sign," he said.

"Sign," she said.

"This will get him out once and for all," he said.

She was silent.

He formed her fingers around the pen. His fingers were cold. She scratched out her name. Then he was gone again, walking out the door without a coat. She saw his head pass across the kitchen window. The snow was collecting on his hair.

She ate in darkness, alone at the table. A few bites were all that was needed. She stood up and cleared the table.

Cuckoos went off at seven o'clock. Still she was alone. She lit a candle and watched as the little bird sounded off, nodding his head to and fro. His house was a little uneven, so she made the adjustment. The key fell out of the back. She picked it up and turned it several times before her gaze, before she unlocked the door. The door! Now she remembered. A childish giggle escaped her. She lit a candle and proceeded. The air was stagnant and damp smelling. Her shadow was cast hideously up against the wall in an exaggerated manner. She passed down the corridor and into a larger room where father used to entertain. Here the ceilings were high and her shadow took on a new form, less grotesque and more oblong, reaching up the walls to the tiles above. Her head and shoulders actually stretched part way across the ceiling, coming up the wall and then bent at ninety degrees, but below, her legs were wobbly and elongated. She passed across the cold, gritty floor. She remembered this room, its spaciousness and the large windows, now boarded up for the most part. Sheets still covered the furniture.

This was at the servants' quarters, a few small rooms and an even smaller kitchen area. The last door was next. Slowly she inserted the key and turned the bolt. The door swung open. This air was warmer and tinged with cooking and smoke. Her bare feet sank into the carpet, pleated, porous, and warm. She passed through a tidy kitchen and out into a living area, where a half open door cast yellow light onto the floor. Voices murmured from the inside. At the threshold, the air took on yet another flavor, both sweet and sour. Flames hummed and snapped in the fireplace. More shadows were on the wall, not hers this time, but theirs. One was kneeling. She recognized the broad back, while the other stood in front of him reading something. At first they did not see her.

She hurried back the way in which she came, back through the door into the darkness. The candle fell, leaving her alone in the darkness. She moved smoothly, effortlessly over the cold tile. She was a phantom of the night. She was back at Daddy's study. She pulled the sheets off his chair, dust flying up her nose, making her sneeze. The leather was cracked and cold against her thighs. She pulled the curtains back on his window. At first she could see nothing, but soon images filtered through the blanket of darkness. It was the final snowfall, collecting one last time on the pines. She shivered and her teeth began to chatter, until she caught the dark, smoky scent, and the soft, warm hands rested first on her shoulder and then on her throat. She was willing to forget everything, even this. Why not?

This spring they would ride the open plains like the buffalo. She would be his squaw and they would go to casinos in Reno, Tahoe and Vegas. He would show her the ocean. The long waves would begin breaking a half mile out, spotted with surfers. They would crash against the rocks and fly up. The mists would soak her body.

He would be known as Chief Pontiac and she would be his squaw, Little Bird. What a pair they would make. They would gain an odd celebrity status at the casinos. Tourists would come up and snap their pictures. She would sell post cards and memorabilia with their pictures on it. He could spend all the money for all she cared. She would just be along for the ride. That was fine. Forgetting wasn't really such a bad thing. Not bad at all.

A House of Stone is Forever

PART TWO:
THE WOMAN WHO FELL FROM THE SKY

O f a time, long, long ago, these things will happen, it is said.

The Great Ice known as Michigan will awaken from its domed sleep and make its southward advance across the millennium, swallowing territories and redefining boundaries on its way, until at last it stands outside the stone house.

1

All of Dee's life The Ice has been there. Even on nights such as this, when the planets are all aligned and meteors shower the skies, he can feel its presence, the deep vibe of its slow approach, coming up through the floorboards, where he now lies wrestling with the angel of sleep. It precedes his earliest childhood memories, The Ice does: getting lost in the Icy Pines, walking stiff-legged home, the sting of poop in his drawers; even seeing his mother and father naked for the first time—his father relieving himself beneath the oak tree, encircling it with his thumb and forefinger before giving it a shake; his mother combing her long hair in her bedroom, the suppleness of her backside with its sudden sweep upward where it connected at the thigh. Before all else, The Ice was.

His first recollections were sensory, auditory to be exact: a scraping that was more akin to some prehistoric screeching or screaming—an awakening, while at other times, a groaning. A struggle was taking place. The earth did not give way easily. These were the sounds that would stay with him long after the stony deafness had set in; sounds that must have been similar to the sounds he could not hear, so many years later on this night, when he is alone, and The Ice is at his door. These sound bytes have become wedged in his brain, and this is how they got there.

He had taken a trip with his father to Mackinac to check The Ice's progress. He was a toddler, then, the last of six children. There was room for one more that day, and he got the lucky draw. He would ride between his father's legs, the sweet and stale smell of whiskey and tobacco would pour over him for the next two nights. But some thought it was more than luck. Even at that young age, he felt the stare of his brothers, Drew and Alfie; the imprint of their hard eyes that would stay with him throughout his days. On this particular day, he was the favored one, but there would be a price to pay.

Midway across the remnant of the Mackinac Bridge, the dogs would go no further. Neither the sting of the whip nor the special cooing sounds of his father could coax them any further. There in the distance, coming across the water was its sound, the snap of pines and the grating of stone. Then they saw it. Shrouded in mist, it sat another level above the land like a ghostly mountain range, moving.

This was Dee's first sighting, but his father, John Dee Sr., had previously made other journeys, while Molly Dee, the mother, had been barely pregnant with C.P., their first. John Dee was the first groundling to measure accurately The Ice's annual rate of progress or ARP. His methods were crude, but remarkably consistent with Communico's, those munificent benefactors of mankind. Their satellites soared across the heavens and measured not only the ARP of the great Ice called Michigan, but also every other imaginable data about it and all else. They were the self-proclaimed guardians of the times, the so called benefactors. And their mantra— beamed down twice daily from the sky to the multitudes below: *What I assume you shall assume, for every atom belonging to me as good belongs to you.* They had tracked it from its inception, a half-millennium before, as it made its southern descent across the territories formerly known as Canada, Minnesota, and Wisconsin, where, with Chicago in its sights—it unexpectedly swung eastward across what had formerly been called "The U.P."

It was at this point, that John Dee became concerned. He had a family to protect, so he conducted his own investigation. He crossed the Mackinac Bridge and swung west along what was left of the Old U.S. 2 trail. Two days he travelled before being forced to stop, when pools of muddy brown water began forming around him. They seemed to be coalescing. In a matter of minutes he was sitting in a small stream. He wasted little time. The dogs were willing to oblige. He made a rapid about-face and raced backward for several miles until he reached higher ground. He settled the dogs down and secured them to a tree. Then he climbed a nearby hill and went further up a white pine until he had achieved the highest possible vantage point. From there he clearly saw and heard the unimaginable. What was most remarkable was the flow of water that poured down in front of it and the salmon flopping and shimmering in the sunlight. This explained the seagulls that constantly circled in front. The Ice was literally redirecting part of the shoreline. The water rushed forward, splashing and washing off the rocks and trees. The front plow-lip was at least twenty feet high, maybe more. It was difficult to say from this distance, but it quickly sloped up to something much higher. Everything was wrapped in a misty veil. He began to take deep strider breaths, causing the dogs to raise their napping heads and pointedly look up at him, on that morning twenty some years ago.

Most would have gone the other way. They would have taken to the sleds and directed the dogs homeward at once. He did not. Had he done so, had he followed his initial instincts and fled, then his own son, John Dee Jr., would not have had the invaluable statistics that would allow him to have calculated his final days and weeks those years ahead—on this very night—when he lies on the floor, wrestling with the angel of sleep, with The Ice just outside his door.

But he did not flee. Instead, he moved forward on foot, following the ridgeline, until he was at the very face of it. The ground shook so and the earth let out such a terrible sigh, just as it would during those final days, though his son would not hear it. The chairs would slide across the tables and the windows would rattle in their frames. Unlike his son, for whom there would be no foreseeable escape, John Dee Sr. had a plan in place that day. He stayed only a few hours and stuffed his ears with rags, while he went about his work, staking out markers and recording its progress. He drove a stake three feet in front of the wall and then set his hour glass. It was just half-empty when The Ice claimed the stake. He performed the experiment a second time, this time measuring off ten paces. Five times he emptied the glass. He ran the numbers. Between a hundred sixty and a hundred seventy feet per day. That was twelve miles a year. That gave him thirty years, give or take, before it could possible threaten the stone house and its community; and for this to happen, it must somehow cross the six mile Straits of Mackinac, assuming that it crossed at the narrowest point. This raised the question of The Ice's relationship to water. During its five-hundred-year trek south from the polar region, it had always gone around significant bodies of water. What had caused it to suddenly swing east and spare what had formerly been known as Wisconsin and Illinois? Rumors circulated. Did The Ice have a mind of its own? Communico had explored this theory, which they labeled as being more of a superstition: Melvillian Consciousness.

His was a family of cosmic balance, with the scales tipping toward science and reason, though not without certain apocalyptic and transcendent tendencies. This balance would change though, when on a cold night in January the whole community would gather on the shores of Mackinac to watch as Michigan closed in on the bridge; and close in it did, turning south and taking with it the Mighty Mac, taking it as a child would take a piece of licorice, twisting it first and then eating it. It slid beneath the waters and for six months created a churning caldron atop, until it emerged on the other side, steaming and hissing in the cold blue light, with the whole Lower Peninsula now before it.

Much of this will be evidenced and prefigured in the archives, those recently unearthed centuries-old boxes, which he, the father, would not live to see, but yet would be aware of—thanks to the oral tradition that had been handed down to him. The son, however, would know and see the boxes firsthand, discovering them by accident, a kind of doomsday capsule from centuries past.

"We were the Jeremiahs of the time," the chronicler had self-consciously proclaimed. These were the words of his ancestors. Strange words, indeed. "Proclaiming to ears that would listen and eyes that would see." Beyond the rhetoric lay the facts. It came from an article entitled, "The Museum of Climate." Highlighted in yellow was the following excerpt:

What came as the greatest surprise was the rapidity of change, though that too had been well predicted from ice analyses at the South Pole. A mere ten years and the average surface temperature for the earth dropped 8 degrees Celsius. This resulted in a shift in climate of approximately 600 miles to the north or south, depending upon which side of the equator one lived. Imagine—a Des Moines, Iowa suddenly becoming a Duluth,

Minnesota, a Madrid, Spain suddenly becoming a London, England. The human species, being always adaptable and ingenious, was able to survive such a change, though not without the high price of a ten-year famine and drought. It was the so called Third World Countries of this epoch who had the last laugh, as the many millions of Western refugees came streaming into their borders seeking heat and food. Things weren't quite so good for the plant and animal kingdoms; many species that were already in danger and fragile, had then become eliminated.

And what caused such a rapid change? As early as the end of the second millennium, Webb and Clark discovered the three modes of climate control, modes that were governed by the northward flow of warm tropical air with ocean currents. For at least 18 K the world had been enjoying the third mode, which brought warm, moderate temperatures in the North Atlantic, caused by ocean water that traveled north and sank in two places—producing a southerly current of warm air from the tropics. We are now certain that the ecological disaster that was taking place a millennium ago had caused a global warming that in turn 'flipped the switch' and caused the rapid change of climate mode, like a rapid countdown: three, two, one...And the new ice age had begun.

One by one, the ice would claim his family. Eight of them there had been, a father, a mother, and six siblings. C.P., the eldest, was the mechanic; Drew, the organizer; Marie, the philanthropist; and Jane, the performer and actress. Even Alfie, with his bad vision and one eye pointed in, could wield a hammer when he wasn't withdrawn in his angry solitude. Where did that leave him, John Dee Jr.? He was the square peg for the round hole, born into a stony deafness that would claim him by his second year. Pertussis or whooping cough was the official diagnosis, not by Molly, his mother, but by Communico, whose "network of love" had learned of this. It was Molly, midwife and mother to all, who would see him through the illness, apply her hot packs to his wheezing throat, keeping the room misted with mint, and dousing him with cayenne, ginger, and honey. His father would teach him the signs, an elaborate system of hand signals used by the Monks of Cluny forest—a shadowy group of mystics that were more legend than fact, who purportedly lived with their mystic leader, far off beyond The Icy Pines. When they communicated this way, through the signs, the words were *like this*. Not really words in the normal sense of discourse, but symbols carved in the air. *They're out there*, his father would signal, going through a flashing, waving routine, which was really more of a dance than a signal, ending with a graceful up-and-under move, that ended in a one-legged stance with palms out and extended toward the black sheet of night, just beyond Dee's bedroom window. He even went so far as to attempt to describe the sound of the horns, long stately appearing instruments that they allegedly blew at certain preordained times to signal something—who knows what.

Dee would distinguish himself in other ways. His father would discover the drawings, between the 2 x 4s in the workshop, tucked away in the back. He loved his father's workshop, the damp, musty smell of earth and stone; the look of the ax and the sickle, hanging on the wall, with their suggestion of power; the vice at the workbench; the various hammers, chisels, and drill bits; the smell of wood and oil; the dankness of it all. The first drawing was made with the leftover clinkers from the stove. It depicted deer standing in an open field, while shadowy figures in hoods gazed on from the circumference. Six months later, during a sudden bout of spring fever and cleaning, he discovered the next drawing, which really was a revised and refined version of the first. This one was much more sophisticated, even to his father's untrained eye. Someone had stretched one of his old deerskins across a pallet. This time Dee had combined the black smudge of the clinkers with some leftover paints. The result was a repetition of the earlier image, though with much more detail. There was an open field with dark woods on the perimeter, shaded in such a way to capture the enchanted, quiet quality of dusk in the winter, when everything is opaque looking and the snow continues to fall. A small herd of deer stood at the edge of the woods. The one in the center had just raised its rack of horns and turned toward something. It was only when he followed its gaze that he saw what. Dark figures in hooded robes were moving across a field toward a building that was camouflaged in the woods.

When Molly saw the picture, a mix of feelings rushed through her. She thought it was beautiful, yet she felt uneasy. Although she was supportive, she lacked words for what she felt. So they asked him about the drawings. It was always best to talk with him about those kinds of serious topics at bedtime, when the womb of covers was snuggled about him, and both parents stood above him like pillars. This time Molly did the hand signs.

You? Father markings shed?

Markings not mother.

Molly felt John's look, the heat from his arm.

Not? What then who?

"Paintings." Sometimes he said words and heard them from the dense, muffled roar inside his clotted head. "Paintings." He said it again. A mystery. "Paintings." Where did it come from? His hands moved through the air. *Stupid paintings.*

Not stupid, beautiful!

Stupid paintings. Drew, Alfie.

Dark figures, who? John said. Who they?

He rolled back over and boldly looked up at his father. His hands moved cuttingly through the air.

The Monks of Cluny Forest.

2

And then there were three: Mother, Father, and him. Alfie was first. Dee saw him packing in the night. *Where go you? What do?* Alfie was not good with the signs. He had no patience. He put his face up close to Dee's ear and shouted, "Monk of Cluny Forest." He pointed to the window. The next morning he was gone. They followed his footprints, which disappeared into The Icy Pines.

Little Jane was next, cutting her arm on a rusty nail, and eventually dying in her mother's arms, but not before sitting up dramatically in bed, with the others all around, and throwing her arms out to some beatific vision, before collapsing. C.P. and Drew would join the others in the great migration south, promising that they would find a place for everyone in warmer climes and one day return. But they, too, were gone. Gone, gone, gone. But John Dee remained, ever faithful to that ancient promise of his blood, which could be evidenced in the engraved words on the ancient slab of wood over the fireplace: A House of Stone is Forever.

The Ice was only three rivers away, at Gwendraeth Valley, two years at most from their door. John Dee began to stockpile provisions, cutting and stacking the wood, enough for two years, maybe more. The animals had long since abandoned the forests, leaving only the shadowy images of the fish lurking beneath the ice of Stone Lake, a natural wonder and creation that time had carved out within easy walking distance. The dogs were gone, set free one morning after days of ceaseless baying. Stone Lake then became the sole food source, and it was in the morning that his father set out toward the center of the lake that the dark clouds began to roll in from the North and the air grew dark damp and cold with the promise of snow. And snow it did.

A foggy mist settled over the land, and at the end of the second day, it thickened and became its own source of light, a glowing opaqueness, a world submerged in milk. Dee felt nauseated, helpless, and trapped. He worried about his father. His dark hands flashed through the white air. *Worry to fear, fear to guilt. Survival. Me not Father.* "Selfish asshole," he said of himself. He knew these words. He kicked the handmade footstool that his father had made and fashioned. Now it lay shattered in a half dozen pieces. Had mother heard this? Probably, just as she had all the others; yet, she remained hidden in one of the other rooms.

Okay, so he would be the hero. He would play the part and try to save the father who could not be saved. If he was lucky, he might kill himself in the process. He stood up and threw on his attire, dressing all in black—black boots, black scarf, black gloves, and so on. Perhaps black would stand out. Molly came out. She ignored the shattered stool, or maybe she didn't notice. She came to him and held his face. Her hands were cold and tired. She needn't speak or make a sign. He could read the words on her tired face. I cannot bear to lose you, too. She was still beautiful, despite the hardships of the past years. She had a face that he had wanted to paint, round with hair pinned up around it, hair that still remained brown with red highlights that stood out in the right sunlight.

In the past, when his father was away, Dee could feel his presence. There was no sense of absence. Even in the early years, when he would take the dogs and be gone for days, it was as though he were only in the other room. He was not there, yet he could feel him and imagine him clearly, if he tried. This time if he shut his eyes tightly and grimaced with concentration, he could only feel him a little. He could not imagine his face, only the outline of it. His whole body was an outline.

Okay, so he would develop this plan. Can't have action without reaction. Here's what to do: he would go out to the storage shed where his father kept the fishing poles. There he would get some line, secure one end to the front porch pillar, and reel himself out to the lake and beyond if necessary. He would take a thousand feet of forty pound test line and tie it together as needed. The shed was situated right next to the house, not ten steps away. He had made that journey from the porch to the shed a million times. He could do it with his eyes closed, he thought. He proceeded out the front screen door with its stiff iron spring that always gave way so reluctantly and brought the door shut with a resounding *thwap* that even he could hear. He hadn't intended that. Now mother would know.

He had not gone three steps, and he felt suspended in a void, a thick white, soupy void of the underworld, a sea of milk. Nausea crept in. He held his breath and groped his way along, till he ran into the wall. He patted down the logs and felt the crease where the mud joint was. This was the storage shed all right. He chuckled at his own sense of doubt. What else could it be? He was developing a headache from the brightness. He had never seen such brightness. He closed his eyes and tried to shut it out. Anything was better than this piercing whiteness, even this mottled brown and black. He found the latch and entered. The inside was dark, yet the windows glowed white. Darkness he could handle. He fumbled around and managed to light a lantern.

He found the badly battered and beat up poles and managed to get the reels free. He took two reels. He fumbled back to the porch and set about his hazardous journey. First he secured one end to the porch pillar. He wasn't the best knot tier, but one that he had learned well was the half-hitch. So he half-hitched the hell out of it: one, two, three, four times; that should do. Then he began taking sideways steps, as if he were moving along a ledge at a great altitude, his back against the wall. This was the way he moved along, counting his steps, while keeping the line taunt. How ridiculous, he thought. What would he do if he found this father? He would probably be dead. He had to do this, though.

He counted the steps. He moved further and further into the void. He did a slide-shuffle step, clearing a path of sorts so he could find his way back more easily, should he drop the line. How smart was that? He was trying to think of every angle. His father would be proud of him. How about this. Instead of the usual winter garb, he had worn his father's rain gear. It was a little small. Granted not the warmest, but the driest, and black as hell. Maybe it would show in this light; it did not. His body was slick with moisture, some kind of weather inversion must have been taking place.

The snow was thick and soggy. He picked up a handful and squeezed it to water.

He knew the path to the lake. It was not long, surrounded by trees on both sides; so he could not go astray. Several times he would bump against that border and readjust, counting his steps: one-hundred-seventy-one, seventy-two. How smart was that?

What kind of world, what kind of light was this? It was like being inside a cloud, one of those white thunderheads stacked up on the horizon, fifty thousand feet high, blocking the sun, but full of light. He must be getting close to the water's edge. He might even be on it. The grade seemed to be leveling out. That was how it was. You walked down a little path for a short distance then out onto the flat surface of the lake. He was over two-hundred steps. He had this figured out too. Father would be proud of him. He slipped off one glove and the inner lining as well. The air was warmer than he expected, not *warm* by any means, but nearly tolerable. Time for the switch. He felt the reel with his forefinger. The line was down to a little core inside. Must be careful here. He brought a knife. He would cut the line of one and connect it to the other, the full one, all in the whiteness of blindness, like taking a piece of his sketch paper and making it three dimensional and going to the center of it, surrounding yourself. Careful now, he reminded himself, slipping the other glove off with his teeth. Mustn't lose the glove. Then pulling a section of the other line, the starter. Tying the quick knot. He must hurry now. He felt the feeling going out of his fingers. One half-hitch, two, and three. Done. The lines were connected.

He could stay out here forever, he thought. He was beginning to lose himself to the light. He was transparent. He was the light. Maybe that was how it was out here. No direction, no barriers. Maybe he would take a nap, but he should call him first. That was why he had come out here, wasn't it? He formed the word and sent it flying. *Dah-ee, Dah-ee.* He really let it fly, over and over, until his throat stung and he could taste the salty tears on his upper lip. He would not give up. He could not give up. *Dah-ee, Dah-ee.* On the last one, he held the "e." *Dah-eeeeeeeeeeeeeeee!* He felt his jaw widen and his teeth bare.

Vertigo swirled. He fell to his knees to steady himself. How smart was that! But he had let go of the line. The nausea returned. Chunks came through his nose, the remnants of this morning's breakfast, French toast and venison sausage that Momma had made. Dear, sweet, loving Momma.

How lucky he was to have a Momma like that. He wiped his face and began to crawl in the direction he thought the line might have been. The snow was mostly water, on top that is, slushy, wet, water.

He began to cry. He didn't want to cry, but the matter was out of his hands. He flashed the signs in the whiteness. *Tried-Daddy. Tried. Again I fail.* He continued to crawl along, feeling his way. Something was tangling him. It was the line. Pretty soon it had his arms and legs, so he rolled until he could go no further, until he was up against something. He took his gloves off and felt the contours, the nose, the hair, the round face, stiff, cold, and caving in to one side. *Not father but mother.*

"Get up, damn you. Get up!" He heard the words and thought they were his father's, but they were not. They were someone else's. "Cut the lines and run. Run!" He realized that he was still holding the knife and he began to slash away. He felt his legs go free and then his arms. Now run. The fog was lifting then, just enough. He ran, flailing his arms wildly as he did, until he hit the front pillar of the front porch and knocked himself out, but not before realizing that the voice he had heard was his own. Daddy would have been proud.

3

He would never forget his first night alone. Provisions were low, and the wood was gone. He had no heat. The last bit of fire had been burnt, the rose of its glow gone. Heavy, still air settled about him. It was a cold, blue Jack London night, the kind of night that slowed things and eventually made them stop.

He had this sleeping bag, given to him some time back by his neighbor, Hobbs. He was joining the mass exodus and was the last to leave. Hobbs did not speak the signs. Instead, he brought a yellow pad and exchanged notes. Dee was spared the clipped British accent.

"Take this." He handed him a rolled garment, olive green in color.

Dee took a pad and scratched out his response. "What is it?"

"A relic of sorts. It's called a sleeping bag." Hobbs had dark playful eyes, surrounded with spidery wrinkles. His salt and pepper beard fell down to his chest.

He wrote something else down, a final note, and folded it. Then across the front, "Don't read until I raise my hand." He demonstrated what he meant.

Dee watched his dark figure slowly diminish, his walking stick pawing at the crusty snow, until he stood at the edge of The Icy Pines, where he turned and raised his hand. He then put both hands to his mouth and called out.

"Use it," he called. His big voice boomed and echoed through the woods. Some snow on top of a Doug Fir gave way and spilled down on him. It stuck to his beard like powder.

"Life can be brutish." He threw back his head and went "Ha-ha-ha-ha-ha!" Then he disappeared into The Icy Pines.

Now he must sleep without heat. It was then that he established his ritual of lying before the hearth. He curled up on the floor, inside Hobbs' sleeping bag. He said a brief prayer just as his family had taught him to do. The words came spontaneously to him, as they always did.

"Lord, grant me a quiet sleep and a peaceful death."

A drowsy numbness began to steal upon him. Was it slumber or death? He couldn't be sure, but he could no longer resist its pleasure. He thought of home, his lost family, friends, and The Ice. He surrendered.

How surprised he had been when the first light of morning began to announce itself and he was still breathing. He jumped to his feet and danced and whooped and shouted. He was alive! He slapped his arms to revive the circulation and wiggled his toes. Tears welled in his eyes and a great tide of joy swept through him, till he fell to one knee and pinched the bridge of his nose, eyes closed in a kind of weak ecstasy.

How great it is to live on, when all hope seems lost. The thick snow and the empty forest absorbed his yelps.

For the first time in recent memory, he was glad to be alone.

And then the visitors arrived.

Three of them there were, scientists, a curious lot, always thirsting to know more. Only they returned; only they broke his solitude. Theirs was always a temporary stay.

The Ice presented an anomaly that still baffled them. They could not rest until an answer was found. They had an absolute need for a total and rational explanation.

They had their humanitarian purposes, too. They were, after all, emissaries from Communico and he was the last person standing in the area. Deeper questions disturbed them: Why would anyone stay behind under such circumstances? Why had this family resisted all attempts at aide and rescue? They had long ago developed a complete profile on everyone and specifically on him, too, ever since their sensors, high above the heavens, had first caught the trace of his smoke—a mix of cedar and spruce, stinging and sweet—stringing out from his chimney and running along the treetops. They zoomed in and imaged the stone house, the lone birch tree in front and the apple orchard and black berry patch behind. They developed their profile of him: "A rare one, indeed. F.I.S.T. Dominated by feeling, intuition, sensory, and thinking, in that order. A throwback to an old era. A rare one, living in a kind of cultural vacuum from the past millennium, filled with all kinds of natural longings and sentiments concerning family, homestead and the land. Has a long procreative breeder-type mentality and family history. Still adheres to printed text. Isolated. But definitely the wrong type for survival-type conditions. The higher reliance on feeling and intuition and the low level thinking and sensing could create problems, especially as conditions worsen.

On a grey afternoon, he finally answered their soft, but persistent knock. He opened his door and beheld them, clad head to foot in their skintight thermos. They spoke the signs, but always it was too fast and with too many words. True to their Communico beneficiaries, they were quite indistinguishable and truly fit the motto: *The difference is no difference.* Third person feminine and masculine had been stricken from their language. All were slender of build, *for eating must sustain life and nothing more*; medium in height, *for happy is the middle flight.* Only the identifying codes that each wore over their left breast gave the particulars, followed by Communico 's infinity symbol: ∞. These identity codes were the last known examples of Communico's use of Common Era's print code, and they were used only for situations such as this, when they visited these few remaining small pockets of inhabitants from that era. The light visors they wore emitted a yellow glow and fit snuggly over their heads, molding to all the contours.

They did not know the nuances of the signs; but the one labeled Yazzie was the best, but even its effort was a textbook diction that was laborious and word for word.

Yazzie lifted the light visor to expose two eyes, one green and the other blue. Next, it removed the mouth filter. A wind-blistered lower lip with a split in the middle delivered words in a low, soft voice, while giving the sign.

Good afternoon. With your permission, we need to run these tests and gather a few samples.

Tests? Dee felt the old caution overtake him. This was not one of his favorite words. *Tests, kind what?*

As you know this is one of the last known stands of North Woods hardwood. We need to get these samples before it is too late. They will be invaluable for our colonizing projects.

Late too?

Yazzie turned momentarily and looked at Elfrin, who was now kneeling before the tree and stroking its white trunk. *Yes, before it's too late, before the end has come. Just a few tests.*

They wanted to dig his earth. They had with them warming rods which they drove into the ground and within a few minutes the area within a six-foot radius would be melted away, the earth soggy and muddy and the snow cleared. Dee caught the scent of false spring, the mud and drizzle.

On the third day of their stay, they made the discovery. It was late in the afternoon, during a rare one-hour patch of unmitigated sunshine that their spades clanked against something metal. He saw them from the back window, gathered together at the edge of the divide between the stone house and The Icy Pines. He sensed their concern. They were having a mild disagreement. The one called Elfrin was rubbing the black top of a box, three feet beneath the ground "Time capsules." The words issued forth in a dreamy sort of whisper. It made the sign: *Messages from the Past.*

Dee jumped down in the hole. He rubbed the frozen earth from the top of two boxes and looked at the emblem. For some odd reason it seemed familiar. He grabbed the shovel and began to dig. For several hours he labored, clearing the dirt away around both boxes and eventually loosening the earth around them so they could be hoisted out. Two of them jumped down into the hole and helped to lift the heavy boxes out.

Later that night, around a campfire, they examined the contents. The one called Elfrin made the signs. *An ancient means of public communication called newspapers and books.* Printed texts had all but disappeared from the earth. Print as a means of communication was nonexistent. Dee's mother and father had taught him to read in the old, outmoded sense, but as for the others—the Communico group—bar translators were needed to understand any chance encounter with print. They adhered to the motto: The Letter Killeth.

Elfrin continued her inventory. *Scientific documents, a musical device called a CD, Eric Clapton, a performer, The Beatles, a geographic locator called a map, an ancient religious relic called a chalice, a ciborium.* Elfrin held up a large plastic bag filled with small white wafers. Of this they had no record. All had been vacuumed sealed in plastic and preserved, except for these, which had survived nonetheless. After a long pause, Elfrin said nothing and put the wafers back in the box.

Such preservation amazed Dee, but the one called Stringer scoffed. *We must control the fantasy. Bread is bread. We're in the beginning stages of an ice age. That's your preserver.*

Some items needed no explaining. He fully understood the pictures. They were watercolors. He immediately recognized the settings, the stone house with the wintergreen and asters leading up to the door, the little pond beneath the bridge, and blue, fluffy skies overhead.

There were other things of interest in the box. He found a book of matches and laughed aloud. He took one and struck it. The little flame sparked to life.

Stringer became even more amused. He angrily flashed the signs: *Ancient, outdated, outmoded, archaic. Know what you are? You're a soppy, drippy-eyed romantic, that's what you are.* Spoken too fast, too many words. Dee ignored them. Instead, he looked on the matchbook cover. It said, The Wel-Come Inn.

On the backside was a picture of a woman in a skimpy red bikini, with a large portion of cleavage showing. She had red painted lips and was licking them in a slow, suggestive manner.

On the back of the cover it said: Grill open until 11:00 p.m. You'll love our buffalo wings

Happy hour every day from 1:00-6:00 p.m.Band every Saturday.

Elfrin began jumping up and down.

He pawed around through the other things, handing them to Elfrin, who made the identifications. There were various odds and ends. A Montgomery Ward's catalogue, a package of Juicy Fruit chewing gum, a package of Tareyton cigarettes, a package of condoms, a Swiss pocket knife. Near the bottom were various bundles of books tied together with handwritten notes in a scrawling sort of penmanship attached to them. One bundle was entitled, "Four Important Books for the Future." It contained a hardbound copy of Stephen Crane's The Open Boat, Henry David Thoreau's Walden, Virginia Woolf's A Room of One's Own, and a copy of The Bible with a red ribbon in *The Book of Wisdom.*

Another bundle simply said "Regional Writers of Some Interest," in the same scrawling sort of penmanship. The Underbark, by Max Ellison, The Hunt, by Richard Erno, and Wolf, by Jim Harrison. The last bundle contained a large stack of notebooks and loose papers that were simply entitled "My Stuff."

He opened the first notebook that was entitled "The Prisoner," and saw with a shock of excitement something that needed no interpretation, something that he recognized immediately. It was a name written across the first page, J. Dee. That had to be his relative. There could be no mistaking the last name.

By this time, Stringer and associates were fully recovered from their labor and were about to leave him there, when he opened the second box and found at the top four bottles of thousand-year-old single malt scotch.

And what have you there? Stringer signaled.

Dee read the label of the bottles. "CAOL ILA."

Elfrin said something to Stringer. *Hold it up,* Stringer signed, *so my colleague can see it.*

He held one of the bottles up. Even in the dim wintry light, it shone in a luster of dark gold.

Elfrin moved in a cautious manner toward him, hesitating at first, and then finally taking one of the bottles and holding it within a few inches of the visor, while rubbing one of the thin fingered hands slowly over the label, and finally saying yet a few more words to Stringer in the same small voice that was barely audible. After listening for a bit, it replied as though it were a medium. "It could be an ancient medicinal recipe, but there is a strong feeling that it could also be something else, something similar yet vastly different."

With that, Dee opened the top. The thick, pungent smell of smoke and peat filled his nostrils and brought tears of longing to his eyes.

I don't believe I've ever seen anything quite like that before, Stringer said. *Let me see it.* Stringer examined the bottle, which still had the original label on it. I do recall reading something about this, a kind of specialty drink from that era. It looked around at the others and made the signs.

Well come on then. Let's get on with it.

It poured some in metal cups. The smell of the smoke and peat surrounded them, almost like a campfire.

Shall we? Stringer said.

Dee stroked his long beard. *Think, I shall we.*

Yazzie and Elfrin refrained while in the true spirit of scientific inquiry, Stringer partook.

They tasted the contents, and felt the golden fire fill their veins. *Quite different, quite unique*, Stringer said.

After the second drink, Dee began to rummage around through the books and various papers. He pulled a copy of Max Ellison and handed it to Elfrin, who began to read aloud, while Yazzie made the signs:

> I know where an old beech tree
> Hid a secret once for me.
> Initials carved within a heart
> Deep into the underbark,
> Time has healed the jack-knife scar
> But I still know where they are.

Elfrin suddenly stood up and walked around to the back of the stone house where a little waterfall had become permanently frozen, like still-action, and in that same deliberate manner of close inspection, Elfrin took a little silver hammer and chisel from the work pack and carefully chipped off three long fingers of ice, holding them up so the sunlight could flash and dance off them.

Elfrin came over and joined the others, speaking in a slow, purring voice, while it made the sign. *You know, I think they did it like this in the old days. The ice served as a solvent, not only chilling but slightly diluting.* It dropped a small nugget of ice into each of their steel cups. *I think I would like to try it also.*

Dee poured more into their cups. Now only Yazzie refrained from joining. This time they waited while the golden liquid melded within. Then they tasted. Stringer drank his right off and sat there staring into the empty cup. Dee poured a little more into its cup.

"Thanks," Stringer said. It didn't bother making the sign. It had become uncharacteristically quiet.

Elfrin drank the contents in a somewhat slow, deliberate manner. "I believe this is how one should proceed. This is how it was done." It didn't bother with the signs either. However, when Dee filled Elfrin's cup a second time, he noticed that the consumption rate had increased.

God, I've been such a self-indulgent, power-hungry, asshole all of my life, Stringer said. *Do you think you could read a little more of that poetry?*

That was how it happened. That was how the archives were discovered and an ancient tradition of The North Woods was restored. They sat there throughout most of the night, while a large fire blazed, and they drank scotch, talked, and read poetry.

The fire was casting off light and shadows in a long-forgotten manner. The fire warmed them. Pretty soon , Yazzie, who had been sitting there passively watching, was forced to pull back the thermo's headpiece and expose long, black hair that fell to her shoulder. Elfrin, too did the same, revealing a light shadow of red hair on her previously shaved head. All things were now known. All things stood in relief. They had become men and women again. Now the four of them, two men and two women sat together and listened while Elfrin read something from boxes entitled "The Prisoner."

During summer nights we would gather, where the gravel roads became two tracks, and the cedars hung over both sides of the trail; far into the recesses of the inner swamp we would go, away from the noisy dispatches of the police and their probing spotlights, surrounded by the minty smell of fern and moss, and the Pembroke River's song, where we would drink our beer, tell our stories, love our women, and occasionally kick ass, if the need for the occasion arose.

My, my, Stringer said. *Such a primitive little society they were.*

Elfrin came over and sat down next to Yazzie and began to stroke her hair.

Just let me have one more, Stringer said. *One more is all I want.* His eyes were small, dark points in the firelight, and they were tear-swollen. Dee poured some more into his cup. *Tomorrow it's all going to be different*, Stringer said. *Just you wait. I've got a lot of fences to mend. Just you wait.*

One by one the others curled up in their thermo-suits and fell asleep around the fire. Dee found himself alone again. This night he didn't sleep in the stone house. He found a place next to the dying fire and lay there thinking about his ancestors of so long ago. Eventually, he too slept, with the smell of burnt cedar in his hair and clothing.

Up above, the satellites had already registered the strange glow and vibration from this last stand of the North Woods. When morning finally arrived, the visitors were gone.

4

So he continues to wrestle with the angel of sleep, but the angel wins. There can be no sleep tonight. These were the times that would drive many to that ancient practice whose name had been lost or forgotten. "A rite of ancient break-breaking" was what Communico called it, passed on from generation to generation. This was partially true. They could find no term, though, for the words, this fountain of language that would suddenly well up from within during these dire times.

He makes the sign: *Lord, heat a little. Warmth a little. Cheer me.* No sooner does his hands shape these in the air than the crescendo comes, the resonating "boom" that he cannot hear but feels, as the sky lights up, and the woman falls to earth; nor will he hear the call at his window, just before dawn. No louder than a dove, it calls: *Wu-hu-hu. Wu-hu-hu.*

He sits up, thinking the light of day has come. It has not, but a peace and silence has settled over things. Even The Ice has been stilled, for now. Drowsiness eases into him. He closes his eyes and floats. The darkness loses strength and thins to gray. The call comes from somewhere inside of him and out: *Wu-hu-hu.* He will forget it by morning, but he will not forget feeling the presence of something at his window, a gaze that met his own.

The air is warm that morning with the smell of false-hope-spring rising. The eves drip. He will take his spear to the lake in search of this morning's breakfast. There is liveliness in his step, until he passes the front window. He kneels for a closer look. His head moves from left to right and right to left, following the trail. The print is large and the gait long and saturated in pink. It is a looping, unsteady trail. *Eyes ache, sky gray split yellow, make.* The spear falls from his hand. Eyes closed, he turns against it, feeling the warmth against his skin. He follows.

Something new, not exactly a "without" as with the fish-need, but something else the thousand cold nights of his past have erased, make his feet move mechanically up the hill, through the pines, following the unsteady trail of the prints; something that grows with each step, until he is moving quickly, fluidly, with purpose, and noticing how much deeper his own prints are than those he trails, and larger, too. He doesn't travel far. A lone hemlock stands above all the other trees. Something is beneath it, curled up and face down. He moves in, through the scrub oak and maple until stopping in mid-step, his left foot suspended in the air, while he balances on the other, arms outstretched. His eyesight has been poor for years, the whites mixed with dull grays and dark lines vertical. And then the focus: sharp and clear now, the lines straightening, distinct; snow, tinged in pink, all around the body, but the body itself has melted through several feet, forming a damp pink bowl.

Salmon snow.

He takes off his gloves. This is a first. The gloves almost never come off and never the boots or the old coveralls. He places a hand beneath the shoulder; it and the back are warm, not just warm, but warm; he rubs his hands together like spark-fire, the shaking and blowing on the palms: hot. He closes his eyes and lets the heat soak into his stiff fingers; he feels the ache of thaw begin to form in his palm and spread up to his wrist. He takes off the other glove and places both hands beneath the arm sockets, intending to lift, but closes his eyes again, caught in the luxury of warmth, sapping his strength. The cold and stiffness of a lifetime are drawn out by the touch— this touch—of a strange body lying beneath the hemlock tree, the day after the storm. He turns his hands over and presses the backsides against the body, until his hands and arms are thoroughly warmed. He has been there for a half hour and the body shows no signs of losing heat. It settles further and further down into the snow, going deeper, perhaps four feet down now, with another four or more to go before reaching the frozen earth.

He rolls the body over, slowly, and deliberately and recognizes the Communico uniform: the infinity sign over the left breast and the usual identification type. Asdzą́ą́. He does not recognize these identification types. The hood falls back unexpectedly; the eyes roll open and then back, closed again. Dark hair pinned up in a queue and wound tightly around with white strings. Square face, high cheeks and rounded, with a trace of a smile. This skin is most remarkable, dark like *leaf fall dead mother ground*. Dee makes the sign to the empty forest. He has never seen dark skin before, so contrasted to the whiteness of his life, to the whiteness of The Ice. She's a woman!

Chest-energy, splitting from the inside, uprooting old, forgotten juices, sweeps through him. His hands weave through the air: *Thaw feel. Good ache.* He snorts the damp air and paws the snow. Then it drops, low and heavy. The sudden need to relieve himself, to either urinate or defecate; he is not sure which, maybe both.

He lifts her body, how light to carry, tall, almost square-featured, falling over his arms like a folded blanket. He begins walking back toward the stone house. The heat spreads. His brow begins to drip, salt-soaking his mustache in a pleasing way that makes him smack his lips continually and run his tongue up and over. *Burny eyes, sting.* He pushes the front door open with one leg and walks to the fox furs, where he places her gently down, as the whole room seems to grow warmer. Something begins to surround him and his home. The rooms seem lighter. The shadows have receded. He makes the sign, this time his hands doing a series of figure eights, ending at last in a cradle motion back and forth at his hips, eyes closed and damp: *Arms of house mother hold me.*

The vigil begins. First night, he parts her lips. The chips of ice instantly disappear on her swollen tongue. He runs to the back yard and chips more off the waterfall. The melt down slows some, but still each one is gone soon after touching the thick, dark, texture of her tongue, which is dark like the deer meat he has not seen or tasted for years. Color begins to return to it, the tongue, a pink, fleshy tone around the edges and the swelling begins to recede. He turns his head sideways and places one ear to her flat breast and hears the fierce pounding. She is turning her head from side to side.

Second night, though still delirious, she makes a sign. At first he cannot believe it and taps her wrist three times with his index finger and she responds, making the sign again. The food sign: *Food, stomach, gnaw.* The only thing he can offer is raw fish. Each time he places a piece near her lips, the spasms increase and she shakes her head no in a violent manner.

Then he remembers the ancient wafers. He hurries to the archives, to the boxes, recently unearthed, where everything is kept. He finds them and brings them to her "bedside"—the fox furs next to the mantle. He places one on her tongue and washes it down with a little water. The effects are almost immediate. The breathing steadies. He tries to place a second on her tongue, but she refuses, shaking her head violently no. Heat continues to radiate from her, though the perspiration has subsided.

The two of them are before the old, forgotten fireplace, which hasn't seen a flame or an ember since his father died and the wood supplies ran out. Her long body extends beyond the fox furs to the mason floors, the hand cut tile, slate, pieced together from generations past. He kneels down and lifts one section of fur. Outside, the thaw is over and once again gray clouds hang low over the earth. Another storm is moving in. Snow has begun to fall in large, floating flakes everywhere. The Ice has returned—as if it had ever been gone, scraping and grinding away, a few hundred meters away at most.

He makes the sign, whirling, flashing, and tapping to his chest: *Let the ice come!*

He lies down away from her and draws a corner of the furs over him. *Heat body glow.* Darkness fills the spaces. The storm worsens. He rolls over on his side and curls up in a ball. Sleep overtakes him. This is good, his body says.

Sleep. Letting go.

This heat, this blossom of warmth soon exceeds its boundaries, until he sits up suddenly, his breathing stopped up in his chest.

He tries to keep his distance, but she unexpectedly rolls to him, though still sleeping, and she tangles her long legs and arms about him. He is entangled, her arms are sinewy vines. She pins him against the wall. Then she explores his body, his beard first, then his hairy throat, his chest, pausing at each nipple, spending time, before moving on. He hears the voice, her voice inside of him as she grew hard and firm to the touch; and the voice said to him, "I am First Woman."

Exhaustion deflates him. Sleep decomposes him. He sinks beneath the fox furs. "Thawing." The word breaks loose from the river bottom of sleep and floats to the surface. A dream, he remembers; bitter smoke curls beneath autumn leaves; he is buried, a child beneath one of the piles, while the raspy rake heaps more upon him, the laughter of children, a snapping flame that refuses to ignite, spinning gray smoke upward.

The burnt smell is still there when he opens his eyes. A new ache pleasurably runs up his belly like a lever pointing northward. This eventually brings him out of his slumber. One hand slung over the empty furs, the other grips himself, his hardness, squeezing it, a slow steady pulse. He wants more of this ache. He wants more of last night; that and the burnt smell in the air.

One droopy eye opens first, then the other. Light rushes in, splitting his head, until he adjusts. Red and black drapes over the mantle; squares of the afghan. Now he remembers, mother's afghan. A painting hangs on the wall, a signature in the corner: Culver; three deer are in an orchard, a stroke of brown sprinkled with white on their backs, one of them looking up, ears alert.

But he must get up. He registers a change in his environment. He gathers himself up and out, stepping into pants. The conformity and order of things frame him. Things have been picked up and put away. New things sit on the mantle, new things framed, taken from the archives. A woman in a long dress sits on a motorcycle, a man in a red flannel holds up a string of fish. A mirror is framed in blue tile. Who has done this? He looks closely at the pictures. He almost recognizes the people. Through the mirror, he looks back at himself. His throat is blotched in blue, little bruises that run up one side and down another. They are on other parts of his body too, his legs, his stomach, and yes—even on that, which is upright against his belly. He has never had such a queer, pleasurable pain. One is swollen, right where the blue vein runs along the side. It is sore to the touch in a way that is pleasing.

The burnt smell laces the air. It is vaguely familiar, not unpleasant. He follows its trail, leading him toward the kitchen, where he finds her standing, her back to him, a lean, tall figure, her head just below the 8 foot ceilings. She is thin and rectangular looking—beautiful in her purple top and tan skirt. Her hair is done up in a queue. A brown leather pouch is attached to her side. Her hands are raised just above her shoulders, as she works corn flower dough, twirling it round and round from hand to hand—and then letting it fall down over her wrists. Old forgotten aromas come to him and put that dividing line in his stomach. Two skillets and a griddle sit on the stove. The griddle is empty but hot. Little bubbles of lubricant stand out on its black surface. One of the skillets is covered and the other is open. She drops the dough into the open skillet. A loud crackling, sizzling sound erupts and then dies down. She turns it several times before taking it out. The dough is golden colored with large wrinkles. She places it on a plate with several others and covers it. She takes the lid off the other skillet and checks its contents. A cloud of steam rises.

She places the lid back on and wipes her hands with a towel. She turns to him and smiles, as though she has known he was there all the time. She walks over to him and takes his hand in hers. He looks down at her grip and feels the heat and suddenly remembers certain things from the night before, causing a color to flush into his cheeks and neck. Her lips move.

"You're awake now." She laughs, a high pitched note on the scale that strikes the air and holds its tonality, a birdsong suspended, erotic and teasing. His head is thrown back, his neck kinked, to look at her. "I forgot," she says, and speaks to him in signs, motioning him to sit at the old oak table, which now shines like new. *Thank you*, she said.

Thank you? His brows knot, a line forms across his forehead.

Life saved me, she says.

Life saved me?

She nods.

Then she tells him about the meteor storm. Her hands move smoothly through the air, touching her breast and then one finger to her temple. *We saw the storm coming for years. But the blackout was totally unexpected. It was like somebody suddenly pulled the plug.* She points to the sky and brings both hands together, touching her fingertips and then making a sweeping gesture away and slowly lowering her hands, her fingers undulating. *A number of things fell the from sky.* She touches her breast and smiles. *Me.*

I am the woman who fell from the sky, and my first gift to you will be the gift of language. I will make you speak and hear. She spit on her finger and rubbed it in each ear.

"It will take time."

She hands him a yellow cup with black liquid in it. The burnt smell he recognizes from so long ago. She puts her soft lips to his ear and speaks the word.

"Coffee."

The brow unfurls. The clouds across his forehead smooth.

"Coffee." He brings the cup to his mouth.

She points to herself. *Áltsé.* These are new signs.

He points at himself. *Dee.*

She waves her hands in the air. *You've been the talk of the Communico Net for years. Akéédóó Hastiin is what they call you, Last Man.* Then she signaled, *Refuse he always.* Her birdsong laugh strikes the air again. This time he laughs back, his like hers now, filled with playfulness, teasing, and the other.

He has nearly forgotten about Communico. The mentioning of the name makes make him cross his legs. His brows once again begin to knit and knot. The names Stringer and Elfrin, pop up not in sight, but for the first time, in sound. And now this new visitor. She doesn't seem like a Communico member. She has shed the thermo-suit.

Woman you, he says. This time her eyes will not meet his.

He brings the coffee up, smelling its aroma, sipping its steaming contents. He can still feel her warmth, standing next to him like that.

Hot you why?

She pulls two white pills from her pocket and shows him, they are small with a cross on one side. "Metab pills."

He looks at them in her brown palm. He puts his finger to one. She puts them back in her pocket and begins to explain, moving her hands rapidly through the air, a long sequence. This will take a lot of explaining. It will not be easy.

Pills speed up for space travel, kept warm, keep going. Unexpected reentry, what Communico calls THE ENIGMA, sky split, time split, everything split, forced reentry, no orientation, and no problem. She takes his hand and presses it to her cheek and neck. His eyes immediately fill with tears.

"I will be like this for a few more days. I don't remember much about the last few days. Hope I wasn't a problem."

Problem-no-problem.

She is back at the stove again, her long, lean back to him. He holds the blue cup in his hand and slowly brings it to his lips. The kitchen has been transformed. The brass fittings on the old wood range shine and the stove hums with an internal blaze. The sink as well as the windows are sparkling and the floor has a clean, anti-septic smell.

A question crosses his brow, a look toward something that he can't quite remember, something terribly important and relevant to the situation at hand, the fire, the food.

Her hands form looping figures. *Communico supplies, air, soon help.*

Soon help?
She shakes her head yes.
Here?
She shakes her head yes again.

Back at the sink, she begins mixing up a batter in a blue bowl. "The first thing is to get some food into you." She drops four white circles onto the griddle and watch as the bubbles form across the smooth surface. Then she turns them.

One plate already has golden wrinkly things on it. "Fry bread," she says, and holds a piece up to him before pouring honey over it. She puts the plate in front of him. "Try this." She tears off a small piece and drops it into his mouth. More tears come to his eyes.

"It's okay," she says softly. She flips two pancakes onto his plate. "I found this here." The old gray earthen jug, the label still intact, 100% Pure Michigan Maple Syrup. She pours some over his pancakes and then spoons a heaping pile of scrambled eggs and sausage on his plate. She sits down across from him and watches him eat.

He can only stare at the steaming plate. She crosscuts the pancakes and mixes in the eggs and puts a large forkful into his mouth. From there on, he is on his own. No coaching needed. He dips his head low and cleans his plate.

"Next, we've got to clean you up."
He blinks.

"I figure with everything, we've got enough to last a couple of weeks. Somebody should be here by then." She walks to the kitchen window and pulls back the new white curtains. The scene outside is sculpted: white figurines in wind-swept designs, heaped up high—the storm's aftermath. Behind that, The Ice. Baldy Hill is half-swallowed. Only the brief clearing and a small stand of trees between it and the house.

"That is, if our friend doesn't get here first." There in the distance, he sees it, though the snow flies in all directions. In his new found warmth, he has nearly forgotten it. The white sheet is moving around them, like a pair of hands at the end of a long pair of arms, reaching out and at long last about to pull them in.

She made the sign. *One thing us.*
What?

Asdzą́ą́, the First Woman, smiled and took him by the hand. She put her mouth to his ear.

"I will show you everything."

Dee stood up.

Why?

Now woman I am, you make.

Me?

"Yes, you. And now I will teach you what it means to be a man again."

She pulled him up from his seat.

"Let us begin here."

His chair made a scraping sound against the floor.

Her hands flashed figure eights and slicing motions: *Clean the kitchen.*

5

The Ice will not rest; the stone house trembles with its approach, pictures fall from the mantle; windows vibrate. She moves about his house, sprinkling pollen on the doors and singing ancient songs.

Dee has his old routine. He tries to continue it. He goes to a small room at the back of the house, where his father used to sit and smoke during the old days, when he ice was still a remote dream. The ceilings are low and the lighting poor. He runs his finger along his forearm, where the hairs are still dark, but the skin is waxy colored. The window is nothing more than a peephole, a waist-high view of a trail cutting through sumac, rising up a knoll and disappearing. He likes the closeness and narrowness of this room. Here he can enjoy the large flakes drifting forgetfully to earth.

He would like to close his eyes, but there is this vibration in other parts of the house. Doors are slamming and cupboards rattling; and these footsteps, he feels them up through the floor. A steady, determined tempo moving about the house. Fingertips are at his shoulder, tapping gently, and then making the sign.

Hurry, not much time.

What now?

Come. Sit too long. Learn must do.

She takes him by the hand. He can see himself through the peephole following her. She is in front, taking long graceful steps through the snow, while his are short and choppy from behind. He carries a large rug, folded and drooped over his left shoulder.

He follows her up the knoll and onto a clearing next to The Icy Pines, where two fires burn, one to the north and the other to the south, both within about ten feet of each other. She motions for him to spread the blanket on the ground. She tends the one fire and adds a few sticks of cedar to it. A white finger of smoke rises to the air and disappears to the cracking and snapping of the flames, until, at last, it is burning well. Next to the fire sits an empty brown basin that rises up to a narrow neck. She signals for him to fill it with snow.

He signals a question, but she shakes her head no, making a small circular gesture with her hands, *question no, important, talk no*. He fills the basin with snow, packing it down inside the narrow neck with a stick, until it is filled tight. Then together they lift it onto the big fire, hanging it from a hook and cross beam over the fire. As the snow begins to melt, she adds more snow onto to it, until eventually it begins to steam.

She signals, *take off clothes*. His knees automatically come together at the thought of such, a reflex. She holds up a pink colored cloth. Reluctantly, self-consciously, he steps out of his pants, one leg at a time, then his underwear, holding his hands over his private parts, shivering, until the urine begins to spill down his leg. She has made a blanket of cedar boughs for him to lie on. Once he is down on them, she draws pitchers of hot water from the basin and pours them across his shoulders and back.

Next she takes the basin down from the beam, using cloths to hold it. Once it is on the snow, she begins adding a few things from the buckskin pouch tied to her waist—some dried petals and fine yellow dust. Next she breaks off some of the cedar needles and adds them also. Then she dips the yellow cloth into the hot solution and begins washing his back in a slow, circular motion. He takes in the scent of the cedar and flowers, feeling his nasal passages open and his inner cavity expand. A light, pink suds coat the top of the water and his skin. It reminds him of the snow color on that day he found her beneath the hemlock, the way it had melted away around her body. She works the suds into his scalp, massaging it in, slow, circular motions and pulling his black hair up into a single horn.

She dumps more hot water over him and begins on his shoulders and back. She uses the same slow, circular motions. The porous cloth scratches his skin, making red marks beneath the slick water marks. She takes another cloth from her bag, this one of soft white cotton and she wets it down, before adding the same ingredients to it directly, the flower petals and the yellow powder.

She moves around to the front side of him and kneels down to wash his front side. His penis has become erect, but he isn't aware of it. Carefully, she washes the underside of it, then the top side, and finally the end. Then she does each testicle, rinsing each clean. She finishes off with this legs and buttocks, until every inch of his body is clean and pure.

Next she combs his hair straight back and trims inches off the back and sides, including his beard, giving him a precise, manicured look. She pins his hair up in a queue like her own. She holds his square chin in the palm of her hand and turned his face from side to side.

She places the blanket next to the second fire to the south and has him lie down on it. She takes white powder from her bag and sprinkles it over his naked body and rubs it in until his skin glows. Next, she takes white and yellow powder and mixes it together in a small bowl, adding a few drops of water, until she has made a paste. She applies the paste to the inside of each ear, using her finger until each ear is entirely covered. Then she rolls him up in the blanket so that only his head comes out from one end. She adds more cedar to the fire. Then she begins to sing softly, *hey-yah-hey-yah-hey-yah-yah-yah*.

The fire cannot yet penetrate the blanket. He is enveloped within it, rolled up tight like a smoke; yet it is looser around his face, allowing him to breathe. He loves the closeness and the warmth, which comes in from all sides and begins to spread across his body. He could sleep here, even die. The trees paint a pretty picture above him, bowing beneath the white weight coating that decorates the boughs. A small piece of blue sky lies between them with wisps of clouds.

The comfort is soon gone. Sweat begins to ooze. His eyes fill. He has gone liquid. The blanket is wrapped in such a way that the seam runs up the middle of his back, a line that divides him and holds him secure. The heat grows around him and penetrates down to his organs, his heart, lungs, liver, kidneys, stomach, and intestines, making them stand out from the rest. He begins to wiggle and kick his legs and arms, slowly at first, but more aggressively with each passing moment, until he is wiggling and twisting away against his bondage, struggling to be free.

He feels himself roasting beneath the blanket. His brain is a burning center that begins to expand. Language erupts. "Somebody is trying to kill you, man!" And with these words come a wild outburst of energy, kicking and twisting. "Let me go! Let me go, goddamn you."

She rips the blanket open and rolls him like a steaming log into the snow. He keeps his arms to his side like a mummy, and she keeps on rolling him over and over, packing the snow onto the red body. He jumps to his feet. Midsection she sees a part of him awakened, long and straight, with dragonfly wings. A pitched whistle comes from afar and gains momentum until it is whining and screaming at unendurable levels. He clamps both hands over his ears and looks at the Icy Pines, which are swaying in the breeze. Plus there is The Ice, always before a background drone, a dull vibration, now more like a heavy motor that turns at the center of the earth. She rushes to him and whispers. "Of course. It is all too much." She rubs the yellow paste into his ears and makes a soothing sound. She traces the contours of the inner ear, round and round with her finger, first one ear and then the other, applying the yellow pollen, cooing with her voice. She speaks to him in the merest whisper, accompanying her words with signs.

"Now you hear what a noisy place the world is." She continues to rub his ears. "I will teach you to say the words. I will teach you to listen. I will teach you take action. I will teach you to reclaim your life."

And she did. His father had taught him the ancient signs and to read, but he read without voice. Much of the background was in place; the association of the sounds to the symbols came quickly. At first it was echolalia.

"You are Last Man," she says.

"You are Last Man."

Then she points at her chest. "I am First Woman."

"I am First Woman."

She shakes her head no. "You are First Woman."

"You are First Woman."

This is how it went at first. Back and forth with the pronouns and tenses and so on, but he was at apt pupil.

She has warmed his home. The stones retain her heat. The eves run. Smoke once again curls from his chimney. At night the fireplace hisses and snaps. Though the house continues to shake and a new storm rages, he is happy. She is his teacher.

Overhead, the Communico modules sail noiselessly through the heavens; they have sent their voice probes to her; the warnings go unheeded. The Ice inches closer. At night they can hear the tearing of the trees and cold scraping, which now sounds like an audible groan.

The storm rages. However, each afternoon, they enjoy a one-hour reprieve. It has become predictable, nearly to the hour. The snow stops and the wind ceases it plaintive wail. Even the gray clouds part to expose a patch of sapphire-colored sky.

He selects one of the journals from the archives that they will take "on location." These notebooks contain fairly detailed maps of the region, all apparently drawn by the same careful hand. Each map has a series of anecdotal narratives that accompany it.

At first these readings have had a great and somewhat polarized effect on him. Sometimes they bring tears to his eyes and other times he laughs loudly. As of late, though, their impact has seemed to fall somewhere in the middle, producing an amused, thoughtful look upon his face.

"Where shall we go today?" she asks him.

"Is today our last day?"

She takes his arm and they begin to walk. "Today is another day. That's all we ever know for sure."

She has changed into a warm, hooded parka with snowsuit, pink mittens and black buckled boots. He has selected one of the notebooks and now randomly turns to a page, as he is often wont to do. He recognizes the drawing: a sketch of a pointed tower with an illuminated clock that juts up from the center of a large square building with angled roofs. The clock is numbered in Roman numerals. All of the hands point to XII. A bright moon shines in the background between two clouds.

"Let's go there."

They pack a lunch and strap on their snowshoes. They slog along to what once was the Main Street of the small Northern Michigan village known as Blackwood. They move through an imaginary location as she reads to him.

"Here was Red's Café, there the Moby Hardware, here the Community Hall; there Jensen's Drug Store; here Dino's Delicatessen."

It continues like this with the two of them standing at the site of a life that has been obliterated by a thousand years of winter and cold, known only on the printed page, until they come to the last item, The Court House. Here there is more than the world of imagination and print. He stands next to the old belfry, lying on its side, still exposed, which somehow, like the stone house, has managed to endure.

Dee walks up to the clock, the glass now gone and shattered in the past. "Read to me."

"I still recall the strike of midnight, the smells of the warm summer's song coming through my open window, the radio's soft song drifting across the darkness and your scratch at the screen. Into the gypsy night we would steal, never thinking that God in His infinite mystery would someday separate us."

She stops reading.

"What kind of people were they back then, Áłtsé? What kind of life did they have?"

She takes the hand of the old clock and sets it to "XII." "It's hard to say. They seemed happy. They still believed in love."

6

The time has come. Plates are crashing to the floor and large cracks splinter the floors. Yet, the stone house continues to stand its ground.

"Come, it's time." She takes him to the edge of The Icy Pines. "I don't want to go in there," he says. He turns and takes a last look at the stone house, which is nearly consumed by the gaping mouth of the glacier. "I don't want to leave my home." She turns him around and puts a finger to her lips, the sign of silence. *Speak signs now.*

"I don't want to speak in signs. I don't ever want to do that again."

She only looks at him in a way that goes beyond words. She makes no signs but he gets the message. She takes his hand, but he pulls away. *No more follow.* He walks beside her. His steps are brisk and short. She moves in a long, curvy S-pattern weaving in and out of the pines that hang low with their snow dressing. Sweat pours from him. His clothes are soon soaked and his chest is about to explode, when she slows and then stops.

Her breathing is unaffected but his comes in long, panting intervals, like what the dogs must have had after they'd pulled to capacity, and he would spell them; and their tongues would hang out and their eyes would stretch back wildly. That is how he felt and imagined himself, sitting there on his rump in a small open area, his shoes standing up on their heels, the gray sky low overhead.

She gives him a minute. Sweat soaks his beard and drips to the ground. The heavy silence of trees absorbs everything. The grind and hum of The Ice is behind them. The sting of cold settles on his nose and forehead.

Flecks begin drifting down. She pulls him to his feet. *Begin now. Soon dark.* He wants to protest, but she gives him the look of quiet. She pulls him along. They move back into the thick of the woods. The snow gives off its own kind of milky light, dimming slowly as they go. She is beside him now, where he can see her and draw strength from her linear features. She makes the sign: *Further, a little.* But he is not sure he can go on. His hope is fading right along with the daylight.

Finally he stops again and squats down, his face clamped between his two hands. *Home gone. Past gone. Away hope.*

She brushes the snow from his hair and turns his face upward. *Yes, yes, yes.*

He looks back at their tracks, which are already filling with snow. *How? Back no more.*

She nods. *Back yes! Forward back.* His brows knit together. She presses her hand to her heart. *Trust. Forward back.*

He is about to say something back when he hears a sound in the distance. He stands up to listen. Again it sounds, faintly through the growing darkness, just as he had imagined it when he was a little boy. Just as his father had described it, the trumpet: three notes sounding with a pause, followed by three more.

They move toward the sound. Soon they are standing at the edge of a clearing. She turns to him and makes the quiet sign. Her figure is straight and dark like the trees around her. Her back is to him on the edge of a clearing. He looks in the direction of her gaze. It is just as he imagined it all of those years ago, in the drawing. There in the distance, three small bushes moving, though he knows they are not. For a short distance they move, and then stop. The trumpet sounds and they pause for a short while and then begin to move again, only this time they are coming toward Áltsé and him.

She tries to take his hand, but he shakes loose and moves on his own, alongside her. Out across the ravine they go, moving toward the three approaching figures, all of whom are now close enough in the gathering darkness, so that the hooded tunics that drape over their faces can be seen. All is not covered. The flash of smiles and white teeth come out of the darkness. They shake Áltsé 's hand and then Dee's. They speak in signs, inviting Dee and her to follow. They lead them back across the opening to a log structure that lies just inside the covering of the trees.

They step inside to a room whose floor is covered with straw mats. Candles burn low from the floor, where others are sitting. A whispering sound fills the room, though he cannot make out the words.

The gentle, firm pressure of hands pulls him down into a chair. They undo and remove his footwear and place a pan of warm water next to him. A solitary individual kneels down and begins washing his feet. Next the individual dries each foot and applies oil, before standing and pulling the hood back. His face glows in the darkness. Dee recognizes those ears, how they sit low on his head. Alfie makes the sign, *Go in peace*. He points toward another room and quickly exits. Once again the hands are upon him, gently nudging him through the door.

In this room a solitary red candle burns before a tabernacle. Seated in front of it is a very old man pleating rope. His hair is thick and white and comes across his head smoothly from a left hand part. He sits in an upright position, though his shoulders are stooped. He is clothed in sackcloth and his left hand seems to tremble violently as he fusses with the ropes, but his eyes are steady and alert.

"Please be seated," he whispers kindly.

Dee sits down. He feels the warm presence of her body pressed up behind him, against his back, where her two small, firm breasts are.

"You may ask your question."

Dee turns and looks at Áltsé and she nods her head. He thinks for a moment. What question? Then she wraps her arms around him and presses more firmly against him. Now he understands.

"What should I do?"

For a moment the ancient holy one looks at both of them and a trace of a smile crosses his time marked face.

"Go in peace," he whispers. "Be fruitful and multiply."

They were obedient.

It is said that at that exact moment the scales tipped in humanity's favor. The Ice stopped, just as it was about to consume the stone house, and thus began its long, slow, but inevitable withdraw, and she felt the new child that was within her leap for joy.

The couple, known from then on as First Woman and First Man, made their way back out of Cluny Forest to their new home and because of their love, the weather warmed and the animals slowly migrated back into the forests.

Of a time, long, long ago, these things will happen, it is said.